ANGELS UNAWARE

Late nineteenth century: After the death of her young husband, Rebecca must return to her parents' home because women are not expected to work. Feeling she has to do something, however, she trains with the missionaries to care for the sick. But even they have restrictions on unattached females and will not allow her to go into field service. Remaining with her parents until their deaths, Rebecca, now aged thirty-two, decides to go to a remote part of Oklahoma to care for the sick. Yet again, though, she is thwarted — the superstitious hill people will not accept a newcomer. But things change when Rebecca meets Ole Woman . . .

Priscilla A. Maine was born and raised in Atoka County, Oklahoma. She is an active member of Women Writing the West, EPIC, EPPRO, EQUILD, Oklahoma Writers Federation, Inc., McWriters and a graduate of Writer's Digest School. Priscilla A. Maine has been published in several magazines and lives near the foothills of the Kiamichi Mountains with her husband.

PRISCILLA A. MAINE

◆

ANGELS UNAWARE

Complete and Unabridged

ULVERSCROFT
Leicester

First published in the
United States of America

First Large Print Edition
published 2003

The moral right of the author has been asserted

This is a work of fiction. While reference may be
made to actual historical events or existing locations,
the characters, incidents, and dialogues are products
of the author's imagination. Any resemblance to
actual persons, living or dead, is entirely coincidental.

British Library CIP Data

Maine, Priscilla A.
    Angels unaware.—Large print ed.—
    Ulverscroft large print series: general fiction
    1. Large type books
    I. Title
    813.5′4 [F]

    ISBN 0–7089–4803–0

Published by
F. A. Thorpe (Publishing)
Anstey, Leicestershire

Set by Words & Graphics Ltd.
Anstey, Leicestershire
Printed and bound in Great Britain by
T. J. International Ltd., Padstow, Cornwall

This book is printed on acid-free paper

To my husband Russell,
whose faith in me never wavered.

Acknowledgments

To Gina S. Fields who walks in my soul.
Thanks for finding all my mistakes and
pointing me in the right direction.
To Kelley L. Pounds for her encouragement and inspiration.

You ladies are truly amazing.
Thank you both for being there when
I needed you most.

Be not forgetful to entertain strangers: for thereby some have entertained angels unawares.

Hebrews 13:2

1

Rebecca couldn't remember a time when she hadn't done exactly what was expected of her . . . until now.

'James, you and Louise act as though I'm going into the wilderness to live in a tent. Have you forgotten I have a house there?' Rebecca glanced out the window. A rented, covered wagon, loaded with her possessions, stood at the end of the walkway, ready for her departure. Now all she had to do was say good-bye to her brother and sister . . . again. For even at this late date, her siblings were still trying to talk her out of leaving.

'It's been years since you've seen that place. How do you know it's still standing?' A frown creased her brother's brow. 'Besides, those people are different from folks you've always known. They're clannish, superstitious, and suspicious.' He stacked his objections like a barricade.

'What will you do for entertainment, Rebecca?' Louise chimed, twisting her linen handkerchief about her index finger. 'You're leaving at such an awkward time. The bridge tournament is next week. Whatever will we do?' The handkerchief became damp and limp as Louise's agitation grew. Louise could always be counted on to get to the heart of things. One more set of whist or one more garden social, and Rebecca would scream. Love for her sister stifled her protest. Instead, she laughed softly. 'Where's your sense of adventure?'

Noticing the stricken looks on their faces, Rebecca realized they were like two slices of plain white bread, filling and nourishing, yet tasteless. And she'd been sandwiched between them since birth. Then, taking pity on the pair, she tried to reassure them.

'James, you have control of my business affairs. You've agreed to find renters for the house, to forward my mail and bank drafts. You've made excellent investments with the remainder of my funds. What else is there?'

'Family,' her sister replied.

'Family, Louise? You have a family. James has a family. I lost my husband thirteen years ago. Now, with Mama and Papa gone, I have no . . .'

'You have us. You know we love you,' James reminded her.

'Then wish me well.'

Social blinders firmly intact, they skirted the real reason behind Rebecca's decision to rearrange her life. To do so would give it credence, and that, neither was willing to do. Guilt was their weapon of choice and they dished it up in double portions.

'What will our friends think? Judge Rice's daughter going God knows where, to care for the sick and diseased, handling corrupt flesh, and washing the bodies of strangers.' Louise's plump body shuddered visibly at the thought.

'I don't care what they think!' Rebecca stepped to the window and pulled back the lacy curtain. Jimmy Johnstone, her young driver, waited beside the wagon. 'It's time I started living for myself,' Rebecca said, turning.

'Sister, that's selfish. You should think of someone other than yourself.'

'I am thinking of others! It's for others I'm going to the hill country. There, I won't face the restrictions of social stigma.' She unleashed her pent-up passions and flung their objections back at them. 'No one will know, or care, who I am. They won't have prejudices against a woman nursing and caring for their sick. I'll finally be free to practice what I learned so many years ago. I've waited so long . . . too long . . . to use it.' She looked first at James, then Louise, silently imploring them to understand her need.

Louise busied herself mopping tears with her crumpled hanky. James held Rebecca's gaze, refusing to relent in his attempt to dissuade her. This emotional tug of war would get them nowhere. Besides, they meant well and she didn't doubt they were genuinely concerned for her safety. Maybe she shouldn't have been so blunt with them. After all, even the missionaries, who taught her the truth about faith healing and how to care for the sick, had refused to allow her to go into field service with them. Apparently, even they had restrictions on unattached females. So be it. She would go where she was needed, on her own.

'James.' Rebecca softened her voice, but held her brother's gaze while she spoke. 'Contrary to what you think or say, I don't believe the people of Big Grassy valley won't accept me, once they know why I'm there.' She smiled faintly, hoping to draw him away from his stubborn stance. 'After all, this is 1895, not the Dark Ages.'

In all fairness to her brother and sister, she was also thinking of herself. She simply must share with others what she had learned. 'Please, both of you, try to understand.' She looked at her sister. 'I have to do this. I want more out of life than to be a sponge, soaking up the leftovers of life.'

Louise dabbed at her eyes and hiccuped. James threw his hands up as if in surrender.

Rebecca hugged them both, dropped her house key in James' hand, and dashed out the front door before either had an opportunity to object further.

★ ★ ★

Adjusting her bonnet and straightening the crisp folds of her gingham skirt, she nodded to the freckle-faced young man on the wagon seat beside her. With a sharp flick of the reins and a jolt, they were on their way. Her destination: the hill country of southeastern Oklahoma, Indian Territory. She should arrive there in less than a week, although she had traveled in that direction for a dozen years.

Her rented wagon bounced and swayed along the deeply rutted road. She glanced over her left shoulder for one last wistful look at the house disappearing in the distance. She'd grown up in that house. It held many memories. Within its walls, she had been loved, protected, and sheltered. But she had also been a prisoner there, shackled to a way of life that left her empty and unfulfilled.

With forceful determination, she turned to face the long, empty road ahead and sighed deeply. But not with regret. It was frustration that gnawed at the core of her soul. And lately, it had become her constant companion. Why couldn't her brother and sister accept her decision? James harped about her leaving the security of her home; Louise fretted over the lack of society. Neither mattered to her.

With a mental shake, Rebecca dragged her attention from the past. She longed for their blessings, but with or without them, she — Her thoughts were interrupted when the wagon bounced wildly on the dusty, rutted road with a tooth-jarring jolt. Regaining her balance on the wooden seat, Rebecca placed both feet on the footwell, bracing herself against the impact of the bumps. The glossy tips of her new black boots winked from beneath the hem of her skirt, and she smiled. They were as bright as her hopes for the future.

The morning sun crawled past the treetops, casting soft shadows beneath the white oaks lining the long, empty road. Sounds of spring filled the morning air. Mockingbirds imitated their neighbors with lively notes. Squirrels bounced from limb to limb, barking at the intruders passing beneath them. Oak trees sported lacy new leaves in varying shades of green. Dogwood and redbuds struggled for dominance, providing shelter for the carpet of pink buttercups and lavender lady's-slippers hovering beneath them.

Placing both hands on the seat, Rebecca threw her shoulders back and lifted her face toward the warmth of the sun. Today, she was setting out to fulfill her dream, forging a tomorrow and a future she could be proud of. And she would see it through, no matter what.

'They don't understand that the farm will see my dream set in motion.'

'Ma'am?' Jimmy asked.

Rebecca looked at her companion and saw confusion sprinkled among his freckles.

'Dreams, Jimmy. Don't you have dreams?'

His confusion turned to bewilderment.

'What kinda dreams you mean?'

Rebecca suspected her smile was as warm and radiant as the April sunshine. She reached over and ruffled Jimmy's sandy curls.

'Dreams of life, of living.'

Jimmy's confusion never wavered.

'Never mind, Jimmy. Just keep those horses headed southeast.'

The way he sat, leaned forward, both tanned arms on top of his thighs, the reins held tightly between his strong fingers, told Rebecca his sense of responsibility sat heavily on his young shoulders. He shifted his position as if to ease the strain on them.

'Mr. James didn't look too happy back there.'

'No, he didn't. But time and distance will ease his misgivings. What about your family? Any last-minute reservations?'

'You know Ma. She cried some.' He shot Rebecca a quick glance. 'She keeps forgetting I'm a man now.'

Rebecca hid her smile. A man, indeed. He was barely two weeks past his eighteenth birthday, but she refrained from commenting on that fact.

'I hope your absence won't put too great a hardship on your father.'

'Naw, Billy can help out till I get back. Besides, we can use the extra money.'

★ ★ ★

That evening they camped beside a clear, rushing stream just off the main road. While Jimmy tended the horses and gathered wood for a fire, Rebecca set up a makeshift kitchen and then made up their bedrolls. Inside the wagon, among her sparse but precious belongings, she cleared a space for her bed. Jimmy would pitch his blankets beneath it.

After watching her futile attempts to prepare the evening meal, burning her fingers in the process, Jimmy stepped into the

8

firelight. Puffing out his chest with manly pride, he offered his assistance.

'I can handle that, Miss Rebecca.'

Gratefully, Rebecca retreated from the fire, wiped her flour-coated hands on a grease-splattered apron and found a grassy patch of ground near the wagon to rest. She dipped her seared fingers into the water in her drinking glass before rubbing one of her ointments on them, chiding herself all the while for her lack of outdoor cooking skills. While watching her young companion's efficiency, Rebecca applied her efforts to removing the heavy layer of dust coating her new boots. Her stomach rumbled in response to the aroma of fried potatoes and bacon.

* * *

Each day revealed new and amazing sights to their citified eyes. It also brought stiff joints and bruises. They weren't breaking any records, but progressed steadily onward, traveling until the sun dropped over the western horizon before making camp.

On the third morning, they awoke to gray, heavy skies filled with dark, bulging rain clouds. Rebecca was storing their sleeping gear when she felt the ground shudder beneath her feet. She quickly turned toward

9

Jimmy, who was hitching the team to the wagon.

'What was . . . ?' Earth-vibrating thunder rumbled across the murky sky, stifling the rest of her question. Bolts of fiery lightning momentarily shattered the gloomy darkness.

Glancing up from his chore, Jimmy wiped fat droplets of rain from his face. 'Want to wait it out?'

Rebecca scanned the heavens. The sky was getting darker and the rain falling faster.

'We'll go on. A little rain isn't going to stop me.' She finished folding the last of their bedding. Grabbing her shawl from a nearby box, she draped it about her shoulders, then scrambled toward the front to take her place on the wagon seat and wait for Jimmy to join her.

Mud and mire hampered their progress. The rain continued to fall. For two days and nights it rained. At night, the two weary travelers crouched inside the wagon, wrapped in damp quilts. By day, they suffered the elements on the open wagon seat. Rebecca insisted they go on. Huddled beneath her quilt at night, listening to the ever-present rain, she recalled the driving force behind this trip into the hill country.

★ ★ ★

It started two years after her husband's death. Frightened and alone without Jonathan, she drifted from one endless day to the next. Finally, she relented to her parents' pressure and returned to her childhood home. It wasn't long before she understood the phrase; 'you can't go home again.' Life in her parents' home was vastly different from what it had been before her marriage. They treated her like a little girl, instead of a woman married and widowed.

Soon she felt suffocated, wasted. She had to do something with herself or die. When the missionaries arrived that fall, Rebecca signed up for the nursing classes they gave. She plunged headlong into her studies and found she had a genuine affinity for the work. To see her efforts make a difference brought a joy and fulfillment to her life that had been missing for too long.

Following graduation, she applied for mission work in foreign fields. Even now, she remembered the disappointment that washed over her like waves at the rejection. The reasons given did nothing to ease her anguish. Unattached females, they said, were not taken into the field. Most had proven too unstable, unable to adjust to the rigors of life without the amenities of civilization.

So her life returned to the endless rounds

of social obligations expected of a woman without a family of her own. Sunday bridge, Tuesday whist, Thursday literary discussions, and Friday garden parties. It was like being caught in a spider's web, and the more she struggled to remove herself from it, the tighter she became ensnared.

Then, unexpectedly, her mother became ill and took to bed. Rebecca's nursing skills were needed in a way she had never expected. She assumed the duties of a nurse, and cared for her mother until her death. Then, before the family could adjust to its loss, her papa went into a decline, joining his beloved wife shortly thereafter.

And so it had gone. Until now.

★   ★   ★

On the sixth morning of their trip, they awoke damp and chilled to find the sun weakly forcing its way from behind low, gray-bellied clouds. By noon, the rain ceased, and the sun provided a welcome warmth. Even before the thunderstorms road conditions had been nothing to brag about, now they resembled a washboard. Which did nothing to improve their progress. Still the two travelers arrived at the settlement of Big Grassy just after noon that day.

Rebecca made a valiant attempt to make herself presentable. Searching through her belongings, she found an almost-dry skirt and shirtwaist. She changed inside the wagon before they entered the settlement. Her hair, though still damp, was pulled back and tied with a matching ribbon at the nape of her neck. Stray tendrils escaped the ribbon and curled about her ears, making her appear younger than her thirty-two years. Her blue-gray eyes sparkled with jubilation when she stepped down from the wagon.

Above the dusty boardwalk, a sign reading BERTHA'S MERCANTILE AND POST swayed in the wind.

'We'll ask directions to the farm from here,' Rebecca said. 'I'll get a few supplies, too.' She gazed up and down the well-rutted road that ran through the little community.

At the far end of the street, the clang-clang of the blacksmith's hammer rang through the midday air. Wood smoke belched from the round hole in the roof with each whisper of the bellows. Off-key notes from a tinny piano *plink-plonked* through the split-door of the tavern across the way.

Her attention was drawn toward the feed and seed store where a lone worker was loading several wagons. Circles of sweat marked his shirt, as well as the red bandana tied about his forehead. Without a pause in his labor, the swarthy-skinned worker appeared to take inventory of the two strangers

Rebecca ignored his rude perusal and let her gaze drift farther down the street to a church bearing a sign that proclaimed, 'Welcome to the Baptist Church of Big Grassy.'

Both, she and Jimmy, were exhausted and eager for the chance to stand and stretch their stiff, cramped limbs. While Jimmy placed a feedbag over the nose of each horse and tied the reins securely to the brake handle, Rebecca entered the store, hoping she didn't look as wilted as she felt.

A bell attached to the door set up a clamor at her entrance. Halting just inside the door, a variety of sights and smells assaulted her. Every available inch of space was utilized for merchandise. Shovels, hoes, rakes, axes, and picks lined one wall near the entrance. Brooms protruded from a barrel sitting next to the door on the left. Tables laden with bolts of fabric, from corduroy to gingham, nestled next to tables heaped high with overalls, work pants, blue chambray shirts, brogan shoes, boots, calico dresses, and poke bonnets. Barrels brimmed with crackers, beans, flour, and pickles, and tins of sardines and buckets

14

of molasses nestled side by side. Slabs of bacon, smoked and salted, hung from the rafters. On the counter, rounds of golden, tangy-smelling cheese perched next to rows of glass containers filled with tempting penny candy.

Behind the counter were numerous rows of tin containers of food. Bins of potatoes, turnips, onions, cabbages, and squash lined the back wall. The pleasant aroma of the leather harnesses hanging on the wall mingled with the spicy scent of cinnamon, clove, allspice, and garlic.

A cast-iron potbellied stove, encircled with cane-bottomed chairs, dominated the center of the crowded room. Near the back wall, next to a stairwell, a small table and two chairs nestled almost out of sight. Sitting in the center of the table was a fruit jar overflowing with pink buttercups. It was a cozy little area, but somehow out of place with the other items surrounding it. Just behind the counter, a wooden shelf divided into small squares served as the post office.

Jimmy joined Rebecca, and she watched his nostrils flare as the aroma of baking bread pervaded the room, creating a welcoming atmosphere.

'Jeez, it's big, ain't it?' he whispered, shoving his hands into his pockets and glancing about the room.

As if his remark conjured her up, a woman stepped from behind the green and yellow striped curtain covering the doorway at the rear of the store. Jimmy's eyes bulged at the sight of her.

A large woman with a jovial face and large, brown, cow-like eyes stood before them. Her fiery red hair wound into a loose knot on top of her head trailed stray wisps about her crimson cheeks. She wore a bright flowered dress and a limp white apron that reached her shoe tops. Her playful smile seemed to say she found life hilarious. Large hoop earrings swung from her thick, pink ears.

'Howdy, I'm Bertha Callahan. You folks lost?'

Damp, travel-worn, and eager to be on their way, Rebecca and Jimmy stood slack-jawed and pop-eyed, gazing silently at the smiling, florid-faced woman.

Bertha appeared accustomed to the startled reaction the first sight of her five feet seven inches and two-hundred-pound frame evoked. She waited for the shock to pass while she, in turn, scrutinized the strangers.

The next half-hour passed swiftly and pleasantly with introductions and generalities while Bertha filled Rebecca's order of supplies.

Bertha Callahan glided effortlessly about the abundantly stocked store with a natural grace unexpected in one so large. Genuine laughter and an earthy humor laced her lively banter. She regaled the newcomers with the problems of a woman alone, along with her current marital status.

According to her tale of woes, Bertha had gone through four husbands. This bit of information was imparted with a gleam in her lively brown eyes and a hint of suppressed mirth. 'Seems if I don't work them to death, I just purely love them there.' Pausing, she glanced over her right shoulder at her speechless customers and added. 'Except the last one. He just up and run off one day. Said he needed a rest. I ain't seen nor heard from him since.' Then, with a laugh that vibrated her mountainous frame, she proclaimed, 'They just don't make men like they used to.'

The shocked silence only seemed to fire Bertha's mirth. With a mischievous gleam in her eyes, she turned and spoke to Jimmy.

'I need a replacement for that last worthless excuse for a man. You interested, youngun?'

With a bolt and a sprint, Jimmy was out the door, red-faced and muttering something about seeing to the horses. Rollicking laughter trailed behind him.

Bertha turned to Rebecca and placed her ham-like arms on the table, a definite change of mood in her eyes. She leaned forward in her chair. 'What you want with directions to the old Williams' place? Ain't nobody living out there.'

'I intend to.'

'You got a man coming to join you later?'

Rebecca noticed lines of concern creased Bertha Callahan's broad brow. 'I'm a widow,' Rebecca replied, drawing herself up in her chair. 'I'll be living alone.' Those words still caused pain to rip through her heart.

'The boy, he ain't staying with you?'

'Jimmy will return home once I'm settled.'

All trace of the storeowner's former frivolity vanished while she prodded the newcomer. 'You got kin in them hills?'

Rebecca shook her head, wondering what prompted all the questions.

'Then, I'd turn around and go back where I come from, if I's you. Them folks out there don't cotton much to strangers, and a woman alone . . . '

Noticing the emphasis placed on 'alone,' Rebecca abruptly stood, interrupting the woman's objections.

'I appreciate your concern. But I did not travel six long, miserable, wet days to turn around in defeat before I've even arrived.'

Her voice trembled with her barely controlled emotions. Taking a deep breath in an attempt to regain her calm, she continued, 'It's mine, and I intend to live there. If faith can move mountains, surely it can make friends and neighbors of strangers. Good day, Mrs. Callahan.'

The screened door slammed behind her but didn't block out the words that followed her. 'I sure hope you're right.'

2

Their wagon topped a ridge and Rebecca got her first view of her new home. She placed her gloved hand on Jimmy's arm.

'Wait,' she said. 'Let's look a minute.'

Jimmy brought the wagon to a halt beneath the canopy of newly formed leaves of a huge red oak. Nestled at the base of the hill, trees circled the house like a cup in a saucer. The land sloped gently toward a quick-flowing ribbon of water known as Ten Mile Creek.

Behind the house, adjoining the creek, she saw an orchard of fruit trees. The front of the house faced a wide, green meadow bordered on the far side by a pecan grove.

'I'm finally home.' Joy filled her voice. 'I can hardly wait to get moved in. And I promise you a real home cooked meal tonight. Hurry, please!'

'Yes, Ma'am. I could go for some regular grub.' Jimmy snapped the reins. 'Real pretty place, ain't it?'

Only when they drew closer were the scars visible. From the distance it had been impossible to see the holes in the roof, or the rotten places in the porch which spanned the width of the house, or the broken windows. Like vacant eye sockets staring out of a scar-battered face, those pane-less windows gaped accusingly at their approach.

The wagon swayed and bounced across what once had been the front yard. Most of the split-rail fence lay scattered in the weed-choked area. Climbing off the wagon, they stood side by side, gazing at the dilapidated house. This possibility hadn't occurred to her. In silence, they carefully made their way up the rickety steps, cautiously picking their way across the porch to the front door.

'At least it has a door,' she muttered softly.

Hesitating a moment, Jimmy turned toward her. 'You sure you want to go in, Miss Rebecca? We could maybe go back to that settlement and find you lodging. This place is gonna need a lot of work.' His young face wore a mask of concern.

'It's my home. I'm staying.' She felt hot tears of frustration sting the backs of her eyelids, but refused to let them spill over. 'Surely it's not all like this.' She swiped at her eyes with the back of her hand, admonishing herself as she did so. This was no time for a pity party.

With her shoulder, she nudged the door open. Its rusted hinges groaned in protest at the disturbance. She stepped slowly inside and halted. To her dismay, it was even worse than the outside.

Determination and willpower thrust her forward.

Working together, she and Jimmy displaced a litter of infant squirrels scampering in the big fieldstone fireplace in the kitchen, and a family of field mice in what had once been a bedroom. The large room at the front, thankfully, was varmint-free, but shrouded in a dense layer of spider webs and dust.

'We could have spring planting right here.' She ran the toe of her boot across the floor.

Glancing first at Rebecca as if to judge her seriousness, Jimmy smiled with a grin that spread across his ruddy face.

'Can't be too bad if you found something to joke about. Besides, you didn't expect to find it spit and polished, did you?'

'I didn't expect to find the south forty in the parlor, either,' she shot back, following his example of light-heartedness. She might as well laugh as cry.

Closer inspection of the three large, airy rooms revealed that the front room had fewer leaks from the damaged roof. They could unload the wagon of furniture and supplies in there. But not today. First they would clean it.

So began an afternoon of sweeping ceilings, walls, and floors, of cleaning out the huge fireplace in the kitchen. A grown man would have no difficulty standing upright inside that fireplace, even with the iron rod embedded about three feet above the fire area from which to hang the cook pots.

'Jimmy, if you'll locate some kindling and dry wood, I'll start a pot of stew for our supper.' Rebecca wiped her brow with the back of her hand. 'I'll get some water.'

Striding briskly across the yard with a bucket in each hand, Rebecca headed for the creek. The late afternoon sun warmed her straight, narrow back, and the new carpet of meadow grass, sprinkled with flowering clover, cushioned her steps. A gentle breeze whispered through the canopy of leaves overhead. A feeling of happiness wrapped itself about her, and she hummed under her breath.

She was returning with her buckets brimming with water when she spotted smoke surging from the gaping, pane-less windows, and pouring from the holes in the roof.

'Jimmy! Jimmy, where are you?' she screamed, dropping both buckets and dashing up the rickety steps. Just when she reached the door, Jimmy darted out of the smoke, coughing, and rubbing his tear-filled eyes.

'I'm okay, ma'am. Chimney must have been stopped up. It ain't drawing. Smoke's just coming right back down in the house.' Apparently noticing the stricken look on her dust-streaked face, he tried to reassure her. 'Soon as the smoke clears out some, I'll check it out. Should have thought of it before I started a fire. It's my fault. Guess I had my mind on that stew.'

'Oh, don't worry about that. I'm just glad you're all right.' Glancing behind Jimmy at the smoke-filled house, she smiled. 'Besides, maybe the smoke will run off the rest of those spiders.'

Taking his arm, she guided him away from the house, out of the smoke. 'I'll get you a dipper of water, if I didn't spill it all. It's about the only thing I've found so far that's clean around here.'

After drinking his fill of the cool, sweet-tasting water, Jimmy asked, 'Suppose that creek's got any fish in it?'

'I don't know. Why?'

'Just thinking. Baked fish and cornpone be mighty tasty. Seeing as how we can't have stew, on account of the fireplace not working.' Handing her the empty dipper, he added, 'If its awright with you, think I'll try my luck.'

24

He set the buckets of water on the edge of the porch and started across the yard.

'But you don't have a pole, or line; how will you catch fish?'

'Noodling. Don't need a pole or line for that,' he answered with a wide grin splashed across his freckled face.

'Noodling?' she mimicked. 'What in heaven's name is that?'

'Noodling's when you run your hands under the edge of rocks or tree snags under the water till you find ole Mr. Catfish laying up, sleeping. You ease your hand along his side real easy-like, so's not to spook him, and then run your fingers inside his gills and jerk him out of the water.' His freckles sparkled as he demonstrated his method of fishing. 'Done it a lot of times. If there's catfish in that creek, we'll have them for supper. You just have a rest and I'll be right back. Shouldn't take long.'

Rebecca leaned back against the house and watched Jimmy trot off toward the creek like a young buck in the late afternoon sunshine. When he stopped at the edge to roll up his pant legs, she glanced toward the house and judged it free enough of smoke to continue her cleaning. She took the remainder of the water and set to scrubbing the floor of the front room. It would be too late to unload tonight, but she would have it ready for tomorrow.

Rebecca had always been physically active; she had to be to care for someone bedridden. And she had cared for both her parents during the long years of their illnesses. Yet by the time she finished scrubbing and rinsing that one floor, she was weak with exhaustion. Riding on the wagon seat for days had clearly left her out of shape.

Leaning wearily on the mop handle, she gazed at the sparkling clean room and spoke her thought aloud. 'I definitely have a lot to learn. But, I've got lots of time.'

By the time she finished storing her mop and dumping the dirty water, Jimmy had a fire smoldering in a pit dug in the yard and was busy cleaning a medium-sized catfish. He glanced up and watched her cross the porch. When she stepped gingerly around the weak, rotten places, he grinned broadly.

'Supper will be ready soon.'

So much for the home-cooked meal. But tomorrow was another day. Only one thing remained to be done today. This was her first night in her new home, such as it was, and she intended to sleep in comfort. With Jimmy's help, her feather mattress was unloaded and placed on the floor near one of the windows of the front room.

It was late and they were both exhausted, so instead of trying to locate her bed linens, she made her bed using the bedroll she'd used while traveling. Jimmy spread his bedroll on the front porch where it appeared to be solid enough to support him, and they retired for the night. Just before sleep claimed her, Rebecca wondered once more why Bertha Callahan had hinted she shouldn't stay here alone.

3

Rebecca awoke slowly. An uneasy feeling of being watched crawled along her nerves. Without moving or opening her eyes, she lay quietly, listening, attempting to locate the source of what awakened her. She was certain she hadn't heard anything, yet that feeling of being watched persisted.

Turning her head slowly toward the shaft of light filtering through the window, she cautiously opened her eyes. Rebecca couldn't have said what she expected to find, but it wasn't what she confronted.

Bolting upright from her mattress on the floor, she clutched a quilt protectively to her chin, her mouth flew open to scream. At the same instant, realization dawned on her: the creature peering in the open window was as frightened as she was.

Fear danced across the face before it withdrew quickly from sight.

'Wait!' Rebecca frantically scrambling into her robe. 'Who are you?' She stumbled, almost falling over Jimmy when she dashed from the house onto the porch, just in time to see a figure disappear into the woods at a run.

'Hey, what's going on?' Jimmy stammered. 'What's the matter?' He tumbled out of his bedroll, rubbing sleep from his eyes.

'We had a visitor.'

'Who?'

'Probably a curious neighbor.'

Rebecca snatched a quilt from Jimmy's bedding, then wrapped the coverlet about her shoulders to ward off the morning chill. Her gaze darted to the distant tree line. What if she was wrong about the prowler? What if it ... no, she refused to dwell on other possibilities. The Lord would protect her; she had to remember that. Shrugging her shoulders, Rebecca turned toward the sleepy figure beside her.

'Let's have breakfast before we get started on the rest of the cleaning. With luck, we could be through by noon and start on the roof.'

Noon came and went and the cleaning continued. By mid-afternoon the ceilings, walls, and floors sparkled. Rebecca was pleasantly surprised when the layers of filth disappeared to reveal the warm, rich woodgrain of knotty pine floors throughout the house.

Cleaning the fireplace included removing a squirrel's nest from the flue. Then Jimmy built a fire to check the draw. When the smoke rose lazily up the chimney, he looked up from the hearth and said, 'My stomach thinks my throat's been cut. How about taking a break and grabbing a bite to eat?'

Their meal was cold cornbread and baked sweet potatoes. Jimmy had taught her how to bury potatoes beneath the hot coals and ashes of their breakfast fire in the yard. Relishing the gentle breeze as it cooled her sweat-soaked body, Rebecca heard Jimmy say, 'We need shingles.'

'Can we make them?'

'Naw. It'd take too long.' Pausing a moment, he added, 'We'd need tools, too.'

'I have tools.' Excitement filled her voice at solving the problem so simply. 'I brought some of Papa's.'

'What have you got?'

'A hammer, a saw, and an axe.' She smiled as she called off her list. 'Oh, I almost forgot, a small bag of nails, too.'

'It would take too long, Miss Rebecca. We got to think of something else.'

She felt a sharp thrust of despair. Though she rarely felt despondent, it was like a grieving in her bones. Her mouth went dry. She sat, slump-shouldered, on the edge of the porch, contemplating the problem of the roof. Her body sagged wearily. It seemed that bleary eyes of defeat glared at her from the weed-choked yard. The dirt, grime, and varmints, the holes in the roof, the rotten porch, and the pane-less windows taunted her.

What next? Was the whole venture doomed before it started? Self-pity flexed its muscles and crept closer, tempting her.

'Why don't we wander around some? Maybe we can find something to use to fix the roof,' Jimmy said.

By the tone of his voice, Rebecca knew his suggestion was meant to pull her from the doldrums. Well, why not? She had nothing to lose in the effort. And they just might get lucky. With renewed determination, she forced the frown lines from her sunburned brow and straightened her shoulders.

'Watch where you step,' she cautioned as they rounded the house. 'It's warm enough for snakes to be moving.' Weeds had long ago claimed the debris-littered yard. A jolt slammed through her body when she collided unexpectedly with a solid object among the waist-high weeds.

'You okay?'

'I think so,' Rebecca grunted, pulling the weeds back from the offending barricade in her path.

'I'll be blamed!' Jimmy muttered once the weeds parted. 'It's a well. And we been toting water from the creek.'

'Our luck seems to be changing. Look over there.' She pointed beyond the tangle of brush. 'Isn't that a shed? Maybe there's something in it we can use on the roof.'

'We can pry these shingles off for the roof, and these wallboards ought to fix the porch. Maybe we can make some shutters for the windows, too. What do you think?' Jimmy industriously scrambled about the shed in search of material.

'Shingles first,' Rebecca announced, rummaging through the shed's treasure of usable materials. There were wooden crates filled with moldy fruit jars, crock containers of various sizes, a rusty garden hoe, and a rake with a broken handle. Certain she would find a use for each of the items, she stacked them neatly in a pile to collect later.

They fashioned a makeshift ladder using boards from the shed, stripped and trimmed the used shingles, and commenced the patch job on the roof. The sound of hammer against nails rang across the valley floor. If the folks of the area hadn't been aware of her arrival before, they were now.

It was a new experience for Rebecca, but one she relished. With each nail driven home, her self-esteem soared upward a notch. It was her sweat and her labor going into this project; she couldn't help but feel pride in her accomplishments. Rebecca tried to imagine her sister with her skirts tucked between her legs, squatting on top of a roof, nailing on shingles. The image started laughter bubbling up from deep in her stomach and bursting forth in a gush.

Jimmy tore around the house, yelling at the top of his lungs, 'What's the matter? You okay?'

'I've never been better.'

She watched him return to the shed for another armload of used shingles, shaking his head. She imagined Jimmy mulling over the odd notions of adults. She smiled and shook her own head.

The afternoon sun was sliding across the treetops on its western decent when the roof repairs were finally completed to their satisfaction.

Rebecca was jubilant; her spirits soared, her despair forgotten. Leaning back on her heels, she wiped her sweaty brow and gazed about the valley from her rooftop perch. The peach, apple, and plum trees were in full bloom, their pink and white blossoms tempting the bees whose droning hum filled the surrounding air. A doe and her fawn grazed near the far side of the creek. She watched in awe as the doe left her feeding and proceeded to give her baby a bath, first licking its face and ears, then traveling the length of the spotted body to its white flag tail.

Watching the bath brought home the realization of how hot and sweaty she was. The sound of water in the creek, crossing the rocks in its path downstream, whispered to her temptingly.

'I need a bath. I think I'll visit the creek,' Rebecca called over her shoulder while gathering her tools.

She rummaged through her trunk until she found a suitable skirt and shirtwaist and a change of undergarments. Grabbing a towel and a bar of sweet-smelling lavender soap, she strolled off toward the creek. Since the well bucket needed a new rope, she took a bucket to carry water back to wash their supper dishes.

First she filling her bucket with fresh, clear water then, located a secluded spot on the bank, out of view of the house, where a huge willow grew near the water. Its overhanging branches dangled like lace curtains over the top of the water, dipping low and creating a screen of privacy.

It was sheer luxury to feel the cool, clear water rush over her tired, aching body. She lathered her hair twice to be sure the dust and clinging cobwebs were removed. Then she did the same to her body before lazily floating on her back, allowing the water to wash away the stiffness in her muscles.

Suddenly the mood changed. Icy fingers slithered up her spine. It was the same feeling she'd had that morning when she'd awakened to find the strange face peering in at her. Quickly, she stood in the water, edging slowly toward the bank and her clothes.

'Who's there?' She forced the words past her lips, doing her best to control her trembling limbs. 'What do you want? I know you're there, so say something.' Rebecca continued her retreat toward the creek bank. Once on dry ground, she snatched up her clothes and hastily dressed, not even bothering to dry off. While wrapping the towel about her dripping hair, she called out once more. 'I know you're still there. Show yourself.'

She jumped like a startled doe at the sound of snapping twigs and leaves in the underbrush and tangled vines growing near the water. She whirled about, and was momentarily speechless. Before her was the same face she'd seen spying through her window.

Rebecca's gaze locked on arresting green eyes. Green like expensive emeralds, densely fringed with dark, dusty lashes and arched brows like gleaming, golden wings above a narrow, upturned nose. Hair the color of ripened wheat framed the face. Her gaze dropped lower. Unironed creases revealed an altered hem in the faded pink dress that exposed bare feet and slender ankles. Rebecca looked up. Fear and uncertainty filled the young girl's eyes, and the two emotions tugged against each other. Rebecca saw the indecision of whether to run away or stay reflected in those amazing eyes.

'Who are you? Why are you watching me?'

The willowy frame remained poised for flight. Her fingers twisted apprehensively at the coarse fabric of her faded frock.

Rebecca saw the fear and recognized it, though she didn't understand it. Softening her voice to erase that trepidation, she again inquired, 'Who are you?'

No reply.

'Do you live around here?'

Silence.

The possibility of the girl being mute, or deaf, or perhaps both, crossed her mind. Slowly, Rebecca removed the damp towel from her hair, fluffing and combing it as best she could with her still-trembling fingers. She sat on the grass, her back toward the girl.

Talking as she worked, she slipped on her shoes.

'My name is Rebecca. I live over there.' She pointed toward her house. Unsure of what else to do, she continued to talk nervously about anything that came to mind.

A light touch on her hair was her first indication that the girl had moved. She'd approached without making a sound. Did Rebecca dare move? Unsure how to handle the situation but, certainly not wanting to frighten the girl, she continued to talk.

The hand drifted from her hair to her blouse, and Rebecca allowed the hand to explore. As it slid down the sleeve of her blouse, she said, 'Do you like it?'

'Pretty.'

The single word jolted Rebecca to her feet. At the sudden movement, the young girl leaped backward, her eyes nearly swallowing her face.

Rebecca reached for the girl's hand, took it in her own. 'Please, don't be afraid. I won't hurt you.' Smiling to soften her words, she added, 'I want us to be friends. My name's Rebecca. What's yours?'

'Girl.' Again, only one word.

At least she wasn't mute. Puzzled, Rebecca prodded. 'Girl? Is that your name?'

The stranger nodded once before dropping

her emerald gaze to her bare feet.

'Do your folks know where you are?'

An expression leaped across the girl's face before she turned quickly to look toward the creek, but it was gone when she glanced back at Rebecca. Had it been fear Rebecca saw dart across those lovely features? If so, what on earth was she afraid of? Who was this stranger? Where did she come from? Why was she so fearful?

There were no answers to her questions. Not now, at least. Perhaps she would find out later. For now, there was the girl who just stood there, as though frozen in time.

Rebecca still held her hand. She hadn't moved and hardly seemed to breathe. Surely this stranger wasn't afraid of her? 'Would you like to go up to my house and have some cookies?'

Green eyes darted a quick glance across the creek. Whatever she saw, or didn't see, seemed to satisfy her, for she smiled and nodded.

Rebecca gathered her discarded clothing and bath articles. Together they crossed the lush, green meadow. Rebecca was glad, not for the first time, that Louise had insisted on packing not only enough baked goods to see her through her trip, but enough to last until she was able to do her own baking. There was still a loaf of bread, a tray of gingerbread and a tin of sugar cookies. Glancing at the young girl beside her, she blessed her sister for her forethought.

It would have been hard to say who was more surprised when they came face to face, Jimmy or the girl. He bounded off the end of the porch just as they approached from the side of the house, landing smack in front of her.

The girl jumped like a frightened rabbit, darting behind Rebecca.

Jimmy's mouth flew open like a trap door. 'Who's that?'

Gently tugging the frightened youngster from behind her, Rebecca explained. 'This is our neighbor from across the creek.' Their guest stood with her head hanging down, peeking at Jimmy through her unkempt hair. 'My dear, this is Jimmy Johnstone, a friend of mine.'

There was no reply forthcoming.

Rebecca left the two young people shyly taking stock of each other and prepared the promised cookies on saucers. Rejoining the silent pair, she placed the treats on the porch in the shade.

They'd barely taken their seats when an eerie, high-pitched noise broke the strained silence. All three flinched in reflex to the sound.

'What's that?' Rebecca asked.

The girl bolted off the porch in a sprint. Quickly she returned, snatched the remainder of the cookies from her plate and stuffed them in the pocket of her none-too-clean faded dress. Glancing over her shoulder in the direction of the noise, which was repeated at short intervals, she sprinted off again. Stopping momentarily when she reached the edge of the creek, she turned and waved shyly, then splashed across the water and disappeared into the forest.

Jimmy watched until the girl was out of sight. With a baffled expression, he asked, 'Wonder what that was all about? Someone blows a horn, and she's off like a shot.'

'A horn?'

'Yeah. It's made out of a cow's horn. You hollow it out and cut the tip off, then blow on it to call your dogs and such.'

'Whatever it was, it certainly upset our new friend.'

'What's the matter with her, anyhow? Can't she talk? She didn't say nothing.' The boy brushed locks of his sun-bleached hair from his brow. 'But, she sure liked them cookies.'

Rebecca ignored Jimmy's remark about the cookies. 'She can talk. That much I know. Apparently, she chooses not to. When I asked her name, she said, 'girl.' ' Glancing briefly in the direction their visitor had departed, Rebecca continued. 'Something's very peculiar here. I suppose we'll find out what it is in time.'

'I reckon so.' Jimmy's eyes followed Rebecca's gaze. Then, with a slight shrug of his broad shoulders, he dismissed the stranger from his thoughts.

'I'll start some cornbread to go with our stew. You hungry?'

'I could eat a bear!'

4

Rebecca awoke the next morning before the first golden rays of the sun cleared the horizon. She wrapped a long robe about herself, padded barefoot to the kitchen, made a fire, and a pot of coffee. Then she took her steaming cup and slipped quietly out the back door. The air was crisp and clear. Dewdrops glistened like jewels on the grass. Pulled by an irresistible urge, she crossed the damp yard to the orchard. Standing beneath the blossoming trees, she breathed deeply of the perfumed air. Peace flooded her and she hugged herself with the joy of it. She felt more replete at this moment than she'd felt since her husband, Jonathan, died.

Somewhere in the distance she heard a haunting call. Wolf or coyote, she couldn't be sure. An answering yowl sent shivers dancing up her arms. She crouched beside an apple tree and watched the sun complete its ascent above the treetops, tinting the valley floor a rosy gold.

Her thoughts turned to the strange young girl who appeared and disappeared without warning. What sort of family did she come from? Why was she so reluctant to speak? Recalling the moment when callused fingers had touched her sleeve, she remembered they had been gentle, almost reverent. Not grasping or grabby. The girl's eyes, though filled with fear, had been warm, seeking.

Rebecca felt an immense desire to get to know this young woman. Not for curiosity's sake. No, it was more than that. It had no name; rather, it was something she felt but couldn't explain. She had seen her own need for acceptance mirrored in those brilliant green eyes. At that moment, resolve to know more about this young girl rooted in her soul.

Leaving her place beneath the blossoming fruit trees, Rebecca returned to the house and prepared a quick breakfast. It would be a long day.

After breaking their fast, she and Jimmy unloaded the furniture and together assembled the enormous four-poster bed. A massive affair, hand-carved of cherry wood, it belonged to her parents. The posts stood five feet in the air like sentinels above the feather mattress, which they fluffed before placing it on the frame.

Once the bed was made with fresh linen sheets and pillow slips and covered with her grandmother's hand-crocheted spread, Rebecca gazed at the effect lovingly. It truly felt like home now. She could sleep in a real bed tonight.

She heard the rusty creaking of the well-pulley and knew Jimmy was still working on attaching a rope and one of the water buckets to the pulley, so they could use the well instead of carrying water from the creek.

For the first time since her arrival, she felt in control. Everything was going perfectly. Just as she wanted.

While she was unpacking crates of dishes and cooking utensils and humming under her breath, a shadow fell across her shoulder. Glancing back, expecting to find Jimmy, she saw instead the girl with the haunting green eyes standing outside the screen door.

It was always the same, this popping in unannounced and unexpected. Rebecca's smile of welcome was genuine. So was the trembling in her knees, but she did her best to hide that. She wanted the girl to feel welcome to visit her any time.

'Good morning. I hoped you'd come by today.' Wending her way among the crates and boxes to the back door, she pushed open the screen. 'Please, come in. I was about to fix lunch. Can you — ?' Her words lodged unspoken in her throat when the girl stepped past her into the room. A dark, purplish bruise marred her left cheek. Rebecca's hand reached to touch the spot. 'What happened to you?'

The girl's hand flew up and brushed Rebecca's away, side-stepping out of reach. Dropping her head shyly, the girl stood silently dragging one dirt-encrusted foot across the other.

'Someone struck you.' Rebecca's voice was husky with emotion. 'Who?'

Silence was the girl's only answer.

The frenzied motions of the young hands twisting the pocket of her faded frock tore at Rebecca's heart. Realizing her attitude was upsetting her guest, Rebecca changed tactics. Moving slowly across the kitchen, she finished her earlier invitation. 'Will you stay for lunch?'

Inwardly, Rebecca fumed as she set out their lunch. The idea that someone, anyone, would strike this child with sufficient force to leave her face in that condition was unthinkable. Watching her visitor while she worked, Rebecca couldn't help but wonder again what sort of family she came from. She noticed how attractive she was, or could be, with a bath, clean hair, and a clean dress. Those eyes! And when she smiled, her face glowed like an autumn moon.

'Here, you set the bread on the table while I dip up our stew.'

The meal was a strained affair. Rebecca did her best to ease the tension at the table, receiving only an occasional non-interested reply from Jimmy, who was more absorbed in the girl than in eating.

Their guest devoured her meal with a singular devotion. She looked neither right nor left while she consumed an amazing quantity for one so slender.

They were having dessert on the porch when Rebecca heard sounds of a horse approaching in the distance.

Glancing over his shoulder toward the ridge, Jimmy commented, 'Looks like you got company coming, Miss Rebecca.'

An expectant silence settled about the trio like a foggy mist. They watched a lone rider approach. The breeze, which only moments before had caressed them gently, ceased as though it, too, waited. The birds stopped singing. No one moved. A shadow crossed the yard. Glancing up, Rebecca saw a dark, ominous cloud obscuring the noonday sky. Only moments ago it had been sunny and clear.

Another change was taking place as well. The girl beside her was noticeably agitated. Green eyes darted to and fro, from the approaching rider to Rebecca, then back again, like a rubber ball. Her fingers absently worried the seam of her dress, twisting it into a tight knot. Her behavior reminded Rebecca of a cornered fox with the hounds at bay.

Standing, Rebecca placed her hand gently over those fidgeting fingers. 'Do you know this person?'

The frightened young girl darted behind Rebecca as if placing a barrier between herself and danger then whispered timidly, 'Preacher.'

As though he'd been shot at, Jimmy whipped his head about and stared open-mouthed at the girl. He'd never heard her speak, and like Rebecca, he'd apparently thought her mute.

'Why would you be afraid of a preacher?' Rebecca broke the awed silence with another question. She turned fully to face the trembling girl. A tangle of wild, blonde hair sprouting from the bowed head shielded her from Rebecca's probing eyes.

When Rebecca turned to face her impending visitor, trembling hands reached out and grasped hers in a death grip. Rebecca pulled the girl closer to her side, patting her slender shoulder reassuringly. She watched him draw nearer, wondering what would prompt such a violent response at the sight of this man.

The lone rider entered the yard and walked his horse to the porch. Tipping his hat, he introduced himself.

'Howdy-do, ma'am. I'm Zakeriah Daniels, the preacher in these parts. Heard back in the settlement you'd moved in.' Relaxing in the saddle, the man pushed back his hat. 'Thought I'd drop by and welcome you to our neck of the woods. Don't reckon you'll be getting much of a welcome from most folk around here; they don't cotton to outsiders. Where's your man?' His gaze swept the area. 'Surely a fine figure of a woman like you's got one. Ain't you?' He boldly looked her up and down as if she were a horse he was considering buying.

Rebecca suspected his attitude was no ruse and had little, or nothing, to do with her. Zakeriah Daniels obviously thought well of himself. He no doubt officiated at the services for those that married and those that died. He'd probably baptized a few of them. He would know them well, be acquainted with their sins. She had met his type before and suspected he showed no sympathy for them. Their sufferings, both spiritual and physical, probably evoked no emotion in him.

Rebecca didn't care for his arrogance or his audacious examination. 'I thank you for your welcome, Mr. Daniels.' Her words were measured and spoken slowly lest she lose the fragile thread of her self-control. 'I don't have a man. I'm a widow.'

The girl took a step backward as though she would flee. Rebecca reached and took her hand and smiled reassuringly at her, then turned back to her visitor.

'I'm called Brother Zake by my friends, ma'am. You can call me Zake.' Again, his bold gray eyes traveled the length of Rebecca's frame. 'Widow, huh? Well, you won't be long, I'll wager. Won't take long for you to hook yourself a man. Yep, might even be interested myself if you're a Christian lady and a good cook.' A leering smile tugged the corners of his hard mouth upward. 'Course, I'd settle for the good cook, and take worry about the other later.'

'Say, ain't that the Penny girl behind you?' Ignoring Rebecca, he leaned forward in the saddle. 'What are you doing here, girl? Your Pap know where you be?' Pointing a stubby finger in her direction, his next words were an order. 'You better be getting now, before I tell him you was loafing around over here. You know he ain't gonna like you hanging around strangers. Get on home now, and I might not tell on you.'

'Mr. Daniels, I thought you said you're a minister,' Rebecca said. 'I've never met a minister quite like you, who goes around threatening and frightening children. Furthermore, I'm not looking for a man to get my hooks in, as you so rudely put it. But if I were,' she paused and took a deep, calming breath, 'be assured, you'd never be a candidate. Good day to you . . . Mr. Daniels.'

Turning her back on him, still clutching the girl's hand, she started for the door. A throaty laugh halted her retreat. The irony in her voice was apparently lost on him. Rebecca turned around. He was leaning his forearm on the saddle horn, watching her with a curious frankness and a leering smile.

'My, my, what a temper. Yessirree, I do like a woman with fire. We'll make a fine team, you and me. Course, you'll take some taming, but I can handle that. Look forward to it, even.' He straightened and motioned with his hand. 'Don't worry about what I said to the girl. She probably don't understand half what I said, anyhow. She's half-witted, you know. Frightened of most things.'

Throwing his arm in a wide arc, he rushed on. 'Besides, you got to keep these people in line, else they get above themselves and start sinning.' Bringing his outstretched arm forward, his hand doubled into a fist, he struck an imaginary pulpit. His voice rose to the occasion. 'A heavy hand, that's what's needed. Put the fear of God in them.

Yessirree, the fear of God.

'Now that we got that out of the way, tell me what a little thing like you is doing out here all by your lonesome.' Daniels leaned back in his saddle. 'Say, this young feller here ain't your son, is he? You don't look old enough to be his ma.'

His was a ruthless, dominant look, from his black, coarse hair and cynical, cold gray eyes to his prominent dimpled chin, and hard, cruel mouth. Rebecca gazed at the firm, inflexible planes of his dark face. Noticing his hands, square, thick, and large, she felt icy chills clambered up her spine.

A little thing like her? She simmered inside. Her patience was as thin as ice in a spring thaw. Gritting her teeth, Rebecca pulled herself to her full height of five feet nine inches. This man was undoubtedly the most arrogant and conceited person she'd ever met. She lifted her chin so she was looking down her narrow nose at him.

'Mr. Daniels, this young man is Jimmy Johnstone, a friend of mine. And for your information, though it's none of your business, I'm here to share with my new neighbors the love of God, not the fear of Him. And to help with the sick, if they'll let me.' She glanced at the timid figure beside her.

'I sincerely doubt this child is simple-minded as you say. Now, once again, good day to you. I have important things to do.' Turning quickly, she stepped inside, leading the girl with Jimmy following close behind.

Laughter and the clatter of departing hooves filtered through the open door where they stood in the center of the front room, gazing vacantly at each other. Rebecca was caught by surprise when the girl suddenly threw both arms around her neck and kissed her cheek. Then she quickly withdrew, dashed out the front door, across the yard, and then the creek.

'Wonder what made her cry?' Jimmy was the first to speak. 'She was crying when she hugged you. Wonder why?'

'I don't know, Jimmy. It seems there's a great deal I don't know about our little friend. Like her name, or why that so-called preacher frightened her so. But at least we know her last name. He called her 'the Penny girl.''

5

A thunder of suspicion rumbled through the area. The hills within a fifty-mile radius of Ten Mile Creek vibrated with the news. Strangers were in their midst. Questions abound. Who were these strangers? Where were they from? What did they want? Speculations varied. Suspicions rose. The inhabitants of the hill country were distressed by the intrusion. But, being cautious, they waited and watched.

★ ★ ★

The mystery surrounding the girl nagged constantly at Rebecca. As anxious as she was to meet her neighbors and begin the work she'd come here to do, she couldn't concentrate on anything but the Penny girl.

She kept busy to still the questions tumbling through her mind. The boxes containing her food staples were unpacked. Rebecca mixed bread dough for a couple of loaves of yeast bread. Setting the dough aside to rise, she buried sweet potatoes beneath the ashes and hot coals of the fireplace to bake for supper.

Jimmy had gone off earlier to set traps for quail, and to try his luck at squirrel with his slingshot. He'd promised to show her how to set game traps before he left for home. Rebecca didn't care to dwell on that eventuality. She'd grown quite fond of the freckle-faced youth, and knew she would miss his lively company.

The smell of yeast filled the kitchen with aromas from her childhood. Memories from her childhood replaced her concerns about the Penny girl momentarily. Rebecca's mood lightened at the images. Finally, gazing about the room, she was satisfied with her afternoon's labor.

Wiping her hands on a tea towel, she nodded in satisfaction. Taking cookies from a tin, she dropped them in her apron pocket and stepped out into the warm afternoon sunshine. She needed a walk, a breath of air.

Jimmy had gone toward the pecan grove, so Rebecca strolled in the opposite direction. No need to hinder his hunting. Her swift, sure strides reflected her mood as she crossed the creek. A soft, gentle breeze whispered through the leaves overhead and rippled the silver glitter of the water's surface. The woods were alive with sounds of spring: cooing of the mourning doves, creaks of tree frogs, the shrill call of a rain crow.

Enthralled with her surroundings, distance and time were of no consequence. Slowly, a whimpering sound penetrated her awareness. Rebecca tilted her head to one side and listened, attempting to locate the source of the sound. To her right, in a briar thicket, the whimpering sound was repeated. Without conscious thought, she left the animal trail she'd been following to push her way carefully through brambles, weeds, and briars, knee-high and clinging, toward the cry. Rebecca felt the prickly thorns grasp and snag her skirt, impeding her progress.

Pushing aside a large, dangling grapevine the size of a man's arm, she gained the center of the thicket. With an audible gasp, she froze at the gristly sight before her.

Two furry bodies lay side by side in a crimson pool of blood. The smallest animal lay snuggled near the lifeless body of the larger one as though seeking protection. A gaping wound ran the length of its body. Its life pumping away with each beat of its heart, it lay whimpering, watching Rebecca's approach.

Recovering from her shock, she knelt down beside the bloody figure. When her hand reached to stroke its head, she was stunned by the reception she got. Desperation born of fear and pain overpowered its weakness, and the furry animal bared its teeth and snapped at her outstretched hand. Realizing her mistake, Rebecca drew her hand back lightning-quick.

Talking quietly, she attempted to ease its fears. 'I won't hurt you, little fellow. I want to help. What did this to you, huh? Won't you let me help you?'

Remembering the cookies in her apron pocket, she slowly withdrew one and held it out toward the animal. Suspicion and pain filled the furry creature's eyes as it watched her. Cautiously, Rebecca opened her hand and held the cookie under his nose and waited.

Once more she reached out slowly to stroke the shaggy head. This time he let her touch him without a sound, appearing too weak from loss of blood to resist further. If she was to help him, there was no time to lose.

Warily, the injured animal inspected the hand holding the treat, sniffing it on both sides. Then, seemingly satisfied, he snatched the treat between his teeth and lay his head back on the ground, exhausted from his efforts to defend himself and get the food.

Working quickly, Rebecca removed her apron and spread it on the ground. As gently as she could, she eased the small body onto it. Wrapping the apron snugly around the bloody body, she gathered him up and started back to the house.

On the way home, the animal whimpered and opened his eyes briefly. Rebecca crooned softly to him in reassurance, wishing her own fears could be as easily soothed. His wound would require stitches. She could only hope there was no damage to his intestines, because repairing them was beyond her training.

She placed the bloody bundle on the porch then went in search of her sewing kit. She dropped a threaded needle and her embroidery scissors into a pan, then poured boiling water over them. Next, she found clean linen rags to cut and use for bandages. After scrubbing her hands, she was ready to begin.

Her patient lay where she'd left him, too weak to move, and barely able to whine as she took the first of many stitches down his left side. It didn't seem at all strange that the first one she'd helped since her arrival was an animal with its side ripped open. He'd been in need, and she was there.

Rebecca applied an herbal salve to the stitches and was wrapping the linen bandage around the small body to hold the delicate stitches in place when Jimmy rounded the corner of the house. Two young fox squirrels dangled by their hind feet in his left hand.

Her young hunter froze when he saw what she was doing. Dropping his squirrels to the ground, he blurted, 'You know what that is, Miss Rebecca? Get rid of it, quick!'

'Of course I know, Jimmy. It's a puppy. I just finished sewing him up.' She saw the color drain from Jimmy's face.

'That ain't no regular pup. Nosirree, it's a wolf cub, and it's dangerous. Besides, its mammy will follow its scent here to find him, and then you sure enough got trouble. Better let me take him back where you found him, before she finds him here. She-wolves are right mean about defending their younguns.'

'It's all right, Jimmy. His mother's dead. She was slashed to death and this little thing was lying beside her, near death, when I found him. What do you suppose did this to them?'

Color returned to his freckles and he visibly relaxed. He watched while she continued to wrap the bandage. 'Probably a wild hog. Lots of them around. I saw tracks while I was hunting. Yep, probably a wild hog. What you gonna do with him? Can't keep him! They're too mean to keep.'

'I haven't thought about it . . . what I'm going to do with him, I mean. I only wanted to fix him up. He was in pretty bad shape when I found him. I suppose I'll decide that once he's stronger.'

'He'll leave. Soon as he's able, he'll sneak off. Best that way, anyhow. They's too mean to keep. Never heard of one staying around folks no how.' Seemingly satisfied that he'd settled the issue, Jimmy's attention returned to his stomach. 'Hey, I almost forgot. Look what I fetched for our supper.' He bent to retrieve his squirrels.

'Manna from heaven, meat for supper.' Rebecca gathered up her sewing equipment and went to wash up on the back porch.

They both ate with a ravenous appetite that evening. Rebecca had baked the bread in the fireplace, and they pretended not to notice the ashes on the tops of the loaves, or that the bottoms were brown on one end and black on the other.

Jimmy had soaked the squirrel in salt water for half an hour before cooking to remove the gamy taste. They were young, tender, and cooked to a fine turn, spitted over the fire. Both were crispy outside and juicy and delicious inside.

Rebecca removed the ribs and put them on to boil for her patient's supper. He would need to eat if he was to recover from his ordeal with the wild hog.

After supper they sat on the porch. She

de-boned the ribs and fed the cub. He lay quietly, eating from her hand as though it were natural to do so.

'If that don't beat all,' Jimmy said, watching the feeding. 'I never would have believed it. A woman feeding a wolf cub. Sure do beat all.'

Rebecca saved the broth to make mush for the cub's breakfast. Jimmy made a bed for the cub using a wooden crate with a burlap sack for padding. Rebecca placed it beside her bed.

They were awakened sometime during the night to the sound of rolling thunder, and lightning cracking, and rain blowing in all the pane-less windows.

Jimmy dashed inside, dragging his bedroll pallet. He was already drenched to the skin, his hair plastered to his head. He dropped his bedding and scrambled to help Rebecca move her bed to the center of the room, out of reach of the blowing rain, then moved the cub's makeshift bed. 'Got to do something about them windows first thing in the morning,' Jimmy mumbled, shaking like a dog to free himself of the clinging rain.

'You'll get no argument from me.'

Together they scrambled about, distributing pots and pans to catch the rain. Had there been any doubt, the rain confirmed that the shingles needed additional work.

Dodging the moisture, Jimmy explained how he could fix the leaks with tar.

'We don't have any tar,' Rebecca reminded him.

'We can make it. I seen Pa do it lots of times.' He pushed a lock of damp hair from his forehead. 'All you need is a pine tree heavy with resin, a wash pot, a big rock, a small piece of tin, and a good hot fire. I'll show you tomorrow if it quits this raining.'

'You make it sound so simple. What would I have done if you hadn't agreed to come with me?' Tugging at the rain-splattered hem of her robe, she glanced toward the young man across the room. 'In case I haven't told you so before, I'm truly grateful for all you've done for me. I don't know how I'd have managed without you.'

Apparently embarrassed by her expression of thanks, Jimmy lowered his head to hide the blush creeping slowly up his neck to his freckled face.

'Aw, shucks, weren't nothing. Besides, I was glad to come.'

'Nevertheless, I do appreciate it.' Her gaze swept the ceiling, checking for additional leaks. Finding none, she dried her hands, ready to retire once more to her featherbed. However, the cub had been disturbed by the move and started whining. Leaning over his box, Rebecca made soothing sounds and checked his bandage for drainage or signs of fresh bleeding, talking soothingly as she worked. The wolf cub raised his head and licked her hand. 'Are you hungry, little one? Is that what you're telling me? Okay, then, I'll see if I can find you something to eat.'

Fishing the remaining few bites of meat from the pan of broth, she fed her hungry patient. He immediately returned to sleep. She noticed Jimmy standing in the doorway watching her. A puddle formed on the floor where he stood.

'You'd better go dry off and change out of those wet clothes,' she told him. 'You can make your pallet in the kitchen by the fireplace. It's warmer there.'

She returned the bowl of broth to the kitchen and picked up the lamp from the table, adjusting the wick. 'Before something else happens, I think we'd better try to get some sleep. Good night.'

'Night, ma'am.'

6

Rebecca awoke the following day to the bright morning sun filtering through the open window, casting rays across her bed. She stretched leisurely, enjoying the feel of the mattress caressing her. Her sleep had been the sleep of contentment.

The ring of an axe slapping wood and the cub whimpering to be fed reminded her of the day's work awaiting her. She also remembered they hadn't worked on the porch yesterday. Instead, she'd worked on the cub. She put on a pot of coffee and a pan of water to boil for their breakfast mush, then went to investigate the sounds of the axe.

Jimmy glanced up when he heard her approach. He waved, then wiped the sweat from his flushed brow with the back of his hand. 'Morning, Miss Rebecca. Thought I'd get an early start on them leaks this morning. I found a big rock down the creek a ways that'll be just fine. And there's a couple pieces of tin under the wagon seat. Now all we need is a lot of wood for a hot fire, and this here tree cut up in chunks to fit the wash pot.' He stooped and retrieved one of the big chips he referred to. 'See the resin running out of the bark here? That means it's fat with resin.' When her expression remained blank, he dropped the block of pine and wiped his hands on the damp grass. 'Oh, well, I'll show you when I get it cut up.'

'What can I do to help?'

'You could maybe fetch lotsa dry wood along the edge of the woods there, and take it down to that big rock by the creek. I done took the wash pot down. I'll be done here pretty soon.'

Rebecca gathered what she considered an adequate supply of dead limbs and branches, and was resting from her labors when Jimmy arrived with an armload of cut and split pine wood. The smell of pine resin permeated the air.

'What do we do now?'

Brushing the sticky bark from his bare arms, he looked sheepishly at her woodpile and shyly replied, 'Get more wood. That's enough to start with, but we're gonna need lots more.'

'Oh.' Wearily, she resumed her chore. There was an ample supply of deadfall in the area. By the time Jimmy felt they had sufficient wood, she was drenched in sweat and had discovered muscles she hadn't known existed. They all ached. 'Now what?'

'Well, I got the pine chunks packed in the wash pot. Now we put this here piece of tin on this big rock. I've already bent it so's it'll make a trough to form a runoff for the tar. If you can help me lift this pot of pine chunks up, we'll turn it upside down on the tin. Ready?'

After considerable straining and re-shifting their load, they got it in place.

'Now what?'

'Find some clay. Can you get me a bucket or a big pan to put some clay in? I seen an old lard can out by that shed. I need it, too.'

Rebecca went in search of the lard can, hoping her young friend knew what he was doing because she certainly didn't.

When she returned with the requested items, Rebecca found Jimmy jubilant over his success. He'd located the clay. Grabbing the pan, he dashed off down the creek to collect his prize. Jimmy used just enough water to form a putty-like mixture to seal off the rim of the wash pot with the clay, leaving an opening over the bent trough in the piece of tin. Beneath the lip of tin, he placed the lard can near the edge of the rock. Next, he broke up the limbs and branches Rebecca had gathered, piling them on and around the iron kettle. Then he set fire to the mound of wood.

'Now, we just keep that fire hot and wait.'

Gathering his tools, he started toward the house.

'You're a wonder. You know so much for one so young,' Rebecca complimented him.

'Aw, shucks, ain't nothing.' He gazed back at his handiwork with a self-satisfied grin stretched from ear to ear. 'I could sure use some grub. How about you?'

Oh no! She'd forgotten the coffee and the pan of water.

Jimmy could only watch and wonder when she broke into a sprint.

Both pots had boiled dry. The coffee grounds were scorched. 'Oh, bother! What next?' she muttered aloud, knowing she shouldn't have asked when the cub set up a weak howl and started whimpering. 'I know, little fellow, you're hungry again,' she crooned, carrying his box-bed into the kitchen so she could watch her coffee and mush cook while she fed him.

Breakfast was a hasty affair, with Jimmy rushing back to tend the fire and keep it burning hotly. Rebecca relaxed over a final cup of coffee before she joined him.

When she rejoined him, she noticed a thin trickle of liquid dripping from the tin trough into the bucket. Red-tongued flames licked the air, consuming the wood while heating the wash pot to a glowing amber.

While the tar cooked off, Jimmy worked on making wooden shutters for the windows. He pried off usable boards from the old shed and dressed them out, saving the larger pieces for use on the porch. Rebecca busied herself with scrubbing cabinets and lining shelves with the old newspapers from her packing. Then she unpacked her dishes and kitchen supplies.

By supper, they were both pleased with their joint accomplishments. Jimmy had completed and hung the shutters, which were a bit crude but adequate, dressed out enough boards for the porch repair, and collected a lard can of tar for the roof.

Rebecca had her kitchen set up and ready for use, which she proved by making a dried apple pie for their desert. It was to have been a pie, but it ended up a cobbler. Since she didn't have an oven, she had to cook it over the fireplace. That experience convinced her to invest in a cookstove. At any rate, they relished the cobbler while relaxing from their day of labor.

Jimmy offered to feed the cub while she straightened the kitchen and cleared away the supper dishes.

'What the . . . ? You little devil!'

What could be wrong now? Drying her hands on a tea towel, Rebecca went to investigate the commotion. 'What's wrong, Jimmy?'

'That little rascal snapped at me when I reached in to pick him up. He's a regular devil.'

'Did he break the skin on your hand? Here, let me look at it.'

'Naw, it's awright, but I reckon you'd best feed him. Looks like he's gonna be a one man, excuse me, a one woman cub, don't it?' Glancing up at her, he asked, 'By the way, what are you gonna call this vicious little critter, anyhow?'

Watching the cub, he leaned back on his heels and pushed an errant lock of hair from his forehead. ''Peers to me he ought to have a name. You thought on a name for him?'

'To be honest, I haven't really considered it. Besides, I don't see any point in naming him. As you said earlier, he'll leave as soon as he's well.' Retrieving the object of their discussion from his makeshift bed, Rebecca sat down beside her young companion.

'Yeah, but we need to call him something till then,' Jimmy persisted.

'I suppose you're right,' she replied, sensing that naming the cub was somehow important to him. Besides, what harm would it do? 'It seems to me you've already given him a name.'

'Me? I ain't named him.'

'Sure you have. You've called him 'devil' at least twice tonight.'

'Aw, shucks, ma'am. You can't call the critter 'devil.' Fitten, mayhap, but not much . . . much . . . what's the word for it?' He scratched his head in distraction, fumbling for the right word. 'You know, somethin' what means 'special'.' Jimmy glanced from the cub to Rebecca. 'He is, you know. But what's the word for that . . . special?'

'You mean class? You think he should have a name with class?'

'Class, yeah, that's it.'

'Well, let's see. How about Diablo? That's got class, and it's also fittin', as you said.'

'Diablo. What's it mean?' the young man asked, a puzzled expression creasing his brow.

'Diablo is a Spanish word. It means devil. So, you've named him after all. What do you think of it?'

'Diablo.' He rolled the word across his tongue, considering it, testing it. 'Yeah, it's got a nice sound to it. Yeah, I like it,' he replied, gazing fondly at the young wolf pup.

'Well, let me see if our Diablo is ready for his supper now.' She checked his bandage before feeding him and found it clean, with no sign of infection. 'So far, so good, little one. You may make it yet.' The remark slipped

69

out without conscious thought; still, she instantly realized how negative the statement was.

She had come here intending to help heal and teach faith for healing according to the Word, and she sounded like someone with either no faith, or no knowledge of it. This, she realized, was the result of becoming so preoccupied with everyday things that she had neglected the things of the Spirit. This thought only served as a reminder that when you feed your body three square meals a day and toss your spirit a cold snack in your spare time, your spirit becomes weak, which results in a weak faith. And she knew that without faith, it was impossible to please God. Rebecca resolved then and there to resume her daily devotions and meditations. She couldn't afford to have a weak spirit, or faith. Not now. Not ever.

With that decision firm in her heart she began to pray, in the spirit, for the healing of the young cub's weak and torn body. She placed her hands on the bandage covering the many stitches down his side as she prayed, and immediately felt the power flow from her hands into his battered flesh. The young cub became very still, ceased his whimpering and slipped into a peaceful sleep.

Though he hadn't been fed, the cub rested.

Jimmy squatted beside her. His expression was one of awe and bewilderment.

'I ain't never heard nothing li — like that before, Miss Rebecca. Wh — what's it mean?' Jimmy stammered his question.

'It's okay. I've never done that before, pray for the healing of an animal, I mean.'

'You was praying? Didn't sound like no kinda praying I ever heard. I couldn't understand a thing you said. Was it that Spanish like you said Diablo was?'

'No, not exactly. It's a prayer language. An unknown tongue, some call it. I don't even understand what I've said when I pray in the spirit.'

'Praying lingo, huh? And it were for healing the cub? Do it work? I mean, how come you thinking God gonna heal that wolf cub when there's so many sick folks and He ain't healing them? Does God love animals more than folks, you reckon?'

Rebecca knew his question reflected his confusion. She could almost see the questions bumping into each other in his head. Questions forming faster than he could voice them as he sat wide-eyed and silent. She returned the sleeping cub to his bed, then stood. Shaking the wrinkles from her skirt, she tousled Jimmy's hair playfully.

'Let's get another helping of that apple

cobbler and a cup of coffee, then go sit on the porch. I'll try to explain it, as I know it.'

So Rebecca explained to Jimmy about healing, as the Word of God told it. 'You see, Jimmy, God wants us all well and healthy. And He provided the means for that. Just as Christ died on the cross for our sins, He also died for our healing. It says in First Peter Two, verse twenty-four: 'Who Himself bore our sins in His own body on the tree that we, having died to sins, might live for righteousness — by whose stripes you were healed.' Also in Isaiah Fifty-three, verse five, it refers to our being healed by His stripes.'

Glancing at the silent figure beside her, she asked, 'Did you notice, Jimmy, it said were healed, meaning we are, not will be, healed?'

'What for it say that, you suppose? I know lottsa sick folk. How come they's sick if the Bible says they's healed? I don't rightly follow all this.' Setting his cup and saucer aside, he sat silent for a moment, his brow furrowed in thought. Gazing back at Rebecca, he voiced his concern. 'Besides, the preacher back home says all that healing and miracle business done gone and passed away. You know, with the early church, whatever that means. How you gonna explain that one?'

'He's been deceived by Satan, Jimmy, who wants us to believe that lie. Then he'll be able

72

to dump his sickness and diseases on us. Satan deceives all who listen to him, and sometimes it's very easy for him to deceive those with a religious spirit, even pastors. They mean well, I suppose, and for the most part, they are sincere. But according to the Word, they're sincerely wrong.' Rebecca stood and stretched the cramped muscles in her back, giving Jimmy a moment to consider what she'd just told him.

'At any rate, that's why I've come to the hill country. To prove that God is still in the healing business, just as He was when Christ walked the earth, healing all those who were oppressed by the devil. And for those who don't know yet, or don't have the faith to receive their healing . . . ' Rebecca perched on the edge of the porch beside Jimmy before finishing. 'Well, I'll help them get well with man's medicine. After all, God uses man to do His work here on earth.'

A gentle breeze filled with the sounds of evening cooled their tired bodies. A calm peace wrapped its arms about the two sitting side by side in the twilight.

'I just don't know about all this. Gonna have to do me some studying on it, so's I can get it straight in my mind.'

'That's an excellent idea. I'll give you some more Bible passages before you leave for home that refer again and again to God's healing power, and how we know that we, His children, are to use that power. But for now, what do you say we retire? It's been a long and tiring day.'

★ ★ ★

At last, the repairs to the house were completed. The leaks in the roof were coated with tar. All the weak or rotten boards were replaced on the porch. The days were full of activity, but the house was now comfortable and livable. It had become their custom to retire to the front porch for a last cup of coffee following their evening meal, to discuss the day's accomplishments.

This was the first chance, since last night, for Rebecca to check on Diablo's condition. She'd fed him twice during the day, but as soon as he'd eaten, he drifted off to sleep again. So as they sat with their coffee, she lifted Diablo from his makeshift bed and gently unwound his bandage. The young cub did not whimper tonight, as was his usual response to her disturbing his wound. Instead, he tried to lick her hands as she worked gently to remove the linen strips binding his stitched side.

Once the restrictive binding was removed,

the pup began to wiggle and attempted to stand in her lap. Though his small legs were shaky from inactivity, after a couple of tries he managed to stand and immediately began licking her hands again and wagging his tail happily, much as a small dog would do. He was obviously glad to be free of the constraining dressing.

Rebecca, fully aware of the power of prayer, was nonetheless overwhelmed by the manifestation of the results. To see a miracle was always a blessing. What she found beneath the compress was indeed a miracle. Not only was there no evidence of drainage or signs of infection, there were no ragged edges of raw flesh visible. Just the neat row of stitches she'd sewn.

Jimmy, who hadn't been too attentive to the cub, was startled by the sudden and unexpected sharp yelps from the animal. 'What's the matter with him? He hurting or something?'

'I don't think so. Come see for yourself.'

Jimmy examined the cub. 'Hey, I don't believe it. He's up, and feisty as can be. He's been so weak. He hardly ever moved at all. And now look, he's feeling frisky as a colt in spring. His side is all well, too. I can't hardly believe my eyes. It's so ... so ... ' His freckled face turned from the animal to

Rebecca. 'Hey, wait up a minute. Is this here what you's talking about last night? 'Bout that praying and healing and power and such? Is this it?'

Jimmy's excitement was genuine. His eyes were bright in the twilight as he rushed on. 'If it is, it sure enough works. I ain't never seen nothing like that before.'

'Yes, Jimmy. This is the result of last night's prayer. I tried to explain it, but I suppose this is the best example, the results. What do you say we let our young patient try his legs?' Rebecca set the furry animal down and immediately he scampered across the newly repaired porch, yelping and wagging his tail. After exploring from edge to edge, he bounced over and scrambled onto Rebecca's lap where she sat next to his bed. His frail, tiny body shook all over as he licked her hands and face and yelped softly.

'I think he's saying thanks, ma'am. Just look at him; he's right happy. Sure enough wouldn't have believed it if I hadn't seen it.'

'That's not faith, Jimmy. Seeing is not faith. Faith is believing what you can't see.'

'I don't know about all that. I just know what I'm looking at, and its got to be a genuine miracle.'

'That it is, Jimmy. That it is.'

They sat in silence, watching the frolicking

cub and pondering the joy of it. The darkness edged closer. Sounds of evening filtered through the night.

'Kinda a shame the girl weren't here to see it, though.' Jimmy's comment broke the serene silence between them. 'Wonder where she's been lately? Ain't seen her in a day or two, and she was here most every day before that preacher man come by. Suppose he spooked her off?'

'I certainly hope not. I'd like to get to know her better. I hadn't realized how long it has been since her last visit.'

'Sure hope she comes again before I have to leave. Like to say bye to her. She's kinda strange, but sort of nice, too, ain't she?'

What's this? Was Jimmy infatuated with their odd guest? His comment sounded like more than idle curiosity. But then, stranger things had been known to happen. Her musings remained her own. No need to embarrass him.

'You mentioned leaving. When do you plan to go? I hate to even talk about it; I've enjoyed your company so much. I'm going to miss you.'

'I was thinking about tomorrow. 'Less you need me to fix something else, or you need to go down to that settlement and maybe get supplies. I ain't got to go tomorrow, it's just I told Pa I'd come on back home soon's you got all set up. Matter of fact, I kinda hate to go. I like this here place. Real pretty country, too. I'll miss it.' He hesitated only slightly before adding, 'And you too, ma'am.'

'I don't need supplies, and I can't think of anything else I can't finish up myself.'

'Then, I guess its tomorrow. Might as well get to bed. I'll start bright and early in the morning. Be a long, lonesome trip home, I expect.'

'Good night, then. I think I'll put our sleepy friend to bed and retire myself.' She looked down at the cub resting comfortably in her lap. A miracle indeed.

7

After an ample breakfast of fried salt pork, sour dough biscuits, water gravy, molasses, and coffee, Jimmy departed with the first glow of the sun.

Rebecca stood on the porch watching as he drove the team and empty wagon out of the yard. The horses had fattened up, she noticed. Grazing and roaming at will for the past six days had done wonders for them.

As she stood gazing at the disappearing trio, she lifted her hand to wave good-bye and realized Jimmy's attention was on a figure standing near the timber line at the edge of the creek. It was the girl. The young man lifted his hand and waved, and the girl echoed his action.

Rebecca stood pondering this latest development in the mystery of the girl while she watched her last tie with home disappear from view. It struck her that she was truly alone now. On her own. Succeed or fail, it was up to her. No more relying on someone else to do it for her, or even to help. No one to give advice. No one to say, 'It can't be done.' 'Okay, Lord, it's just you and me now.

Show me the way and I'll follow.'

'Huh?'

The sound jerked Rebecca from her thoughts, and only then did she realize she'd spoken aloud. She turned to find the girl standing at the edge of the porch gazing up at her with doe-like eyes. Wonder of wonders, her hair was washed and combed. The early morning sun set golden highlights winking through the glossy strands.

'Did you say something?' Rebecca asked, trying not to show her surprise at her visitor's changed appearance.

'You was talking and ain't nobody here. Why?'

'Oh. Well, actually I was thinking out loud.' She swung her hand toward the doorway. 'Have you had breakfast? There's plenty left. I was just going to have another cup of coffee. Join me?'

'I ate already.' She gazed wistfully down the lane. 'Where's he going?'

'Jimmy? He's returning home. He only came to help me move in.'

'He coming back?'

'I don't know for sure, but I hope so.'

'Me, too.'

'You're very talkative this morning. I don't believe I've ever heard you talk this much.' Her natural curiosity got the better of her

80

manners and she asked, 'Why?'

'Nothing to say. No one to talk to. I like talking to you. You don't yell at me, and I ain't afraid of you. You's kind to me.' The soft-spoken reply seemed to come from the top of her head as she stood dragging her toes in the dirt, staring at the ground.

'Well, I'm glad you're not afraid of me. You have no reason to be. I hope we can be friends. I need a friend. You're the only person I know here. Would you mind showing me around and maybe introducing me to some of the families in the area?'

'Folks around these parts don't much cotton to strangers. But, I'll show you around if you like. Wanna go now?'

'Why not? I'll get a shawl.'

They walked for endless hours, sauntering through the woods which the girl seemed to know well. Rebecca was sure she'd have become lost on her own, yet the girl always knew exactly where she was, and how to get where she was going. The areas they traveled were isolated, and filled with wondrous sights.

They observed squirrels frolicking from tree to tree feeding on the young, tender tree buds and leaves just forming as spring arrived in the back country. They flushed several covey of quail from the underbrush during their walk. The girl showed Rebecca berry patches, wild plum thickets, wild cherry, and mulberry trees. Rebecca tried to remember their locations for future use. They'd be great for jellies, jams, and pie making.

She also pointed out an unusual plant she referred to as 'poke greens'. It had pinkish-green stalks about three inches tall with pale green leaves.

'They's best ate when small like this, but can also be eaten when bigger, except they ain't as good, and don't never eat the berries from the big plants,' she instructed her fascinated listener.

Along with this bit of information came the warning that the plant was poison if not cooked properly. Rebecca wondered why on earth a person would want to eat such a thing. Yet she was assured the plants were quite delicious, and even good for you. Her guide promised to show her how to prepare them properly. Rebecca decided to wait to form a final judgment until then, but she couldn't say she was overly anxious for the lesson, either.

Though the sun was out and the sky cloudless, the air was chilly in the shaded areas beneath the trees where they walked. New grass and wildflowers carpeted the ground. The girl stooped to examine the blooms. Her lovely face reflected her pleasure. She touched one of the snowy white petals with her work-worn finger.

Kneeling beside her, Rebecca reached out to the flowers nestled in the grass. 'They'd look nice on the kitchen table. Help me pick a few.'

Before she could snap the first stem, she felt a restraining hand on her arm and heard the pleading in her voice when the young girl said, 'Don't. They're too pretty to kill just so we can fancy them a short spell.'

Rising, Rebecca smoothed the front of her dress. Gazing intently at the girl, she was surprised to find tears glistening in the corners of her expressive eyes. What a gentle, bewildering creature she was. Smiling, Rebecca took the girl's hand, giving it a gentle squeeze. 'You're right. We'll leave them.'

As their walk progressed, Rebecca concluded that this young, mysterious girl was neither simpleminded nor slow as that so-called preacher suggested. She chattered almost non-stop with a wealth of information on the plant and animal life. It amazed Rebecca at the difference between her behavior of today and that of her previous visits.

'By the way, I still don't know your name.'

'They calls me Girl.'

'But, you must have a name.'

'That's it, Girl,' she replied softly.

'Who calls you Girl?'

'Everybody. Pap and the boys.'

'I see. Well, what about your mother? What does she call you?'

'Ain't got no ma. She died when I's born. That's why I ain't got no name. Pap blames me for her a-dying. So, he just calls me Girl.'

Rebecca heard a painful cry of hurt in her reply. 'You poor child! Well, I can't just call you Girl. What if you and I give you a name? Would you like that?'

'Pap won't like that, not a bit.'

'We could keep it our secret, just between you and me. Would that be okay, do you think?' Even as Rebecca asked, a quiet voice inside reminded her it wasn't right to encourage this young person to be deceitful. Yet, she was suggesting she keep something from her father. At the same time, Rebecca couldn't help believing the good would outweigh the bad in this situation. She had seen the quick glimmer of hope dance in those eyes at the mere suggestion of a name. She needed and wanted a name of her own. Imagine being called Girl all her life, because her father blamed her for a death she had nothing to do with. The risk and any consequences would be worth it, she resolved.

'You think it be awright?'

'I do! What would you like for your name?'

'Don't know.'

'Well, let's see, how about Mary? No.' Rebecca cupped the girl's chin with her hand and tilted her face upward, toward the morning sunlight. Such a lovely face.

'Martha? Abigail? Rose? Wait, I know. How about Megan? You remind me of a Megan I once knew. She was pretty and bright like you. Do you like the name Megan?'

'You think I'm pretty?'

'Yes, I do. So, would you like that for your name? You know, not everyone gets to choose their name. Our parents choose it for us and we go through life being called by their choice, whether we like it or not. So, you're lucky. You can pick your own. How about that?'

'Megan.' She rolled the word across her tongue as if tasting, sampling it. 'Yeah. I like it. I be called Megan Penny.'

'How do you do, Megan Penny? It's nice to make your acquaintance,' Rebecca said with a smile.

Megan lit up like a sunbeam with a grin that included her eyes. Eyes Rebecca noticed were almost always sad.

'What do you say we go have lunch? We've walked for hours, and I've worked up an appetite. How about you?'

'Lunch? You mean dinner? If it be dinner time, I best be getting home. Pap be mad as a hornet if I'm late fixing his dinner.' Unconsciously, her callused hands twisted the fabric of her faded dress. Already her joy of the morning was fading as if she had only now recalled she shouldn't be with an outsider.

'Can you get back on your own? You just go straight that-a-way.' She pointed in the direction Rebecca was to take.

'Sure, I'll make it fine. Don't get in trouble because of me,' Rebecca cautioned.

'See you,' she quipped, departing at a lope.

8

After a leisurely walk back to the house, Rebecca spent the remainder of the day sorting through her memory of the events of the past week. Storing information, recording it, sharing in her journal with her beloved Jonathan, this new life. It had been more than thirteen years now since that senseless accident took him from her, yet she still couldn't accept it. She knew he was gone, that she would never feel him hold her again. Never hear his laughter or see his smile. Yet, it was all so needless. She went over the incidents of that fateful Fourth of July repeatedly, to no avail.

Why? Why was it him crossing the street that day when a drunk started firing his gun into the air to celebrate the Fourth, and spooked the unattended team of horses hitched to a wagon loaded with lumber? The frightened animals ran over Jonathan before he could get out of their way.

Their one year together wasn't enough, not nearly enough. Yet, that single year held more happiness than some couples knew in an entire lifetime.

Being a widow at nineteen had been difficult to bear. She supposed though being a widow at any age wasn't easy. She felt her life had only begun when suddenly her beloved had been taken from her, and she was left an empty shell. The light of her life was snuffed out and she roamed in a dark world, searching for herself.

Rebecca had always been someone's daughter or sister, and for a very brief time, wife. Then she was alone, on her own. Needless to say, she'd been ill equipped to deal with such a situation. In the end she returned home to live with her parents, their little girl again. To be fair, she'd needed that comforting cocoon existence for a period. Time to adjust, to grieve, to . . . what? That became the next question. To what? She could only attend so many teas, plays, cricket matches, bridge games, quilting bees, and literary readings. Was that to be her life? Everything within her screamed, NO! Surely there must be more to life than that. But what?

Then the visiting missionaries came and told her church about the need for missionaries in foreign countries, a work that required willing workers. Well, she was willing, and probably needed to do the work as badly as the missionaries desired it done.

So, she attended the nursing classes they taught in preparation for field work. Not a lot of detailed nursing, just fundamental, basic training. The rest would be done by trained doctors and nurses. The trainees were to be helpers only.

She completed the course, very excited about the opportunity to use a skill needed by others. At last she could become more than a fungus on society. Rebecca could do for others, instead of being done for. Then came the unexpected blow. Unattached females weren't allowed by their group to go into the field. They were considered unstable and unreliable, soon giving up because of the heavy demand of the work, or getting married and leaving.

She supposed the Missions Committee felt justified in their reasoning, but it seemed unfair to her. She knew she could handle the work and responsibility. And never, ever would she again consider marriage. She'd given her heart to Jonathan, and just because he was gone didn't mean she'd ever stop loving him. For her, love was forever. Jonathan would have her heart forever and always.

The missionaries were unshakable on their policy, and she returned to square one. What now? That question was soon answered in a most unexpected way. Her mother took ill and then took to bed, never to leave it until she died. Following the death of her mama, her papa lost his will to live and soon joined his beloved wife.

Yes, she'd cared for their needs during those frustrating years, yet she was never able to convince either of her parents of the healing abilities of the Lord. That had been the most important thing she'd learned from the missionaries, that God was still in the healing business.

First Peter Two, verse twenty-four, says, 'Who Himself bore our sins in His own body on the tree that we, having died to sins, might live for righteousness — by whose stripes you were healed.'

'Yes,' her Papa would say, 'but the preacher said all that went out with the early church.'

'But Papa, what about the verse that says, 'God is the same yesterday, today, and forever'. And, 'He is no respecter of persons'?' she would reason with him.

'Daughter, I don't like the new ideas those folks have filled your head with. Your mother and I have been believing it this way too long to change now. So, you just keep those notions to yourself. If it were true that our Lord still heals folks today, I'm sure our pastor would tell us.'

So, she had cared for and buried them both. It was after the loss of her parents Rebecca made the decision to do something with that wonderful truth she'd found. She knew in her heart of hearts that God still healed today, just as He did when He walked the earth. He healed those who were oppressed by the devil. And for those who couldn't, or wouldn't, believe for their healing, you treat with medicine, man's way. But she knew she must try, and if not in China or Africa, then the hill country.

Her friends and most of her family thought she'd gone off the deep end. They couldn't understand her decision to go to the southeastern corner of the territory of Oklahoma, Indian Territory, to minister to the sick in body and spirit. After all, they reasoned, she would be leaving behind her a life of ease for a life of uncertainty, hardships, and goodness knows what else. They constantly reminded her of the type of people she'd be dealing with: superstitious, suspicious, and uneducated. Some even suggested that she suffered from the complaint of women at a certain age, and surely was not responsible for making her own decisions.

She supposed she deserved that type of comment. After all, she hadn't made a decision of her own in over thirty years, with the exception of choosing to marry Jonathan. Yet, she knew this was something she must do. She was tired of being an empty sponge, soaking up the leftovers from other people's lives. She must live for herself, not through others, not through books. She must do this for herself. And she knew she would never be alone in this undertaking, God would walk with her every step of the way.

9

April 21, 1895, my thirty-third birthday. It isn't the age I regret, it's all those wasted years. But I intend to spend at least the next thirty-three years making up for all that useless time.

Rebecca set the pen aside and re-read her journal entry. Through the open shutters sounds of morning floated across the valley as the countryside greeted the dawn. Leaning forward, she watched the big, bright orange sun, as it broke above the scraggly shoulders of the hills in the distance. Birds sang, and frogs formed a choir as they serenaded the morning. Squirrels barked one to another, welcoming the new day.

She pulled the robe closer about her body and listened to the joy of the world around her. Glancing once more at the journal entry she'd just made, she closed the book. *Wasted time. No more*, she thought.

Rebecca remained faithful to her journal, recording her thoughts and actions daily. Since Jimmy's departure, her chronicle had been her only companion. For the first time in her life, she knew what it meant to be physically alone. She had been lonely, but never alone. It was a new experience, and one she found she enjoyed. She uncovered depths and facets of herself she had never known before. This was a time of getting acquainted, of learning who and what she was.

I have so much to learn, she thought as she put the leatherbound volume away. But how was she to know others if she didn't first know herself? The question haunted her. It wasn't knowing herself that disturbed her. Her problem was more complex: how was she to meet her new neighbors?

Before her work here could begin, she had to meet those she came to help. Daily, she explored the surroundings of her new home, hoping not only to familiarize herself with the region, but to meet its inhabitants. Anyone.

Her excursions provided plenty of fresh air, exercise, and vistas that delighted her sense of adventure. Nothing more. Except for a short visit from Megan one afternoon, she hadn't seen a living soul. There was plenty of evidence that people resided and worked nearby, woodsmoke trailing above the tree-tops from chimneys, felled trees, neat stacks of wood, cut and ready to move, but no people.

'This wouldn't have been a problem back home,' she muttered as she dressed. 'I would have been met by the welcoming committee and introduced to the community.'

Dragging a comb through her long tresses, Rebecca laughed aloud at the thought. 'So much for the social amenities of the locals. Maybe I could give myself a party.' Pitching the comb onto the dressing table, she frowned. 'You sound like Louise now,' she mouthed at her reflection in the mirror. She grabbed a shawl from the hook beside the door. It was time for her daily walk.

Today turned out different from her other trips. She'd roamed farther afield than she was wont to do when she became aware of a most peculiar odor. Not unpleasant, but different. It wasn't a smell she associated with anything she was familiar with, nor could she relate it to the surroundings. She took a deep breath, filling her nostrils with the scent. Leaving the animal trail, she followed the telltale odor until she located its origin.

Surprised at what she found, she studied the contraption emitting the unusual smell. It appeared to be a large, copper soup kettle partially covered with mud, an oven of an odd type beneath it, and a fire made of long ash logs that protruded from the oven. A copper pipe extended from the top and coiled into a keg of water, then reappeared at the bottom of the barrel, dripping clear liquid into a funnel cradled atop a gallon jug.

Rebecca stood within the small confines of the laurel thicket surrounding the contrivance and observed that the center of the shrubbery had been masterfully cleared away to form the roomy setting where she stood. Only the odor wafting from its leafy walls had given away the secret within. Otherwise, any passerby could walk within feet of the hideaway without detecting it.

She noticed other unusual objects contained within the odd thicket-room. There were several hogshead of white corn that appeared to be sprouting, as if left in the rain. Who would have been so careless to allow good corn to get wet and germinate? If cared for properly, those brimming casks could have produced enough cornmeal to feed several families.

Someone had spent a great deal of time and energy on the concealment of this area, and it was obviously well cared for. Everything was orderly, even the several dozen quart fruit jars that were neatly lined up. Even the logs, approximately six feet long, took up one side of the cleared area were stacked with care. Yet the disregard and neglect of such an amount of good corn didn't fit into the picture.

Another mystery.

The abrupt sound of branches and twigs snapping jolted Rebecca from her wool gathering. Someone was approaching, probably the owner of this hidden hoard of puzzles. Instinctively knowing her presence wouldn't be welcome, she made a hasty retreat, her heart thrumming in her ears.

Several minutes later, and at a safe distance from her latest source of bewilderment, she roamed aimlessly in a dazed condition. Her attention was so absorbed she even forgot her ever-present companion, Diablo, who trailed along in the timberline.

Her foot encountered an unseen bundle on the ground. In mid-stride, she attempted to check her progress and nearly fell when she tripped on the small pile of bones, covered with a much-washed, oft-worn dress. With an exclamation of startled surprise, she righted herself and observed the bulk in her path. Leaning closer for a better look, she noted it was human, and surprisingly alive.

'I'm sorry, let me help you,' she stammered gently helping the aged woman to her feet. Rebecca felt her jaw drop open and her eyes widened. The aged woman appeared nothing more than a collection of bones loosely covered with deeply etched leathery skin. Rebecca couldn't begin to guess her age.

Then Rebecca met her eyes. Her eyes

belied age: they were young, filled with peace; sad, filled with knowledge of life; laughing, filled with joy. Oh, what eyes! Rebecca stood transfixed in silence, her mouth still agape like a dolt.

'Chil,' you be awright?' The query stroked her ears like smooth satin. What a contradiction, the body reflecting an age to match original sin and the eyes and voice of springtime.

'Yes. Yes, I'm fine,' Rebecca sputtered, struggling to compose herself. 'Are you okay? Did I hurt you?'

'Bah! Take more than a little shake up like that to hurt me.' Her age-spotted hand smoothed her apron and brushed twigs from her dress. 'Who you be, chil'? Where you come from?'

'I'm Rebecca Rice. I just moved into the Williams' place.'

'Reckon we be neighbors of sorts, then. Folks here about call me 'Ole Woman.' I take care of their ills.' Her fragile hand brushed at loose blades of grass clinging to the hem of her white apron. Her eyes never left Rebecca's face. 'When folks get sickly, they send for me, Ole Woman. That's what I's doing now,' she gestured toward a basket, 'collecting herbs for my medicines.'

When Rebecca failed to respond to her

comments, the satin voice asked, 'You sure you be awright? Look a mite peaked.'

'I-I'm sure.'

'Well, then, you can help.' It wasn't a question. She pushed a woven container toward Rebecca. 'We'll talk while we work.' Thus, the two women spent the remainder of the day.

As the old woman gathered herbs and plants, she explained the purpose of each and how she stored and prepared them for use in her home remedies. There was chamomile for cramps, headaches, and digestive disorders; horehound for sore throats and as an expectorant; lavender and lemon balm for sedatives; peppermint for indigestion and gas, toothaches and gum pain; thyme, which had antiseptic and expectorant properties; sassafras for tea and blood building; wild cherry barks, willow bark and leaves, roots of the mayapple, bark of the persimmon, red oak and white oak. The list appeared endless.

Rebecca noticed during her discourse that the main additive to most of the concoctions was whiskey. Being naturally inquisitive, Rebecca asked, 'Where do you get the whiskey for your remedies?'

'There are ways, and then there are ways. Why you wanting to know?'

Rebecca unexpectedly found herself telling

the aged healer her own dream of helping the people here with her nursing skills, and concluded with a request for the old woman's assistance.

'With your knowledge and my training, plus what you could teach me, we could be quite a team. And if I'm to make your concoctions, I'll need a supply of whiskey.'

'I see.' The gnome-sized figure stood, gently rubbed her forehead as if deep in thought. 'Let me think on it. I'll see what I can do.'

'Thank you,' Rebecca replied, then found herself sharing the other part of her dream, that of the Lord's healing power by faith.

At the conclusion of her tale, the tiny woman gently shook her head.

'What's the matter, don't you believe in faith healing?'

'Oh, yes, chil', I believe. I always has, but folks around here won't believe it. Besides, you gonna have a powerful enemy working against you, even if the folks wanted to believe.'

Rebecca frowned. 'An enemy? I don't understand. Who?'

'You will. You will, chil'. Wait 'til you meet up with the preaching man. He won't cotton to the idea of you teaching the folk about healing and love and forgiveness and such.

Nosirree, he ain't gonna be a bit happy about this.'

'Why? I thought perhaps he'd help me.'

'Chil', you got a lot to learn about folk around here in general, and about the preacher in particular.' She paused a moment and wiped her gnarled hands on the edge of her white apron. With those knowing eyes, she held her listener's attention. 'Preacher Zake got a good thing going here. He ain't gonna want you to go tearing down his playhouse.'

'What do you mean? I've come to help, not hurt.'

'Well, like I said, he's got a good thing here. He makes a right comfortable living off the folk here abouts. He feeds off their natural fear and superstitions. In this way he controls them. He don't pay me no mind, 'cause I don't interfere with his message of 'Hellfire and Damnation.' I just tend to their bodies and don't tamper with their spirits.' The old woman wagged a finger at Rebecca. 'But you, gal, he ain't gonna ignore you and your message of love and healing. You best be fearful where the preacher be concerned.'

The old woman stooped to gather up the basket of herbs. When she straightened her diminutive body, her aged bones creaked in protest. 'Now, then, how about us going back to my place and having us a nice cup of hot sassafras tea, and you can tell me more about these plans of yours.' Linking her frail arm through Rebecca's, she smiled warmly and said, 'I'm thinking I be for helping you, girl. Ain't been in the midst of a good fray in a coon's age, and this one has the makings of a good one. Never did cotton to that preaching man myself. Too self-important, he be. If he had the love for the people what he got for himself, it would be a different kettle of fish.'

Less than a half mile later, the women left the dense timber of hardwood sprinkled with wild plum thickets. When they encountered a split-rail fence of cedar logs snaking crookedly about a cleared area, Rebecca instinctively knew they had reached their destination.

Rebecca's steps faltered as she approached the dwelling, noting how it huddled in a small hollow between two low hills. In the quiet of the peaceful setting, she heard the unmistakable sound of a bubbling spring flowing somewhere behind the two-room log house.

She followed the old woman through the arched gate and up the winding path of flat, lichen-splattered river rocks. Everything was immaculate, wearing the signs of loving care. Halfway down the walkway, Rebecca stopped to admire the beauty and serenity of the place. She noticed the flower beds overflowed with early spring blossoms: asters, hollyhocks, larkspur.

Chickens and guineas scratched industriously near the porch, while a spotted cow grazed peacefully behind the house. Three long clotheslines were loaded with clothes flapping in the afternoon sunshine. Long, narrow strips of bleached linen dangled like limp noodles beside yards of spotless white aprons. Rebecca turned to inquire about this oddity and found her hostess patiently waiting a few steps away.

'That's the badge of my trade,' the old woman informed her. 'Always wear a white apron. It makes folk comfortable, makes them think you know what you're about.' She flipped one gnarled hand toward the clothesline. 'And them linen strips, they be bandages. Always make your own, that way you got them and you knows they be clean.'

Rebecca was rudely reminded of her constant shadow when she heard a commotion behind her and whirled around to investigate the source. In the midst of flying feathers, she spotted the fluffy ball of fur. Rebecca had completely forgotten about the wolf cub. Since her unexpected meeting with the amazing old woman, she hadn't given him a thought.

Whatever his intentions had been when he

approached the hens, he surely didn't expect to be the recipient of the vicious flogging he received. Rebecca didn't know who was most frightened, but Diablo was protesting the loudest, with full-throated yelps of pain and fright.

Rebecca quickly dashed into the center of the hen pecking to rescue the cub from his own folly. Just as she retrieved him and stepped back to a neutral zone, the guinea fowl became agitated by the sudden movement, sending up their alarm of 'putt-rak, putt-rak,' which only served to frighten Diablo more. Snuggling into the curve of Rebecca's arm, he hid his head and vibrated like a leaf in a storm. Her soothing ministrations to the cub were interrupted by a gleeful outburst of laughter.

'Chil', you gonna be right good for me. I ain't had so much excitement in — I can't remember when.' She swiped at her moist eyes. 'Been meaning to ask . . . ' her gaze dropped momentarily to the trembling animal. 'Where'd you get the wolf cub, and how come he stays with you?'

Rebecca related the story of how she'd found Diablo. She finished with the fact that the young pup slept in a box by her bed, and accompanied her everywhere.

Those knowing eyes gazed at her as if they

were looking into, instead of at, her when she said, 'Yes, indeed, Rebecca Rice, you'll do the Lord's work awright.' Her head bobbed toward the small animal. 'Even that critter trusts you, and that's not a natural thing for a wild creature. But he knows, he senses, as only animals, or the very young and old can, there's love and peace in you. Welcome, chil'. Welcome to the hill country. I've waited a long time for you.'

She embraced Rebecca with her spidery-thin arms, and Rebecca knew she'd acquired something very precious, a friend. She was left to wonder what the old woman meant by saying she had waited for her.

Rebecca had no way of knowing then as she stood gaping at the apparition, that she had just blundered into the greatest source of help in her undertaking of healing here in the backwoods.

While her hostess prepared the tea, Rebecca scrutinized her surroundings. They fit Ole Woman; everything was aged, yet showed loving care and attention. She was the jewel, and this was her mounting.

10

The bud of friendship formed in April blossomed in May. The old healer insisted Rebecca spend part of each day making rounds with her to families in the area. Her excitement matched Rebecca's. The plan could have been her own.

'No time like the present. Sooner they get to know you, the better.' Eyeing her new friend, Ole Woman gauged the response to her next remark. 'Be patient with them. It'll take time for them to warm up to you.'

'Well, I've got plenty of that.'

If Rebecca didn't receive the warm welcome she hoped for, she struggled to hide her disappointment from her new friend. Her brother, James, might have been right after all. Maybe these people didn't want her here, interfering in their lives.

Rebecca trudged along, the silent partner. If they weren't receptive to her presence, the same couldn't be said of her patron.

'Get that flea-ridden hound out of the house and keep it out.'

'Yes, ma'am.' Eyes downcast, a sheepish grin on his stubble-shadowed face, the owner of the offending hound backed out the door, hat in hand. The scenario had become a familiar one by now. The hill people's response to this dwarf-sized woman was astonishing. Even the men-folk deferred to her judgments. Everyone treated Ole Woman as though she were the matriarch of these hills. It was evident in everything the old healer did, that hers was a labor of love. And the people left no doubt she was loved in return.

Most of the families they visited appeared to be healthy and happy, with only minor complaints to be tended.

Then she met the Snodgrass family.

When they climbed the grimy steps to the lopsided door, five sore-infested urchins dashed past in a blur. Rebecca's tongue stuck to her teeth, refusing her utterance as she stood just inside the door. The shack was as filthy as its inhabitants.

A narrow strip of sunlight slanted across the room, illuminating the scrawny figures huddled in the center of the floor. From the protective folds of their mother's faded skirt, five tiny faces peered at Rebecca while, like a brood hen protecting her chicks, the weary young mother clutched her young close to her thin body. Wide-eyed and runny-nosed, the towheaded tots were stair-stepped in size.

Shoes were as scarce as hen's teeth; not a shod foot in sight. And if appearances were proof, there hadn't been a face washed, nor a head of hair combed, in heaven only knew how long. The bedraggled young mother didn't appear to be out of her teens, yet the strain of overwork and successive childbearing had already taken their toll.

The old woman took all of this in at a glance. Then, with tiny fist planted on each hip, she unwound like a spring tornado. She snatched up a straw broom leaning against the crooked doorframe, and with arms flailing like windmill blades, swept squawking chickens from beneath the table into the yard.

Figuring he was next, the tomcat wisely chose to leave under his own power. He cleared the distance between the unmade bed to the open door in one leap and hit the ground squalling. Two piglets sunning on the porch were propelled into the grass-barren yard with one quick swipe.

When the dust cleared, the pale-faced young husband willingly toted water from the creek. Then starting with the wash pot, he filled every container in sight. Before his empty bucket hit the ground, Ole Woman slapped a bar of soap in his hand, her finger pointed like a compass needle toward the washboard. Rebecca watched in amazement as the tiny woman took charge.

As though resigned to the inevitable, he lifted his thin shoulders in a half-hearted shrug, then attacked each piece of clothing with his cake of soap, rubbing it generously before dropping it into the wash pot to boil.

It was late afternoon before the meager collection of clothes and bedding were completed. But the goddess of clean wasn't through. Each child was given a turn in the tubs of rinse water. One tub of water scrubbed away the layers of grime, while the other was used for hair washing. Then a bucket of clean water rinsed away the suds. The youngsters found the whole procedure amusing as they splashed about from tub to tub. But their father wasn't delighted when he was sent to tote more water.

Before being released, Ole Woman examined each child from head to toe, then vigorously applied one of her concoctions to each sore, tick, or mosquito bite. When the applications were complete, she gave the remainder of the herbal salve to the young mother with instructions on how, and when, to apply it.

But, Ole Woman didn't stop there.

'Cora Mae, I've told you before, you gotta keep these younguns and this house cleaner. You don't keep them clean, one of these days they's gonna take down with something I can't treat.' Glancing toward the open doorway, she spied two speckled hens hovering in the shadows. A flap of her apron sent them dashing for cover. 'And keep them critters out of the house. Ain't fittin' for them to be inside no how. You hear me, girl?'

'Yes'm, I hear you. I try to keep the younguns clean and the place, too. It's just I'm so tired all the time.'

'Then get that man of yours to help you.'

'Horace?' Eyes big as saucers, the young woman replied, 'Why, that's woman's work. He can't help me.' Shock vibrated her voice.

'He can't, huh? He helped me today. It won't kill him to do a little woman's work. Besides, way I sees it, he helped you get all them younguns. Won't hurt him to help take care of them.' Her eyes narrowed to slits and her voice elevated when she continued. 'And while I'm on the subject, remember what I done told you about no more younguns? Not for a while, leastways. Your body needs a good long rest, or you be in an early grave. You hear me?'

The work-worn young woman's head fell forward, her hair covering her face as she stammered her reply. 'But . . . but my man, he likes . . . ' Her voice faltered. One bare foot idly drew circles on the freshly scrubbed floor.

'I know what your man likes!' the old woman snapped before the girl could finish. 'I'm looking at the results of what he likes. What that young man needs is to be kept busy planting something besides babies. Keep him good and busy all day, mayhap he be too tired come night time for what he likes so often.' Abruptly, she turned and stalked from the room, missing the embarrassed look on the girl's face.

With a shy peek at Rebecca from beneath the limp strands of hair, Cora Mae busied herself with the youngest child, ignoring her visitor as effectively as if she weren't in the room.

In fact, the entire day's work had been accomplished with a minimum of words spoken, and the majority of those were from the old woman.

Rebecca stepped outside onto the uneven porch. The sun nestled in the treetops. It had to be near five o'clock, and they had a long walk ahead of them. They'd have to leave soon or they'd be making their return trek in the dark. In the shadow of trees at the edge of the clearing, Rebecca spotted Diablo, nervously pacing. He, too, realized they must leave soon.

The cub never entered the yard area of any of the dwellings where the two healers visited. He always waited just outside the boundary of the yard space. Once Rebecca remarked on this peculiar habit of his to her new friend.

She'd laughed and replied, 'Wolves never come near humans less they's starving or got the fits.'

'But he comes near you and me, and we're human.'

'Not to him, we ain't. You be like his mama to him, and he senses my spirit's too old to do him any harm. So, we don't count. But he'll shy away from others.'

Rebecca was snapped out of her remembrances by the sound of the old woman's voice. Normally when she spoke, her voice was soothing to the ears, like water trickling over pebbles in a brook, soft and gentle. Now, however, it resembled water gushing from a broken dam. Rebecca glanced around, searching for the uproar, and observed the small woman and young Horace Snodgrass behind a shed back of the house. They were deep in conversation.

Perhaps conversation wasn't the correct term to use. The old woman talked with much finger pointing, and Horace listened intently, nodding his head from time to time, with a whipped-dog expression on his young face. From what she could observe from her place on the porch, Rebecca decided to stay put. She felt quite sure neither party would welcome her presence at that particular time.

Waiting for the matron of the hills to rejoin her, Rebecca stood in the warmth of the dying sun and inspected the surrounding terrain of this pitiful excuse for a house. The yard was all hard-packed earth, no green grass anywhere. An attempt to grow flowers had been made, but the results were pathetic. More weeds than flowers thrived, and the few survivors were sad specimens. The majority became casualties of the chickens, who took dust baths in the center of them. But this feeble attempt at beauty endeared the young woman inside to Rebecca's heart. So young, yet so old, and not yet twenty. Worn out from childbearing; too many, too soon.

If only Cora Snodgrass would talk to her, perhaps Rebecca could help. But as yet, her presence hadn't even been acknowledged. *Give them time*, the old woman had said. *It takes time for these people to accept you, or anyone else from the outside.*

Rebecca stood on the front porch, contemplating. How much time did this young woman have? Three, four, or maybe five more babies before she's used up, and dead before her time. Yes, these were the ones who needed help, the ones like Cora Mae Snodgrass. 'Hurry up, Time, let me in,' she mouthed softly.

'Let's be going, chil'. We's done all we can here, and it be dark soon. If we don't hurry, we'll be keeping the fireflies company.'

Ole Woman's statement pulled Rebecca from her mind-wanderings. Glancing around, she noticed the sun was almost gone from view. They would indeed have to hurry.

They departed the Snodgrass' without a word of leave-taking. When Rebecca commented on this, the old woman replied, 'They know I'm gone. Ain't no sense in telling them.'

The young cub joined them as soon as they stepped into the wooded area where he had waited patiently for their return. He ran circles around them both, licking Rebecca's hands as he passed, his tail wagging so furiously he appeared in danger of being knocked over by it.

'I take it you're glad to see me, boy,' Rebecca crooned, reaching down to stroke his head.

'Ruin him doing that.'

Rebecca straightened. 'Doing what?'

'Petting that critter on the head. It ruins dogs.' Those all-seeing eyes narrowed as they observed the frolicking animal. 'Expect it do the same for wolves. You don't never pet them on their head. You pet them on the back or side, but never on the head.' A distant look appeared in her eyes before she continued. 'My man, he was always saying that, and he had the best hunting dogs in this neck of the woods. Reckon he knew best. Never allowed nobody to pet his hounds on the head.'

'I see.' She didn't, but saw no sense in arguing about it. To change the subject and satisfy her curiosity, Rebecca asked, 'What were you and Horace talking about back there by the shed? He looked like you'd given him a box full of rattlesnakes to hold.'

'Same difference, I reckon. I laid the law down to that one. 'If you don't want to put that pretty young wife of yours in an early grave, you best mind what I'm telling you, son. Work off some of that fun-loving energy you got. Give that little gal in there a break,' I says to him. I says, 'Put some of that energy to use. Raise a garden to feed these younguns you already got. They needs fresh greens and vittles. Not just varmint meat all the time.' ' She stretched her shoulders up and rubbed the small of her back, then went on, 'He could kill two birds with one stone, so to speak.'

'Do you think he will? Raise a garden, I mean.'

With a chuckle, the velvety voice replied, 'Yes to the first, no to the other. He'll raise a garden, cause I can see if he do or don't. I believe I made him understand about the need for greens. It'd help them babies not to have so many sores and infections. For the other, well, he'll probably try for a while, but he's young. I'll no doubt be sent for ten, eleven months from now to deliver Cora Mae of a new mouth to feed.'

Then with a sigh, she muttered, 'It's always the same, the spirit's willing, but the flesh be mighty weak.'

11

They continued in silence for a distance, both lost in their own thoughts. Finally, Rebecca asked about the reception she received everywhere they visited, or rather, the lack of it.

'Like I told you before I took you on rounds with me, you gotta give them time to make up their minds about you. You be an outsider to them, and most folk hereabouts don't cotton to strangers none. They ain't trustful of outside folk. They's waiting to see what you want. Why you're here.'

'But, you didn't mistrust me. You accepted me right off. Why don't they, if you did?'

'Chil', let me explain something. I'm accepted by these folk 'cause I been here longer than most of them been alive. But I ain't one of them. And they all, without exception, will tell you I'm from the outside. You see, I wasn't born here like they was. I was brung here as a bride of fifteen. My man, he was hill folk, but he married an outsider.'

Once more, that faraway look filled her eyes as she recalled the past. 'I don't think they ever fully forgave him for that. Anyhow,

I've lived here ever since my man brung me here. I've born ten younguns, buried eight of them, and my man, too.' Her gaze drifted to her young friend, gauging the response to her words. 'It weren't till after my man died and their ole granny midwife passed on about the same season, that the folks began to act like I might belong here after all. You see, it were known I had some skill with herbs and teas and setting bones, but I weren't never called on by none of them till their own healer died, and then they be needing me.'

Her thin shoulders lifted in a gentle shrug to her confession. 'Most folk I treat now, I helped bring into this old world. The folks what were here when I first come, they's mostly all dead now. I've outlived them all. Now it's me, the outsider, what's taking care of their younguns. Strange, ain't it?'

'I suppose.'

Instead of comforting, Ole Woman's story only disturbed Rebecca more. What if she, too, had to endure a lengthy span of years before she was accepted? Deep furrows creased her brow.

'Doesn't it bother you, at least a little, that they treated you like that until they needed you?'

'That be a queer thing for you to ask. You the one be knowing about the Lord's teaching on love.' She smiled as she said this last statement to let Rebecca know it wasn't said as a reprimand, but as a reminder.

'I know, but somehow things here are so different. So confusing. I catch myself slipping back to man's way of seeing things instead of seeing it through His eyes.'

'Just relax, chil'. Learn to relax. It'll all fit together in time. You can't push it.'

They continued to walk. Both lapsed into a comfortable silence, once again lost in their own thoughts of the day, the events, even the past. In the distance, a cowbell tinkled. The older woman broke the silence to remark, 'Bossie be calling me soon. It's way past milking time, and she'll be ready. You may as well stay at my place tonight; getting too dark to see, anyhow.'

Her bony hand stroked Rebecca's arm. 'Besides, it be a real comfort to this old soul to share the place with someone besides my memories. You be staying?'

Responding to the silent plea in the velvety voice, Rebecca answered, 'I'd like that. I'll feed the chickens while you milk. I never learned to milk a cow, but I can scatter feed.'

'Never mind the chickens.' A twinkle took residence in those eyes. 'Ain't no time like the present to be a-learning to milk. Does a body good to learn something new now and again.'

So, Rebecca got her first experience at milking a cow. Her futile attempts kept her tutor in stitches of laughter. After several false starts, she finally managed to produce a meager amount of milk in the pail before she was gently pushed aside.

'I'll finish it up now. Leastways you got the idea of it.'

They ate a cold supper. Her host explained, 'You best cook enough food in the mornings to last through the day, keep from heating up the house too much in spring and summer. 'Course, winter time don't matter none, fire's a-going, anyhow.'

Together, they cleared away the supper dishes and straightened the kitchen. Then Ole Woman put on a pot of oats to soak for their breakfast.

'Time to set this old carcass down for a bit of rest. Let's set on the porch a spell afore we retire. Bring your shawl, it be a mite chilly at night still.'

Rebecca followed along behind the gnome-sized woman she'd become so fond of in such a short time. Ole Woman was a constant source of amazement. Gazing down on her diminutive height, Rebecca realized that she would make two her size. Besides being at least fifty years older, she often made Rebecca ashamed of herself with her endless energy.

Rebecca was tired long before the older woman suggested a rest. *What an amazing person she is,* Rebecca thought.

Once they were comfortably seated on the rocking chairs on the porch, the old lady busied herself with something taken from her apron pocket. Rebecca looked on while she completed the task, then struck a match. In its glow, Rebecca watched her hold the amber tip to a pipe squeezed tightly in her lined lips. A corncob pipe.

When it glowed to her satisfaction, she held it out to Rebecca. 'Take a draw, it'll help to shut your mouth.'

Rebecca snapped her jaw closed, unaware until then it had fallen open in her utter surprise.

'You smoke?' It was more an exclamation than a question.

'That, and a few other unladylike things.' She took a deep drag on the pipe and released the smoke slowly, then smiled at her companion. 'It comes with age, being able to do what you please without the bother of caring what folks gonna think. You ought to give it a try, loosen up and relax. Learn to be yourself, Rebecca Rice.' Her internal glow was visible even in the twilight.

'Folks'll either accept you for what you are, or they won't. And if they don't, they wasn't going to no how,' she proclaimed with a deep sigh.

In the approaching darkness the evening came alive. Fireflies winked their lights to a rhythm only they knew. Bullfrogs and tree frogs serenaded with their deep-throated bass. A lively pair of coyotes joined the night sounds by howling their secret messages back and forth to one another. It was so peaceful to sit and let the harmony of nature soothe the soul. The fragrance of honeysuckle and roses pervaded the evening air.

Diablo lay curled in a fluffy fur-ball, asleep at Rebecca's feet. It had been a long time since she'd been so at peace with herself and the rest of the world.

12

Rebecca departed early the next morning, declining the invitation to go poke-salet picking.

'I really can't go today. I need to make a trip into town for supplies, and see about ordering a cookstove for my kitchen. I can't seem to master the art of cooking in the fireplace. I also want to order some glass panes for the windows.'

'Wouldn't do that if I's you.'

'What?'

'Go putting in glass panes. Folk around here say it's bad luck to put glass in windows. It'll mean a death in the house.'

'Oh, that's ridiculous. I never heard of such a notion.'

'Nevertheless, folks hereabouts got a lot of superstitious ideas. They believe in them. They won't take to the idea of a neighbor going against their beliefs, newcomer or no.'

'Well, aren't you the one who told me to be myself and if folks were going to accept me, they would anyway?'

'I reckon I was. But they ain't gonna like it,' the woman persisted, a concerned expression on her face.

'They can learn to live with it.' Stubbornness was one of Rebecca's weaknesses. And even though she desired the acceptance of her neighbors, she wasn't about to allow them to make decisions for her.

★   ★   ★

It was a lovely day for her excursion. The sun was warm and a gentle breeze played through the trees, setting the leaves to shimmering and sighing. Birds sang as if in welcome to the new day. The trail was alive with small animals scurrying to and fro: rabbits, quail, even an occasional field mouse darted across her path. At one point, she spotted a doe and her young fawn feeding near the timberline, close enough to dash for cover if they sensed danger.

By the time Rebecca arrived at the Mercantile, she was in excellent spirits.

Bertha was overjoyed by her arrival, though Rebecca suspected it was more a need to satisfy her curiosity than any great desire to see her. Still, it was a nice change to be treated as a welcome guest instead of an intruder. She couldn't help but compare Bertha's welcome with the cold, indifferent treatment she'd received at each stop on her visits with the old woman. It was like stepping from one planet to another. Bertha insisted Rebecca give her list of supplies to the clerk to be filled, while she fixed them a cup of chamomile tea and they had a nice chat.

'Well, tell me all about what's doing at your place.' Glancing past Rebecca toward the open doorway, she inquired, 'Where's that handsome young man that was with you?' Bertha guffawed as she took a seat opposite Rebecca at the small table near the back of the store.

Rebecca suspected Bertha's attitude was mainly for the shock effect, but then, she wasn't certain. The storekeeper kept glancing around as if in hopes of spying the object of her inquiry.

'Jimmy returned home.'

'Oh, that's too bad. He did have a look about him, but then, they most all do, don't they?' She smiled a toothy, good-natured grin.

'Uh, I'm not . . . '

The garish woman interrupted her with a beefy slap on the back and a full-bellied chuckle filled with hilarious delight. Touching the mass of her disorderly red hair, she said, 'Don't let me ruffle your composure, Miss Rice. It's just I speak my mind. And I happen to appreciate a good man, young or old. Tell me, how's it going at your place?' Abruptly, Bertha changed the subject.

Rebecca suspected the switch was for her benefit in a belated attempt to put her at ease. So, she quickly gave an abbreviated version of her arrival, the repairs needed and made, Jimmy's departure, and her current need for supplies. 'I hope you'll be able to get a cookstove for me. How long does it usually take when you place such an order?'

'You're in luck, Miss Rice. Just so happens, I got a dee-dandy one in stock.' Bertha proudly showed her the stove. Its glossy black iron was trimmed in pale lemon porcelain enamel and nickel-plating. It had a copper lined reservoir on the right side for heating and keeping water hot, a two-door warming oven above the cooking area, and a temperature gauge on the cavernous oven door.

'I'll take it,' Rebecca said. 'But how will I ever get it home?'

'The smithy down the street owes me a favor or two. I'll get him and his boy to deliver it for you.' Large, brown eyes held Rebecca in a knowing glance. 'Naturally, it wouldn't be amiss was you to offer them a bite to eat for their time. You know, neighborly like.'

'Of course. I would expect to pay them for their help.'

'Oh, no, you don't understand, Miss Rice. You don't offer pay, just offer a little something sociable-like. Folks here don't take pay for helping out, but it be acceptable to take a meal or a small amount of coins, to help feed the mules, you know.' Turbulent red hair bounced when Bertha nodded in emphasis to her words. 'You'll insult them if you call it pay. Folks be mighty full of pride here about. And pride sometimes gets in the way of an empty belly. You being new around here, I figured to give you a bit of advice. Hope you don't take it wrong or nothing, but I like you, Miss Rice, and I'm trying to help you a bit in my own way.'

'I appreciate the advice, but won't you call me Rebecca?'

'Sure thing, Rebecca. Now, let's finish your order and I'll get that stove loaded so's you can ride back home with it. Save yourself a long trek and some shoe leather.' Taking Rebecca's list from the clerk, the capacious woman checked it over slowly. Then, almost hesitantly, she said, 'Glass panes. You want glass window panes?'

Rebecca's brows arched slightly. 'Don't you have them?'

'I got them. Don't have much call for

them, though, except here in town. Folks out your way got a thing about window glass. Seems they believe glass panes trap the spirit inside the house and cause death to the one living inside.'

'Well, I don't have a thing about window panes, and I certainly don't intend to die because of their beliefs,' Rebecca replied heatedly.

'Simmer down now. I's just repeating what they say. Didn't say I believe it, or you can't have them panes if you've a mind to.'

'Sorry, I shouldn't have snapped at you. It's just that's the second time I've heard that ridiculous idea, and superstitions upset me.'

'Calm your dander down. You best get used to those kinds of ideas, because up there where you're living, they run rampant.'

* * *

It was late afternoon by the time Rebecca and her new stove arrived home. It had been a very quiet, uneventful trip. Neither the smithy nor his son were given to talking much, and after several unsuccessful attempts at conversation, Rebecca gave up and joined them in silence for the remainder of the trip. After the supplies were carried in and the stove set up, Rebecca offered to fix supper for them.

'Thank you, no. Missus'll have our meal ready time we get back.'

They did, however, accept the four bits she offered.

'Thank you, kindly, ma'am. Them mules always appreciate a bite of oats after a long haul.'

13

Rebecca ate a cold meal of leftovers, which she shared with Diablo, who was more than a little upset at being left behind today. He even refused to put in an appearance while the two men unloaded the stove, and sulked under the bed until supper was ready. Hunger won out over hurt feelings, and he joyfully joined her at last with a hearty appetite.

There had been two letters at the post office, which Bertha handed Rebecca as she was leaving. Rebecca hadn't even thought to ask about mail. She really hadn't expected to receive any. Almost everyone had been so upset with her decision to relocate, or as they had put it, 'to bury herself in those backwoods,' she hadn't expected anyone to write.

She should have known James and Louise wouldn't stay upset for long. After all, with their Mama and Papa gone, they only had each other. James wrote that the house had rented for a good price and he had made a few sound investments for her. His missive ended with a note he hoped she returned to her senses soon and rejoined the family.

James, solid and dependable as a rock, had no adventure in his soul.

The other letter was from her sister, Louise. It was filled with news of her family, garden parties, club activities, and the latest social events. This, Rebecca was sure, was designed to fill her with longing for what she was missing. Louise would be shocked to know just how bored Rebecca had been with all those trappings. Her letter ended with the same type of plea, for a return to her senses and civilization.

She reread her letters before tucking them between the pages of her journal. A smile pulled at her lips when she pictured her siblings as they must have looked while penning their letters, being careful to use just the right words and tone to appeal to her better judgment.

James and Louise would make a great pair of bookends, she mused. Rebecca wondered if her being the middle child might explain the differences in the three of them. She didn't know. But at least she was willing to try for what she wanted out of life, even when it meant taking a risk and making great changes in her lifestyle. She'd never been afraid to take a stand, and didn't give up easily on anything she really wanted. Her papa once said she was remarkably like the sign she was born under: Taurus, the bull.

'Rebecca is just like that bull,' he said. 'She's bullheaded, and once she gets an idea or sets her mind to a thing, there's no budging her. She should have been a boy. With willpower like hers, she'd have made a fine man.'

Her Papa's words echoed in her memory and she resolved in her spirit, I'll make a fine woman, Papa. Nothing will stop me from doing what I came here to do. Nothing and nobody! Taurus the Bull, indeed. Well, so be it.

14

The days flowed one into another, nothing of importance setting one day apart from the one before it. The weather grew warmer. Young fruit appeared on the trees in her orchard, though it would be several months before any of it would be ready to eat or harvest.

Rebecca continued to make occasional trips with the old woman, and was still ignored as if she weren't there. From June through September, they were busy gathering and drying leaves, roots, and barks the healer used in her home pharmacy. Her vast knowledge of these many and varied herbs impressed Rebecca.

When she wasn't helping her new friend, she made fruit-gathering trips with Megan, who instructed her on the method of drying fruit for winter storage. She also managed to hot-bath preserve some fruit in jars. She put to good use the cache of fruit jars found in the shed when she and Jimmy stripped it of usable boards for the porch repair.

Through the summer days Rebecca and Megan spent together, Rebecca pieced together bits and pieces of the puzzle surrounding the young girl. It appeared, from listening to Megan talk of her home life; she was a veritable unpaid servant to her father and three older brothers, although she was apparently unaware of this fact. She appeared to accept it as her way of life and her responsibility. No doubt she would be surprised or shocked if Rebecca suggested this was unfair.

The young girl spent her days cooking, washing, carrying water, tending the cow and chickens, collecting the eggs, and gathering fruit to dry and preserve along with the vegetables she raised in a small garden. She did all this in addition to mending the menfolks' clothes and giving them haircuts. The only thing Rebecca hadn't heard her mention was wood cutting. Perhaps the men did that one chore.

At any rate, Rebecca had been afraid to ask about it. She became angry listening to Megan talk, matter-of-factly, of all the work she did, knowing full well there were four grown, healthy men living in that household and none offered a hand with the work load. Yet Megan always found time, at least once, and sometimes twice, a week to steal away from her chores to visit Rebecca. The young girl always stopped off to visit the old woman, too. Until Rebecca's arrival, the healer had been the only female in Megan's life.

Several times during the summer Megan again sported a purple cheek, always saying she had fallen when Rebecca inquired about the bruises. Rebecca didn't believe her accounts, and seethed inwardly at her inability to help this newfound friend.

Rebecca became quite attached to the young girl and was determined to do all she could to teach her about life, life as it was outside these hills. She intended to teach her book learning also, at least the basics of reading, writing, and arithmetic. Megan might never leave these hills, Rebecca reasoned, but if she ever got the chance, at least she'd be prepared. And if she stayed, she might learn enough to stand up for herself by gaining self-confidence and self-worth.

On a morning in mid-September, Rebecca awoke to the sound of music. She lay in her featherbed wondering if she were dreaming, for surely no earthly sound was that sweet and melodious. Even the birds were silent, listening to the wondrous melody. Unable to stand the suspense any longer, she donned her flannel robe and slippers and stepped out onto the porch in search of the euphonious sound. She stood listening, noticing the sun making a valiant effort to struggle from behind a fluffy, white, low hanging cloud. The result of its attempts streaked the morning sky with colors of violet, gray, and pink, reflecting a glow onto the treetops with their leaves of gold, red, yellow, and brown.

Fall flowers were in full bloom. The sound of the creek rippling over the rocks on its journey south blended with the gentle morning breeze whispering secrets in the multi-colored treetops, crowned by the mystical music floating from the grove. Surely heaven must be a bit like this.

Reverting her attention to the music and locating its source, she scanned the area nearest the house. Nothing. Her gaze roamed further down the creek then skidded to a halt. Near the edge of the pecan grove, she saw what appeared to be a wagon with a canvas top. A mule was staked out, grazing on the last bit of green grass within reach of the water. To the left, beneath the trees, stood a man with a fiddle. She had discovered the spring from which the fountain of music flowed. She couldn't actually see the fiddle, of course. But she could see the motions of his arm and that he held something beneath his chin. It had to be a fiddle, but it was being played like none she'd ever heard.

Curiosity consumed her. Who was he? Where was he from? Why had he stopped here? Where had he learned to play like that?

More questions.

Rebecca had found far more questions since coming here than she ever had before, and fewer answers. Almost as if the man sensed her watching, he stopped playing and turned slowly in her direction, then climbed inside the wagon.

She regretted the loss of the music. Could angels sound any sweeter? Turning to go back inside, she almost stepped on Diablo. She reached down to stroke his side with a loving pat, remembering the old woman's remark about not petting him on the head. But this morning, instead of rubbing against her hand in his usual way, the animal seemed impatient with the petting. As soon as she stopped stroking his side, the young wolf turned and strolled off the porch. Then, as if pulled by a magnet, he crossed the yard and raced off in the direction of the new arrival.

'Diablo, here, boy. Come back. Stay here.' For the first time during the five months he'd been with her, the animal ignored her and kept moving toward the pecan grove and the stranger.

Diablo's curious behavior soon became a habit. If she were at home and busy, the cub would amble off to the covered wagon and its owner. If she left the house to go for a walk or to gather dry wood for the stove, he was promptly there to escort her. She wasn't sure how he knew when she was leaving, because after that first morning she never called him, yet he was always there.

Several days after the stranger's arrival in the grove, Rebecca had an unexpected visitor. She was out back emptying a pail of ashes from the cookstove, pouring them into a hopper lined with old newspapers as she'd been instructed to do by her mentor. 'Come spring, we'll make soap,' she'd said. Out of ashes? This, Rebecca would have to see.

Hearing a chuckle from behind, she whirled around, her pail drawn back like a weapon, to find a grinning preacher Zake standing with his big hands on his hips, his feet planted firmly apart, as if he owned the farm and she was the intruder.

'If you had a man about the place, you wouldn't have to be doing dirty chores like that. You could be gussied up, setting on the porch to greet your guest.' He had a cocksure grin plastered on his face.

'You startled the wits out of . . . what guest? I don't recall inviting you.' She fired the salvo like the buckshot she wished it were. 'I have work to do. So if you'll excuse me, I'll get b-back to my dirty chores,' Rebecca stammered, attempting to regain her compo-sure before this arrogant man.

He reached out and took the pail from her trembling hand, as if she hadn't just rebuked his presence. 'Let me, ma'am. Little thing like you ought not be doing a man's work. Leastways, not when there's a man about. Where you want this? I'll put it up for you.'

'I told you . . . are you hard of hearing, or just hard-headed? Give me my pail or I'll . . . oh, just give me the bucket and go, will you?'

'My, my, still got that temper, I see. Need a man, that's what you need. A man to get rid of those frustrations, and your temper would cool down a heap.'

'Will you just go? I don't have time to play games today . . . or any other day, for that matter.' Rebecca reached for the pail.

Zake thrust the container behind his back. 'Now, now, little lady, simmer down. I come by to give you an invite.' He grinned his toothy grin.

'Well, at least now I know why you came. An invite to what?' she grudgingly asked.

'I finally got a female reaction out of you.' He wagged a finger at her in triumph. 'Curiosity. All females are curious as cats.' He placed the bucket at his feet but out of her reach.

'An invite to what?' she interrupted, hoping to be rid of him soon. Ever since their first meeting when he'd called Megan simple-minded, Rebecca hadn't liked this man. And after what the old woman had said about him using his religion to control the people, she wanted to scream at him to leave.

'If you weren't so impatient, I'd tell you.' He quickly snatched the hat from his head as if just remembering his manners. 'I came to invite you to a brush arbor meeting. I usually hold a couple in the spring and again in the fall.' Rocking back on his heels, his grin broadened, exposing his teeth. Lots of teeth.

'Gives me a chance to get the marrying done in the fall before cold weather sets in, then in the spring, I bless the new arrivals. Keeps me from making too many trips out here that way. Kills two birds with one stone, so to speak.' He towered over her, his thumbs hooked in his belt, and an expression on his face as if he'd just explained something very important to an ignorant child.

'You mean, you don't live here or nearby? I thought . . . I mean . . . where do you live?'

'Surely you didn't think I lived out here in the sticks?' He swept his arm outward. 'There's nothing to do out here. No theaters, plays, or socials. You know what I'm talking about. The things you're probably missing right now.' His broad shoulders lifted in a shrug. 'I'd go as loony as they are, if I had to live out here all the time.' A look of disgust marred his strongly chiseled features. A hard, cold glint reflected the enmity he so obviously felt.

Rebecca watched his face as he spoke and felt a knot growing in her stomach. He honestly didn't care a fig for these people. Her contempt knew no bounds at that moment.

'I mean civilization,' he continued. 'No, thank heaven, I don't live here. I just make my circuit couple times a year, then I head back where real people live. Not out here like these hillbillies.' He gave her a knowing look with those cold, lifeless eyes. 'You'll find out soon enough what I mean. You'll leave, too. Mark my word, no intelligent person can stand it out here too long. You'll leave.'

'I see.' And she did see, more than she wanted to.

'Good. Now, will you allow me to escort you to the meeting? Do you good to get out and meet the folks from hereabouts.'

'I think not. I really don't care to attend your meeting, nor do I wish to be escorted by you, anywhere. I have work to do, so if you'll give me back my pail ... ' She found it difficult to control her temper because at this point she would like nothing so much as to tell this person — to call him a man would be an insult to the male gender — what she truly thought of him. He was a miserable excuse of a man, a pastor who had little compassion for the people he was supposed to provide with spiritual guidance. To him it was a lark, a front to serve himself. She wondered if he'd heard of the scripture, 'Go, feed my sheep'?

'You're about the contrariest female I ever met. I thought you'd be glad for a chance to attend meetings and . . . Oh, never mind. But mind you this, Miss High and Mighty, the day will come you'll be glad of an invite from me. Glad.' He turned his lean body as if to leave, then thought better of it. 'It gets mighty lonely living alone, especially way out here. I know these folks. They won't take to you. You haven't got anybody. You get lonely enough . . . well, we'll see.' His bold gaze traveled hotly along her body.

Rebecca returned his daring look with one of her own, filled with all the disdain she felt for this arrogant man.

Apparently correctly interpreting her look, his eyes filled with sparks of contempt. He kicked the pail, turned, and stomped back to the front of the house where he'd left his horse. Rebecca gritted her teeth to keep her mouth shut on the words. *I'll never be that lonely!*

Zakeriah Daniels spurred his mount brutally as he rode away from Rebecca. Back straight, head held high, his eyes shifted neither left nor right as he forced the animal beneath him into a lathered gallop. Until now, he had paid little attention to this newcomer, willing to bide his time. But no longer. Rebecca Rice would rue the day she refused Zake Daniels. One way or another, she would be his.

★ ★ ★

Rebecca spent the next two days fuming inwardly over her confrontation with Zake Daniels. She took her frustrations and anger out on her fall cleaning. She aired her featherbed, pillows, quilts, and bed throws; beat the rag rugs; scrubbed the floors; and re-washed her new windowpanes.

When the realization behind her actions hit her, she sat down and laughed at herself. That man only had the power to upset her if she gave it to him. Well, she would give that last round to him, but no more. From now on she would simply ignore him. That should cook his goose. And what a blow to his self-important ego! She imagined he wasn't used to being ignored. No doubt, he hadn't even considered the possibility. Zakeriah Daniels was the only man she knew who could appear to strut while standing still.

She relaxed her cleaning to an easier pace, a smile tugging upward at the corners of her full lips.

15

Rebecca still wasn't accustomed to waking each morning to the magical sound coming from the pecan grove. Ever since the stranger's arrival she lingered longer in bed, savoring the melody, as a child does a lollipop. She hoped that if she lay very still and didn't move, the music would last longer. It washed over her, seeping into her spirit, making her joyful to be alive, and vibrantly aware of her surroundings.

She hadn't yet met the stranger in the grove, who a few days earlier had removed the wheels from his wagon and set it down on logs. Yesterday, he began building the sides halfway up the canvas top. Today, she noticed he had installed a wooden door in the rear, and a stovepipe protruded crookedly from one side. His nest was now settled, but not permanent.

It appeared the visitor had elected to stay. That was okay with Rebecca, because after the months of silence it was comforting to hear the sounds of saw, hammer, and axe on wood. Even though she didn't know him, she liked the idea of having someone nearby. That thought propelled her into action. She would make a batch of cookies and march right down and introduce herself.

An hour later, bare feet padding across the porch followed by the slamming of the screen door announced the arrival of a guest. Rebecca turned from the table where she had just placed the last tray of cookies to cool and smiled at the figure silhouetted in the ray of sunlight. Her smile widened as she took in the girl's appearance. Sunlight sparkled in her golden tresses, reflecting renewed life. Obviously, she had followed Rebecca's suggestions of washing her hair frequently and brushing it one hundred strokes daily. Though her dress was well worn, faded, and several inches too short, it was always freshly laundered. Since their first meeting, she had undergone changes that were nothing short of miraculous.

Rebecca often wondered how long it had been since Megan had owned a new frock. The abbreviated hemline exposed her bare legs and feet. Rebecca recalled the girl's response when asked about her lack of footwear. 'I'm saving them for town and meetings.' She was really a striking young woman, a bud bursting into blossom.

'What are you doing?' Megan asked. 'Smells real nice in here. What is it?'

'Hello to you, too, Megan,' Rebecca answered, laughing. 'It's molasses cookies. Have one.'

Watching the young girl eagerly devour a freshly baked cookie, Rebecca allowed her mind to drift. If only she and Jonathan had had children, maybe one like this, maybe she wouldn't miss her husband so much. Not only had she been cheated out of a full life with her beloved, but she had been denied the joy of motherhood. It wasn't fair. She had wanted a child so much. Yet here stood a young girl who hadn't been loved enough to even be given a name, blamed by her father for the death of his wife.

'What's the matter? What did I say wrong, huh? I'm sorry, really I am.'

Rebecca's moment of self-pity was interrupted by the bewildered cry in the young girl's voice. Uncertainty clouded Megan's emerald eyes. She stood balanced on the balls of her bare feet as though ready to flee, not knowing she wasn't the cause of the tears Rebecca felt stinging her eyes before they slid down her cheeks. In fact, Rebecca wasn't even unaware until that moment she was crying.

'I'm sorry, Megan. Forgive me,' Rebecca said, wiping her tear-brightened eyes on the corner of her apron. Stepping closer, she enfolded the trembling body in her arms, holding the child close to her heart.

'I'm sorry,' Rebecca repeated. 'I didn't mean to upset you. Just now, you reminded me of how much I've really missed not having a child of my own. A daughter, like you.' There was a catch in her voice. She attempted to halt the tears inside from spilling over.

'You mean, if you had a baby, you'd a wanted a girl baby? Not a boy? A son?'

'Yes. Yes, I would. A very sweet, precious little girl, to love and spoil and teach her things. Like how to cook and sew, and play the piano, and oh, so many things.' Her words gushed forth as she revealed her secret dream. 'A son would have been wonderful, also. But I think it must be something really special to have a daughter. To share things only a mother and daughter could share, like — '

The flow of words formed a logjam in her throat and she nearly choked on her stupidity. 'Oh, Megan, what am I saying? I forgot for a moment that you'd lost your mother. I didn't mean to . . . oh, me and my mouth.' She had to stop; there wasn't anything else to say. She'd blundered badly, talking about mothers when this girl hadn't the faintest idea of what that type of relationship could be.

'It's okay, really.' Her arms encircled Rebecca's shoulders in a gripping hug. Pulling away slightly, the young girl spoke, her words so soft Rebecca leaned close to hear.

'It's just I didn't think anybody would really want a girl baby. I always figured folks wanted boys. You know, if they had a choice. I mean, Pap, he . . . well, he's always talking about his sons and bragging about how lucky he be to have three great, strapping sons. I don't rightly think he likes girls much. I mean, I don't think he thinks he's lucky to be having a daughter. Leastways, he ain't never said so.' Megan fell silent, her lower lip trembling. She hung her head and stood quietly, unconsciously picking at a loose thread in her dress.

Heaven help her, but at that moment Rebecca could have shaken the life out of Jacob Penny. Whether consciously or not, he had put his daughter through hell, making her feel unwanted and unloved. She was emotionally starved for love and affection.

'Oh, I'm sure that's not true, Megan.' Rebecca tried to make her voice sound normal, though she felt rage ripple through her. She didn't want Megan to see that. She must never make the mistake of letting Megan know how she felt about Jacob.

Things were miserable enough for the girl without adding to her misery. Rebecca looked forward to meeting the man, if for no other reason than to tell him what a miserable excuse for a father he was.

'Maybe your father doesn't know how to . . . well, how to talk to a daughter. I bet that's it. He can talk to the boys, but just doesn't know how to talk to a girl.' Rebecca smiled, wishing she could believe it herself. Yet, she offered what comfort she could.

'You think that be it? Really all it be, that mayhap he might love me just a little, except he don't know how to say it to a girl? Wouldn't that be something?' She glowed with hope, maybe her first, as she stood before Rebecca, smiling from the inside out.

Rebecca noticed, for the first time, that she had a very charming dimple in her left cheek when she smiled. She should smile more often. Was Rebecca doing the right thing, planting a seed of hope? If it didn't receive the watering of love it needed to grow, what would be the harvest?

Rebecca changed the subject before she risked making it worse. 'I have a great idea! Why don't you come with me to meet my new neighbor?'

'New neighbor? Who? Where?'

'Whoa! Slow down a minute and I'll tell

you, though I really don't have much to tell. He arrived earlier this week and camped in the pecan grove down by the creek. A few days ago, he removed the wheels from his wagon and built wooden sides all around and . . . oh, never mind all that. You can see when we go down there.'

'Has he got a family? Where's he from?'

Rebecca heard the suspicion in Megan's voice, so typically reverting from youthful enthusiasm to hill country suspicion of the outsider, the newcomer. Rebecca forgot, for the moment, that she, too, had asked the same questions the morning of his arrival. Maybe that's one of the reasons she felt the need to meet this new neighbor. She could relate to the feeling of being left out, of not belonging, that a newcomer felt. Was it the area that affected the people, or the people that affected the area? All outsiders were subjected to the same treatment. 'What do you want? Where you from? How come you come way back here? Who sent you? What you looking for?' Questions. Suspicions. What were they afraid of, these people of the hill country? She didn't know the answers, but she wanted to meet this neighbor. To make him feel welcome to his grove home.

Rebecca stacked cookies in a clean dishcloth to take as a welcome gift. 'I haven't seen anyone but the one man, so I don't know if he has a family, and I don't know the answers to your other questions, either. You may ask him, if you like, when we meet him. Come on, let's go. I'm ready.' Rebecca finished folding the cloth around the cookies, removed her apron, and they set forth to meet the stranger in their midst.

As they crossed the open meadow, which separated Rebecca's acreage from the pecan grove, they saw the man moving about the wagon-home, splitting and stacking wood in a pile near the door. Diablo dogged his every step like a shadow. The stranger seemed very much at home. Spotting them, the cub abandoned his new friend with a bark of acknowledgment and bounded across the meadow to greet them. He ran a circle around Rebecca, then started licking her hand in pleasure, his rear end wiggling in rippling convulsions.

She returned his greeting by scratching behind his ears, which was a particular favorite of his. The three of them proceeded on their way. Nearing the area where the wagon dwelling sat, Rebecca called out a greeting to announce their arrival.

'Hello, anyone at home? I'm your neighbor across the meadow. Hello?'

A glimpse of movement to the right caused

her to turn in time to spot the stranger disappearing into a thicket of wild plums. He quickly hid from view.

'Hello,' Rebecca called once more.

'He be afeared. He ain't coming out. We best be going now,' Megan stated very matter-of-factly, turning to go.

'What do you mean, he's afraid? Of what? Do you know this man?'

'Don't know him, no. But either be afeared of us or he be real shy. I know that much. Us be going, okay? He won't come out 'less we go.'

'Well, I don't know what to do. I only wanted to ... okay, we'll go.' Rebecca deposited the cookie-filled towel near the door, not knowing what else to do but leave them and go. She called, 'Good-bye,' and they retraced their path across the meadow.

They hadn't gone twenty feet when they heard a rustling in the brush where the man had darted.

'So, he sees us leaving. He knew we were there. How odd. Perhaps he doesn't like people.' Rebecca spoke absently, not expecting an answer, and she got none. Just another puzzle.

On the way back to the house, Rebecca discussed her desire to give Megan lessons in reading, writing, and arithmetic. The young woman's reaction was, to say the least, not what Rebecca had expected.

Megan stopped walking and looked at Rebecca as though she'd gone soft in the head. 'What for I need to know that stuff? I be just a girl, don't be needing no schooling. Besides, Pap, he probably wouldn't go for it no how.'

'But I thought . . . I mean . . . oh, forget what I thought! But what do you mean, you're just a girl and don't need to know? Megan, listen to me.' She gently placed her hand under the girl's chin and lifted her head up. 'Being a girl has nothing to do with whether you learn these things.' She looked directly into the girl's eyes, holding her attention. 'Everyone, including girls, needs to know all they can.'

Megan's expression remained unchanged.

'Do you understand any of what I'm saying to you?' Rebecca asked. 'You're a girl, yes, but you're also a person, an individual. You're important.' Rebecca stopped talking when she noticed a play of emotions cross Megan's face. Was it hope, followed by despair, she'd glimpsed? On a hunch, she decided to try a different approach.

'Would you be willing to do it for me? You see, it will be winter soon. I won't have as much to do, and I'm going to get lonely. I probably won't make as many trips with Ole Woman and, well, I'd really take it as a favor if you'd let me give you some lessons.' Rebecca saw Megan waver and rushed on. 'You could even give me some lessons.'

'Me? What could I be teaching you? You shucking corn?' She gazed at Rebecca from her emerald eyes. The breeze whipped a strand of hair across her face while she stood as if trying to figure out what her new friend was up to.

'Why, I bet you know all sorts of things I should know,' Rebecca said. 'Like, uh, well, I don't know how to make candles, or how to braid a rug, or . . . oh, all sorts of things. I'll bet you can do all those things. Will you teach me? Please.' She reached for Megan's hand, which was busy worrying a ravel on her dress. 'It would mean a lot to me,' Rebecca continued. 'I'll even go with you to meet your father and ask his permission. Would you like that? I've wanted to meet him for some time. This would be a good time to do it. What do you say?'

'He won't go for it. Me taking learning lessons, I mean. You don't know Pap.'

'Would you let me give it a try? He might surprise you, you know.'

★ ★ ★

155

'Be a waste a time, that's what it'd be. Girl can't learn. Besides, she's got work to be doing. No. I won't hear of it!'

He wasn't at all what Rebecca had expected. Though, in all honesty, she wasn't sure what that was. Jacob Penny was a tall, broad-shouldered man. He filled the doorway when entering a room, and looked as if he'd just bit into a green persimmon. His appearance was neat and clean. He stood straight like a pine tree, but without its ability to sway when the blows of life arrived. Instead, like the oak, he cracked and splintered. He was a broken man, but what had broken him?

Rebecca's observation of Mr. Penny had taken only as long as his rejection of her request. Although she hadn't expected immediate approval, she also hadn't expected such a forceful, 'No.'

'But, I don't understand, sir. What makes you think your daughter can't learn? She appears to be very bright. If it's only her chores, maybe I could help her.'

'Don't need no stranger round here! Girl can do her own work.'

'Okay, but if she does her chores, will you permit her to . . . ?'

'She be simpleminded. Ain't no use her taking no lessons,' he barked, obviously annoyed with Rebecca's persistence. 'Foolish woman, you don't know when you've been turned away. Just like an outsider.'

'Why do you consider her . . . ' Rebecca forced herself not to glance at Megan when she repeated the hateful word, 'simple-minded, sir?'

'She don't talk, not much anyhow. Even when she do, it be only a word or two. Or after I gives her a cuff upside her head.'

His cold eyes sought those of his daughter. There was a rebellious light reflected in their depths he'd never noticed before. It troubled him. What nonsense was this woman putting into her head? Dragging his gaze away from the defiant figure of his youngest child, he cleared his throat loudly and proclaimed, 'See, I know she can talk, she just don't. Simpleminded or stubborn, and females ain't got enough gumption to be stubborn.' His stinging words were shot directly at the girl. Rebecca wondered if he felt a sense of satisfaction when his remarks hit their mark and her young body flinched visibly.

Oh, haven't they? Rebecca fumed inwardly. Her palms ached to slap that smirk from his hateful face. Instead, she clutched the fabric of her skirt until her knuckles hurt. With all the willpower she could muster, she persisted. 'What if I can get her to talk?' She'd be hung at dawn before she allowed this man to know what a talker his daughter really was. Let him think what he would. 'Will you allow me to teach her then, if I can prove to you she is capable of learning and that she's not backward?'

'How come you want to waste time on her? What's your man gonna think, you neglecting your own work and all?' He scowled at her.

'My time is my own, Mr. Penny. I'm a . . . ' Rebecca paused. She still found it difficult to say the word *widow*.

A look of, what? Was it compassion that darted across his features when he whipped his head around to look at her? Yes, that's what she saw on his weather-tanned face. Compassion. She struck while she had an advantage, fair or not. 'A widow, Mr. Penny. I get lonely. You know what being lonely is like. It would be a great service to me if you'd allow your daughter to take lessons.'

'Oh, quit your jawing, woman. Give your damn lessons. But mind, she don't keep her chores done, that's it. Lessons over. Widder or no, you hear? Widder woman ain't got no business traipsing around the countryside, no how.'

The soft spot she'd seen briefly vanished.

'I didn't choose to be a widow, sir. Would you have me quit living because of it?'

'I did! Now go, before I change my mind.' He stomped from the house, slamming the door behind him.

Rebecca couldn't believe she'd won the battle of wills with this angry man. She realized she'd have to walk softly with this one.

So began their lessons, Rebecca's and Megan's. It was hard to say who enjoyed them more. Rebecca was receiving quite an education herself, and once Megan caught on to reading and writing, she devoured all Rebecca provided.

Megan took to slipping off at night after supper to spend extra hours with her books. Often, she showed up carrying one or more of her 'critters,' as she called them, and stretched out before the fireplace with a tablet and pencil, printing her name over and over.

By Thanksgiving, Megan was reading poetry and Bible scriptures, the shorter, simpler ones. It was like watching a rose progress from bud to bloom. She gained self-confidence, as Rebecca had hoped.

★ ★ ★

Rebecca spent Thanksgiving with her mentor. They had roast goose, a gift from one of her many patients, and cornbread dressing.

Rebecca had attended bigger feasts at Thanksgiving, but none so enjoyable. Apparently, the tiny woman was as glad to have her for dinner, as Rebecca was to be there.

After their meal, Rebecca broached the subject that had been troubling her for some time now, her lack of progress with the people. She came here to share the love and healing powers of her Lord, yet what had she accomplished after seven months? Nothing.

'Give it time, chil'. Give it time. Relax, be yourself. Don't force it. You can't cram something down folks' throats; they'll choke on it.'

'But, I haven't . . . '

'Hear me out,' she cut in. 'Folks hear more with their eyes than with they ears, sometimes. Know what I mean?'

'No,' Rebecca answered, puzzled.

'You say it and do it, now they hear. You see? Folks need examples. They don't need preaching, too. Got that fine Brother Zake, what does enough of preaching. Nope, they need information by example.'

'But how?'

'Simple. You make rounds to the sick with me. You feel a need to pray for one of these folks, do it. 'Course, before you do, it'd be best you ask it be awright. Folk don't like no one, 'specially strangers, laying hands on

160

them for nothing. Not even praying.'

The old healer paused to take a deep drag on her pipe. Her leathery face creased even deeper with concern for the young woman she hoped would be her replacement in caring for her people. It had been a long time in coming, but now that she was here, the old woman was convinced this newcomer was the one she'd been waiting for. She took another drag on her pipe and finished, 'But then most folks, if asked, won't be impolite and say no. Even if they don't believe it'll work, they'll see that you believe it. Example.'

'But, if they don't believe it — ' Rebecca started, only to be stopped by the smile that crawled across the beautiful leathery face, from lips to eyes.

'Chil', relax. I done said they see, they hear. The book says, 'Faith cometh by hearing,' and faith without action won't work.' Waving her pipe in the younger woman's startled face, she added, 'So, you just do and say and they'll hear, and faith will come.' She was still smiling as she made her point and saw by Rebecca's face that she finally understood. 'Just do what you come to do, and don't fret about the results. Remember, His word never returns void.'

And I'm the one who came to teach? Rebecca silently admonished herself.

16

When Rebecca returned home from Thanksgiving dinner, she found two ricks of wood neatly stacked near the back door, and all her new windowpanes smashed out. Surely, the same party hadn't done both? Who? Why? More mysteries.

This wasn't the first time vandalism had occurred. Since her arrival, twice Rebecca had found the well rope cut. And the yard fence was knocked down the day after she finished re-stacking the rails. She had no idea who the culprit was. She never saw or heard anyone near the farm, though she found footprints in the mud, crossing the creek. Why would anyone do these things? To scare her? To convince her to leave?

Well, she hadn't come this far, against the odds she'd faced, to be defeated. So she replaced the well rope and re-stacked the rail fence. She would also replace her windowpanes.

She made another trip to the settlement of Big Grassy for supplies and more window glass. Winter was not far away. Since she wasn't familiar with the weather here yet, she stocked up just in case she didn't get a chance later.

As usual, Bertha gave her a royal welcome filled with questions. In anyone else the quizzing would be interpreted as nosy, but with Bertha Callahan it was friendly concern. At least she had the ability to make one feel so.

Glancing over Rebecca's list, Bertha's eyebrows raised in inquiry. 'Windowpanes? What happened to the last ones?'

After Rebecca explained the incident, the woman replied calmly, 'Told you that would happen.' Gazing intently at her customer, she continued, 'Gonna try again, are you?' At Rebecca's nod, Bertha patted Rebecca's arm. 'Figured as much. Come on, let's sit a spell.'

Just like the last time, Bertha served tea while Rebecca's order was filled, and regaled her with the latest news of the settlement. A drummer selling linens had been through twice, and Bertha felt certain he was about to become husband number five.

'Bit young, but trainable.' She laughed heartily.

Rebecca couldn't help wondering what the ladies of the afternoon tea club back home would think of Bertha. She had to smile to herself at the imagined reaction.

Rebecca guided the talk away from

prospect number five as diplomatically as possible. 'Bertha, where would one acquire whiskey around here?'

Bertha nearly choked, and spewed a mouthful of hot tea across the table. She quickly grabbed a napkin to blot up the mess and overturned her chair; all while mumbling what sounded like an apology. 'Whiskey?'

'Yes, where can I buy some? Surely it's available.'

'Uh, yeah. I . . . I reckon so,' she stuttered, righting the chair.

'What's the matter? You seem upset.'

'Matter?'

'Listen to yourself. What's wrong? Did I do, or say, something to upset you?'

'You . . . yes! No! What I mean is, why would you want to buy whiskey?'

'Why, to mix with my herbal medicines, of course. Ole Woman is teaching me how she prepares her concoctions, and in almost every one of them she uses whiskey. I just thought I should have some on hand,' Rebecca explained, mystified by her host's behavior.

The florid-faced woman immediately exploded into laughter that threatened to burst her corset strings. Her cheeks still crimson, Bertha attempted to control her mirth. 'Lord, love me, but you're a case. I mean, you and whiskey don't appear to go

together. And when you asked, I thought
. . . oh, forget what I thought. Let's just say
it was a surprise, that's all. For medicine,
you say?'

'Yes. But I would very much like to know
. . . what you were thinking, that is.'

'You being a stranger and all, well,' She
glanced about the room as if to be sure she
wasn't overheard. 'You could be one of them
revenoor dogs, or mayhap a secret nipper.
Well, don't look so stunned, it's been known
to happen . . . both.'

It was Rebecca's turn to burst out
laughing. 'Me, a secret drinker? I can't even
have one sociable drink without going to
sleep. A drinker, I couldn't be.' Her brow
wrinkled in concentration. 'What on earth is a
revenoor dog?'

'That's about the worst kind of snake they
be. It be a man . . . ' She paused and glanced
at Rebecca as if for emphasis, 'Or woman,
what works for the law. They hunt out a
man's still and turns him in. It also be a
mighty dangerous thing to do.'

Rebecca felt sure that last was added for
her benefit, as an offhand warning. 'I see. But
I still need a small amount.'

'I reckon you can be trusted. I hope so,
anyway. You get it . . . no questions asked?'

'No questions.'

'Okay. Now, what about the pie supper Saturday night, you coming?' Bertha deftly steered the subject to safer ground.

'What pie supper?'

'You mean you ain't heard? No, reckon you ain't. Out there where you be, you wouldn't.' The large woman settled herself more comfortably on her chair. 'Well, they's to be big doings, they is. We always have two, three a year. Kinda gives folk a chance to get together and have a good time.' The large woman warmed to her subject as she explained to the newcomer about the social event of the season. 'Folk start arriving midday, auction off the pies after dark and then dance till daylight. Lots of fun.' She paused, took a sip of her tea. 'Way to meet some of the folks. Do you good to mix and mingle. Give the folk a chance to meet you, too. You coming?'

'It does sound like fun. Yes, I'll come.'

'Bring a pie, then. The funds from the pie sales goes to the Baptist church here, it being the only church we got. Anyhow, they use the money to provide food baskets for the needy folk. You know . . . man of the house laid up sick or something, can't work. It helps a bit, and folk don't think of it as charity, and no one family ever gets it twice.'

Bertha noticed her guest glancing out the

166

front window and followed her cue. 'I best quit yammering and let you be on your way, or it'll be dark 'fore you get home.'

It almost was, too, so it wasn't until morning that Rebecca noticed all her fruit trees had been pruned.

What in blue thunder was going on around here? Yesterday she'd found two ricks of wood left, and now this. Who could be doing this and why? Rebecca stared in astonishment at this latest development.

Mysteries. Puzzles. She needed answers.

★   ★   ★

The season was unusually warm, so the festivities were held out of doors. If the weather had been cooler, the plan was to move inside the livery stable, adjacent to the blacksmith shop. Instead, the weather seemed more than willing to cooperate for the last big shindig of the season. The stars winked bright as candles and the moon was full and luminous, bathing the area in a warm, radiant glow that cast a magical light on the party goers, causing their work-worn clothes to appear almost festive.

Rebecca thoroughly enjoyed herself and the few people she met. Then Zakeriah Daniels showed up. Though she tried not to let his presence unnerve her, she couldn't help herself. Every time she was around the man, she became angry. Better judgment told her she shouldn't, but that's the way it was.

The bidding on the pies began and almost immediately, Zake spotted her. Rebecca watched him make his way through the crowd of people. He patted backs, shook hands, and kissed babies until he stood arrogantly before her with a lecherous gleam in those gray eyes and a smirk Rebecca itched to slap off his face. His stance reflected confidence and Rebecca had to admit, grudgingly, that he made a remarkable presence in his striped trousers and long black broadcloth coat, black string tie, and starched white shirt.

'Well, well, if it ain't the little widow woman.' Sarcasm laced his words. 'Didn't expect to see you here. Don't worry now, you being new and all. I'll not let you be embarrassed because your pie doesn't sell.' Leaning forward until his face was level with hers, he added, 'I'll buy it myself. We'll eat it together.' His attitude came as no real surprise, but the assault of alcoholic fumes on his breath did. She didn't need to be told; the good preacher had been drinking.

'I thank you for your kind offer, sir. But I'd really rather you didn't.' She turned to leave his repulsive presence and felt a hand clamp down hard on her wrist.

'Wait up! I ain't through with you.'

Her glare should have pierced him when she glanced first at her wrist, where he still had a vice-like grip, then up at him. 'Get your hand off of me!' She nearly spat the words at him. A deadly silence settled over the crowd during their exchange. Rebecca even heard a few indrawn breaths of shocked response, whether at his actions or hers, she had no way of knowing and at that moment didn't care. 'And don't ever touch me again.' She jerked her wrist free. Almost blinded with rage, she stomped off to stand at the edge of the wooden planks laid down to form a dance floor.

Gradually, voices took on a normal tone and activity revived around her where she stood in the shadows, trying to decide if she shouldn't just leave. After that exchange, Rebecca was no longer enjoying herself.

She whirled around when a voice spoke behind her. This was certainly a night for surprises. Before her stood Jacob Penny, Megan's father. He fidgeted with the hat in his hands as he pulled his broad shoulders back and stood straight, emphasizing his immense height.

Without a blink of his eye, or a by-your-leave, he stated, 'I'll be buying your pie, ma'am. Don't fret about the preacher. He won't bother you no more tonight.' His tightly compressed mouth betrayed no sign of humor or friendliness. 'And I want to say straight out, up front like, I be doing this only 'cause you's a widder woman and ain't got no man to look out for you.' His eyes narrowed when he made his statement as if daring her to find fault with his actions, or to misinterpret his intentions. 'No other reason, you understand? 'Cause I ain't even sure I like you none. But, I do know I don't like no man pestering a woman what don't want to be bothered. So now, I done said my say and that's all I got to say. I be buying your pie.' With the situation settled to his satisfaction, he slapped his hat on his head and retreated.

Rebecca's mouth hung open as she watched him depart. He didn't like her, yet he'd buy her pie to keep Zake Daniels from doing so. Would she ever understand these people? In her wildest dreams, she'd never have thought Jacob Penny capable of compassion.

True to his word, Jacob purchased her pie. His determination to be the highest bidder never wavered even when the competition broadened. As the bids soared, she wondered if he could afford the price of his gallantry. She watched when Jacob solemnly claimed the prize he'd bid so heavily for. He brought it to where she stood, shoved it at her, wheeled about, and stalked away. He had no intention of sharing it with her. What a strange bird he was. She wanted to ask about Megan, but decided she'd better not remind him of their conflict over her lessons.

The evening air hummed with the sounds of music, laughter, and voices. Children played at the edge of light reflected from the multitude of lanterns hung about the dance floor. Rebecca joined a small group of women seated off to the side of the plank flooring. 'If you'd like to dance with your husband, I'd be glad to watch the children.' The women tending their young glanced at each other, but not at her. Rebecca ignored the rebuke and made her way to another young woman.

'It's such a lovely night. Why don't you let me watch the little ones for you?' As she half expected, her offers were declined. She was, after all, still the outsider, the stranger among them.

Then about an hour after all the youngest children were bedded down in the back of one of the wagons, Cora Mae Snodgrass eased up beside her and asked shyly, 'You still of a mind to tend the younguns?'

'Yes, of course, I'll watch the children for you, and thank you for asking,' she gushed, realizing she'd been too eager. But at last one person had spoken to her voluntarily. She was pleased and hopeful.

With the children already bedded down, there wasn't much for her to do except be near in the event one of them awakened. She relaxed and watched as the evening progressed. Everyone seemed to be enjoying themselves, some more than others. The liveliest group seemed to be those leaving the lighted dance area to disappear into the darkness. These individuals always returned a bit lighter in mood than when they left. She'd seen Bertha departing in that direction earlier, and wondered if there was a connection between these events. Though she couldn't imagine what.

Rebecca got a glimmer of an idea later when Horace Snodgrass, returning from the suspect area, stopped by to check on his little family. He was less than steady on his feet and reeked of alcohol. So, the mysterious trips were for spirits? But who supplied them? Bertha? After all, she had managed to get a small supply for Rebecca's medicines. So, maybe — ? Rebecca's curiosity ran unrestrained until she chided herself, vowing to mind her own business.

At least Brother Zake had found other diversions. Rebecca was further disillusioned with his ministerial capacity when she observed his less-than-pastoral and ungentlemanly behavior during the festivities. She had seen the good pastor withdraw into the darkness as often as the others, and return with a rolling step. He also made a trip into the dark in the opposite direction with a voluminous redhead whom Rebecca had noticed earlier.

Her attention had been drawn to the woman mainly because she, too, was being avoided, with one exception. The men appeared to be overly friendly toward her. It wasn't too difficult to assess the situation there. So, the preacher pounds hellfire and damnation while doing a goodly amount of hell-raising himself. No wonder the people here were in bondage. They were told one thing and observed another. Rebecca sneaked another peek at the attractive redhead. The evening was turning out to be an eye-opener in many ways.

17

Christmas 1895. It was Rebecca's first Christmas in her new home. Rebecca was particularly lonely during the Christmas holidays. It hadn't been so with Jonathan, their one Christmas together. But since his death, she dreaded Christmas. She especially didn't want to be alone this year, so far from family and friends. She invited Ole Woman to have dinner and spend a few days afterward. She also asked Megan to join them.

Ever since Rebecca's last trip to the settlement, she had been very energetic in preparation of the gifts she wanted to give these two special people. She'd picked a lovely, bright sky-blue fabric sprigged with tiny white blossoms for a dress for Megan. Her other purchase was a soft, silvery-gray yarn.

She had to guess at Megan's size, but using one of her own dress patterns cut down, she felt sure it would be a close fit. She didn't hem the garment. Measurements could be made later while Megan modeled it. The seams were made extra deep, leaving room for growth. Rebecca was very anxious to see her young friend in the new dress.

With the yarn, she crochet a shawl for Ole Woman. On several occasions, Rebecca had noticed her mentor's black shawl was well-worn and raveling in places. She hoped Ole Woman would be pleased with this new one, for each stitch was hooked with love and thanksgiving for her.

Rebecca spent a week making ornaments for the tree, using odd bits of this and that. She strung red berries, gathered from the wild holly and bayberry bushes nearby, and popcorn for added contrast and color. She was quite pleased with herself when she stood back to view her handiwork.

Diablo, puzzled by all this new activity, spent a great deal of his time in the pecan grove with 'the loner.' That's what Rebecca called him in her mind. She still hadn't met him, though the dishcloth she'd wrapped the cookies in had been returned, left on the front porch wrapped around two young squirrels, dressed and ready to cook. He was indeed a strange one, but Diablo enjoyed his company.

She prepared fresh pumpkin and pecan pies, with pecans she'd gathered from her own trees, and a raisin-apple cake, using the apples Megan taught her to dry for winter storage. It was quite a novel experience to use so many ingredients from her own larder.

On Christmas Eve, Rebecca ran her traps, hoping . . . no, expecting . . . to find enough quail for their dinner. Her traps yielded six nice fat quail. A feast for sure. Her harvest pleased her immensely. When she returned from running her traps, she found an unexpected gift for Christmas dinner. A venison ham, wrapped in cheesecloth, swung from a rafter on the back porch. Diablo busily gnawed on a leg bone, probably from the same deer.

While she stood gazing at this bonus of meat, she commenced to piece together the various parts to this newest puzzle. It had to be 'the loner.' The ricks of wood, the tree pruning, also must have been his handiwork. But why?

Safely depositing her quail in the house, she changed her shawl, marched out the front door, and across the meadow toward the wagon-house in the grove. She would try once more. After all, it was Christmas.

As before, she saw a figure dodge into the thicket of brush and out of sight. This time she wasn't going to be put off. Diablo proved to be a help. He dashed past her in a blur, pursuing the disappearing figure with yelps of recognition.

Rebecca trailed them both to the edge of

the thicket. 'You may as well come out. I know you're in there.' Her only answer was the rattling of the bushes as Diablo dashed to and fro. 'I've come to thank you for the venison, and to ask you to join me tomorrow for Christmas dinner. I have no family to spend Christmas with. No one should spend Christmas alone. I'm new here, just as you are. Please say you'll join me.'

No reply.

'I'll expect you tomorrow, then.' She whistled softly. 'Diablo, come on, boy.' Rebecca retreated across the meadow with Diablo following close behind, carrying another fresh bone.

The weather continued to hold onto a remnant of fall and was extremely pleasant as Christmas day dawned bright and clear, promising to warm up as the day progressed.

Throughout the night, the venison baked over hot coals in the fireplace. Wanting everything to be perfect today of all days, she rose early to insure all was ready prior to her guest's arrival. Even before the sun began its slow climb above the naked treetops in the east, the quail were stuffed with cornbread dressing and roasting in the oven.

Ole Woman and Megan arrived early, as Rebecca expected. Each carried a gift wrapped in brown paper and tied with colorful yarn. Megan glowed with excitement, and couldn't sit still for longer than a few minutes at a time. She was like a drop of cold water skidding on a hot griddle, moving from room to room.

'I ain't never had no real Christmas afore,' she said when Rebecca found her standing before the festively decorated tree, touching first one ornament, then another.

Overwhelmed, Rebecca watched the young woman's exploration of joy and wonder; first with anger, then with pleasure. Anger for her father's indifference to his child to the extent that not even Christmas was celebrated in that house of gloom; then pleasure as she watched Megan's expressions of awe and wonder. Her heart melted at the sight of this young girl experiencing for the first time what so many took for granted.

'This can be our first real Christmas together. I haven't had one in a very long time. Come on, now, it's almost time to take up our dinner,' Rebecca said around the lump wedged in her throat. She felt the sting of tears behind her eyelids threatening to flood over at any second.

They'd just placed the last dish on the linen-covered table when a slight rap sounded at the back door. It was such a light tapping at first Rebecca dismissed it as the wind. But

178

Diablo, instantly alert, sprang up from his place near the fireplace and dashed to the door, whining and wagging his tail.

Only one person could evoke such a response from him, 'the loner.' So, he had come after all. Quickly, Rebecca glanced at the two women who stood frozen in place. They were unaware a third person was invited to join them. Half-expecting him not to come, Rebecca hadn't mentioned her invitation to them.

Smiling nervously at the two, Rebecca turned back to the door, where Diablo was busily thumping his tail against the floor, waiting for her to admit their guest.

'Come in, I'm glad you could make it.' Rebecca opened the door and stepped back to allow him room to enter.

'I . . . uh . . . I can't stay.' He rolled his worn hat between his hands and gazed at his feet while he made his excuses. Diablo licked his hand and yelped his own welcome.

'But, I thought you came to join us. I mean, you're already here, why not stay? I would really like you to.' She was at a loss for words, not knowing what to say.

'Sam? Sam, be that you? I thought that looked like your rig down in the grove when I spied it this morning. You get on in here and join us. Come on, sit yourself down here,' Ole

Woman ordered as she briskly came forward and took his hat, then led him by the elbow to the table where she pushed him unceremoniously into the nearest chair.

Sam looked sheepishly around, then dropped his gaze to his hands folded in his lap. He seemed to know Ole Woman would brook no argument.

So, these two must know each other, Rebecca thought as she bustled around, doing her best to cover the tension.

'So, you came back, huh? How long you gonna stay this time? How come you ain't been by my place yet?' Ole Woman fired her questions like arrows from a quiver while she hung up Sam's hat and took his threadbare coat, dropping it on a nearby chair. 'Cat got your tongue? Answer me, man.'

Poor Sam. He must feel like a victim of the Spanish Inquisition.

'Shall we eat now? Our guest can fill you in later.' Rebecca tried to draw attention away from the poor fellow.

'Bah, Sam don't pay no never mind to me. We be old friends, ain't we, Sam?' She smiled and nudged him in a jesting way as she took her seat beside him. 'Say the grace, Rebecca, before this grub gets cold,' the silver-haired woman chided. Rebecca knew Ole Woman wasn't concerned for the food, she just wanted to get on with her questions.

'Father, we thank you for this food You have provided for the nourishment of our bodies. We thank You for the friends gathered together here today to share this day as we celebrate the birth of our Lord and Savior. May each of us follow in His steps, following the examples He set for us, keeping Your commandments always. These things we ask in the name of Jesus. Amen.'

No one seemed willing to break the silence following the prayer, so as host, Rebecca broke it for them, and on a lighter note. 'Well, is this a wake or a celebration? Dig in, everyone.'

The remainder of the meal passed in good-natured banter between the two old friends. Sam finally relaxed and appeared to enjoy himself. Rebecca learned Sam was a frequent visitor to the area, coming and going at odd intervals, sometimes being away for years before returning.

'Tell me, Sam. Did you deliver your usual gifts last night?' Never one to let anything stop her work, the tiny woman asked her question as she passed out slices of pie.

Sam looked embarrassed by this query but he nodded his head slightly.

'Oh, don't go being modest, old man. We all know it be you what leaves all the younguns Christmas sacks of mixed nuts you gather all season.' Glancing up from the pie plate, her knife in mid-air, Ole Woman included the other two in her conversation. 'He fills sacks from his harvesting for each and every chil' in the area and ties it with wild holly and a bit of red ribbon. Each Christmas he be here, that is. Thinks we don't know, I reckon. Got a soft spot for younguns, our Sam has.' This last she addressed to Rebecca then set the pie plate on the cabinet and returned to the table.

'What a wonderful idea. Speaking of gifts, I have a few myself. Wait, I'll be right back.' Rebecca left to retrieve her packages from beneath the tree. When she returned to the kitchen, she was surprised to find two of her guests with a small stack of packages sitting before them.

Laughter and merriment filled the room as they exchanged their treasures. And treasures they were.

Megan had woven a basket of grape vines and filled it with pine cones, dried flowers, and bird feathers for Rebecca's gift. For Ole Woman, she again used grape vines to construct a wreath wrapped in dried flowers with a green ribbon laced throughout the arrangement.

Ole Woman had knitted a pair of mittens

and a scarf for Megan. Rebecca wasn't sure at first what her present was when she removed the wrapping and found a fruit jar filled with a deep, reddish-purple liquid. Her expression reflected her bewilderment and the old woman quickly explained. 'It be homemade elderberry wine, chil'. Good for what ails you, whatever it be.'

'But, I — '

'I know, you don't drink. It ain't for drinking. It be for, well, for relaxing. I recommend a small glass before retiring after a good day's work. Try it, you'll see. Besides, I know about lonely nights, too. I ain't so old I can't remember.'

Rebecca felt a blush rushing up her neck to her face. How could Ole Woman know she'd been having trouble sleeping lately? That she actually dreaded going to bed alone. That her body still remembered and yearned for fulfillment. How could she know . . . unless? Was it possible that Ole Woman, too, still had those desires at her age? Glancing at the woman across the table from her, Rebecca questioned her own judgment on the subject. Or did age have anything to do with it? The two women stared at each other across the gorge of the more than a half-century that separated them, and their understanding bridged the gap.

Hoping her earlier thoughts weren't mirrored on her face, Rebecca quickly gave her friend a hug and whispered, 'Thank you.' She held her tightly, finding yet another bond with this woman.

For a moment, Rebecca thought their male guest was embarrassed by the display of emotions. He left his place at the table and crossed to the door. Before she could react or attempt to stop him, she realized he wasn't leaving but was retrieving something from the back porch.

He reappeared carrying a chair. It was a rocking chair, constructed of willow branches, bent and woven into a fan-like pattern on its back and seat. It was the most ingenious thing Rebecca had ever seen.

'For you. I made it,' he said, his voice so low, Rebecca was left to wonder if she'd heard it at all.

Rebecca's hand flew to her mouth, and still a cry of joy escaped. She dashed across the room and gingerly sat down, though the chair looked too fragile to support her weight. Testing its strength, she realized it was far sturdier than it appeared. 'It's heaven. I love it.' Without thinking, she sprang up and threw both arms about him in a bear hug embrace. 'Oh, thank you. It's lovely.'

Sam turned several shades of red then

mumbled, 'Ain't much.' Stepping from her embrace, he faced the other two ladies and stammered an apology. 'Didn't know nobody else would be here. Didn't bring gifts, but I . . . I'll give you one later.'

'Oh, don't be an ass, Sam. You don't have to be giving us nothing. You just being here's enough for us, ain't it, gal?'

Megan nodded, running her hand caressingly along the back of the chair as she, too, admired it.

'Thank you all very much. Now, for my gifts to you.' Rebecca passed out packages to her guests.

Megan got no farther than the packet containing her dress. 'Can I put it on now?' Megan asked, holding up the frock.

'Of course, use my room.' Rebecca didn't bother to hide the smile prompted by the young girl's excitement.

Everyone put their gifts aside until Megan returned.

She sailed through the bedroom door and twirled around. 'Ain't it the prettiest thing you ever did see?'

'It is indeed, girl,' Ole Woman assured her.

'It fits perfectly,' Rebecca said, adjusting the tie at the back of the dress. 'I'll put a hem in once we get it measured. I'm so glad you like it.'

'Like it?' Megan spun about once more, then threw her arms about Rebecca's neck and kissed her cheek.

Megan's pleasure infected them all and it took a few minutes for the group to resume their gift opening.

Rebecca watched her mentor open her package. Once the pearl-gray shawl was draped about the gnome-sized woman's frail shoulders, she kept running her gnarled fingers across its softness. Lastly, Rebecca handed 'the loner' his gift. His had been the hardest to select. After all, what did she know about this man? She'd only invited him yesterday, and there hadn't been much time.

'I hope you like it. I don't even know if you use a pipe or not. But my father did, and I thought perhaps . . . well, I hope you like it,' she babbled while he took the gift and unwrapped it slowly.

'Ain't never had me a store-bought pipe. Thank you, ma'am.' He ran his hand gently along the stem and around the carved bowl, cradling it between his work-worn hands.

Their festivities didn't break up until almost dark when Megan and Sam departed for their own homes. Megan promised if she could get away, she'd return tomorrow so they could hem her new dress. Before leaving,

Sam presented Diablo with a gift; a piece of rawhide tied in a large knot.

'For gnawing on,' he said with a sheepish grin. 'Dog needs to chew and gnaw on something. Best this, than the furniture.'

18

The New Year of 1896 arrived in an uneventful way. Winter settled in and seemed determined to make up for arriving late. It went from snowfall to thaw in vicious cycles right up until spring. Rebecca spent the time catching up on matters she'd postponed. Having never been one to remain idle for long, she was already looking forward to outside activity again.

Sam, 'the loner,' as Rebecca still persisted in calling him to herself, kept her supplied with fresh game throughout the winter. It was always left on the porch. He never made his presence known, and the gifts of fresh meat were welcome indeed.

Spring finally arrived, and so did the spring rains. Rebecca tended the cheery fire in the big fieldstone fireplace and longed for the rain to cease. Instead, the weather showed every indication of making life miserable for man and beast. It rained heavily all night, and seemed determined to rain even more. Vision through the windows was limited to curtains of water, torn apart by thunder and lightning.

At first, Rebecca wasn't sure whether it was

knocking on the door or the rumbling of the thunderstorm she heard. When the clatter continued, she decided it must be someone outside. In this weather? She opened the door and could only gaze at the drenched creature before her. 'Megan, what on earth . . . ?'

'Come . . . you gotta come quick. It's Pap, he's hurt.' Almost hysterical, she grabbed Rebecca's hand, tugging her forward. 'Hurry!'

'Come inside.' Rebecca pulled the girl inside, shut the door and handed her a towel to dry off with. 'Now, slowly, tell me what's wrong.'

Megan wiped the moisture from her face with the towel, took a deep breath and let it out as a sigh. 'It were the lightning. Pap must have heard the noise and come out to check . . . '

'Let me.' Rebecca took the cotton towel from Megan's shaking hands and urged her onto a chair. 'If we don't get you dried off, you'll get sick.' She fluffed Megan's hair gently. 'Now, finish your story.'

'When the tree fell, it caught him . . . '

'Oh, dear, I didn't . . . what was he doing out in such weather? Is he still trapped?' Rebecca tossed the towel aside.

'He were in the outhouse.' Megan smiled at that. 'Me and Davy dragged him from beneath the tree, but I fear his leg is broke.'

'Have you gone for Ole Woman?'

'She be sick. Said to get you to go. You know same as her how to set a leg.' Her eyes were large as saucers, reflecting her fear. 'Hurry, we ain't got no time to spare. Besides, he be hurting something fearful when I left.'

'Let me get my things together.' Rebecca bustled about, gathering items she thought she'd need. Having despaired of being called upon any time soon, she wasn't prepared for this emergency. Grabbing her coat and shawl, she turned to the waterlogged girl. 'Let's go.'

Diablo on their heels, they splashed their way toward the injured Jacob Penny. She couldn't help but wonder how he would react to his aid coming from the 'outsider' instead of the trusted Ole Woman? That was his problem, she decided, sloshing up the hillside to his cabin. He's the one hurt and in pain. Not a very charitable thought, she admitted. But right now, she didn't feel overly considerate. She was cold, wet, and miserable. And at the moment, she was in no mood to deal with a stiff-necked, hard-hearted man like Jacob Penny.

★　★　★

'Out! Get her out of here, I said.'

'Mr. Penny, I can help if . . .'

190

'Ain't no stranger gonna do nothing for me!' He grimaced with pain as he screamed at her.

Somehow, Rebecca wasn't shocked at his response to her appearance. It was apparent he was suffering greatly. From the bloody flesh of his swollen leg protruded the stark white edges of splintered bone.

'Okay. If that's the way you feel, I'll leave. But if that leg isn't tended properly and quickly, you run the risk of losing it.' She closed the bag containing her medical supplies with a snap, all the while holding the sulking man on the bed with her blue-gray eyes. 'Of course, that's your decision to make, not mine. It's me or nothing. What will it be?' Without waiting for his reply, she snatched up her wet coat and started for the door.

'Fix it, then,' he growled between clenched teeth. His white-knuckled grip on the headboard of his bed never lessened. Obviously, pain raked his body.

'Get me some whiskey!' Rebecca ordered. 'And lots of it.' Her sleeves were already rolled above her elbows as she set about her work.

'You a drinking woman, are you?' Her reluctant patient snarled the accusation. Even in pain, he had a nasty disposition.

'It's not for me, Mr. Penny. It's for you.'

Her eyes became slits when she leaned forward over the perspiring figure sprawled on the bed. With steel in her voice, she proclaimed, 'I promise you, I won't feel a thing when I set that leg, but you're going to need all the help you can get to deal with the pain.'

One of Megan's brothers handed her a quart jar. She slapped a glass into Jacob's trembling hand and sloshed a generous amount of the amber liquid into the tumbler. 'Drink up.'

The musky aroma wafting from the jar jolted her memory. She'd detected the same smell at the contraption in the laurel thicket. She'd almost forgotten it until now, standing beside the bed of this hostile individual. Holding the container closer to her nose, she inhaled deeply. Like a lamp lit in a dark room, she knew instantly what she'd stumbled onto that day, a whiskey still. She'd heard stories of them, of course, but had never seen one. The aroma was identical and unmistakable. She'd stumbled upon someone's still.

'You gonna give me some more, or stand there sniffing the jug?'

'Here, give him as much as he can get down.' Rebecca pushed the jar into the hands of the nearest young man. No one bothered with introductions, so she wasn't sure which one he was. Everyone appeared too afraid of the man on the bed to do anything on their own.

She moved swiftly and deftly about the room, busily making preparations for the job at hand. 'Megan, put lots of water on to boil. Then, get all the lamps in here and light them.' The day remained gray and gloomy, and rain continued to lash the house. The room, lit by a single lantern, was dark as night.

Rebecca turned to another of the young men in the room. 'Get me some clay, lots of it.'

The silent figure peeled himself off the wall where he'd been leaning, observing the scene as though not a part of it. He looked as if he'd like to refuse her request. Then casting a quick glance toward the man on the bed, mumbled something under his breath before snatching a coat from the wall rack and slamming out the back door. His words were partly drowned by the thrumming of the rain and his heels bounding across the rain-washed porch. All Rebecca caught of his grumbled remark was, ' . . . Women, giving orders.'

A third young man sat timidly on the edge of a chair near the huge fireplace, fidgeting with the cap he held in his work-roughened hands. 'Can I help, ma'am?' he asked, looking not at Rebecca, but at the man on the bed.

Rebecca noticed Jacob was still slugging down the liquor. At last he was showing signs of it taking effect.

'Yes, find me a pair of scissors and two flat boards about two feet long,' she replied calmly. He was the only one of the boys who hadn't appeared to view her presence here as unwelcome. He was different somehow, gentler maybe, than the other two.

Rebecca returned to her now quite drunk patient. 'That's enough,' she said, taking the glass from Jacob and handing it to his son.

Even with all the whiskey he'd drunk, it took the two oldest boys to hold him on the bed while Rebecca and the youngest son pulled the leg into place and set it. Rebecca hoped he'd lose consciousness, and blessedly he did, but not until she was almost finished.

Using the two boards as braces, she tied them into place with strips of cloth then, fashioned a homemade cast over them with the clay. They had a bit of trouble rigging up a sling to elevate the leg and barely finished when her patient recovered from his faint.

'What in tarnation you doing to me, woman? Let me down.' Jacob came to in fine fettle, his usual obnoxious self. 'Get my leg out of this contraption.'

'Sorry, Mr. Penny. You'll have to leave it like that for a few weeks, then I'll let it down. For now, you need to rest. Would you like something to eat, or some coffee?'

'I'll have me another drink,' he growled.

'Afraid not. You need to eat. No more alcohol.' She adjusted the pillow under his head.

Slapping at her hand, he snapped, 'You are forgetting yourself, woman. You ain't my wife. I said, I'll have me a drink. Boy,' he twisted his head until he located one of his sons, 'fetch me my jug.'

'Thank heaven for that, sir. Not being your wife, I mean. But I'm giving the orders now. No whiskey.' Rebecca turned to the young man approaching the bed. 'Put the jar away.'

Clearly, this was a new situation. The puzzled young chap started around her with his burden. Rebecca deftly reached out and relieved him of it. 'He needs to sober up now. He must eat to gain strength. I'll give him a sip or two as he needs it for pain. Now, clean up this mess.'

'Me? Get the girl to do it. That's her job,' came the sullen reply.

'The girl, as you call your sister, is already busy. I want you to do it.'

'Pap, you hear that? She wants me to

do the girl's work.' The sniveling young giant appealed for his father's intervention. The room sweltered with crude emotions.

'Do it!' Jacob growled between clenched teeth.

'I'll be staying a few days to keep a close check on that leg. Where can I put my things?'

The silence in the room was explosive, vibrating off the walls.

Megan recovered first and, quickly snatching up Rebecca's parcel, retreated from the scene. 'You can stay in my room.'

Apparently still reluctant to take orders from the stranger, Megan's brother spoke up. 'Pap?' The plea was plainly a cry for assistance.

'Do it!' And with that, Jacob Penny lapsed into an alcohol-induced slumber.

* * *

'I be right tired of hearing that garbage,' her cranky patient growled from his rumpled bed.

Rebecca arched her brows. 'I beg your pardon? What garbage are you referring to, Mr. Penny?'

'You been spouting on for the better part of two days now about that loving, forgiving, and healing God of yours, and I had a belly

196

full. You hear me? A belly full.' His eyes swept the small room, making sure that he had everyone's full attention. With a loud grunt deep in his throat, he announced, 'I know all about God. And He ain't nothing like what you be filling that gal's head with. Nothing at all. Just ask Brother Zake. He'll tell you about what God be like.'

Warming to his topic, Jacob eased his body a little higher in the bed, propping his back against the headboard. 'He punishes His children and teaches them lessons by the trials and tribulations He puts on them. That's the God I know and it be the truth, 'cause Brother Zake be saying so. I don't want to hear no more of these tales you're telling.'

During Rebecca's spare time while at the Penny household she had continued Megan's lessons, of which a part was teaching her about faith, and reading from the New Testament scriptures.

'Mr. Penny, I'm very sorry all you seem to know of God is what some misinformed preacher has told you. Have you never read the Bible for yourself, sir? The Bible is full of God's love.'

'Enough! It were your loving God what took my Leona. She, who was kindness and love itself. And He took her. You call that love?' He spat this at Rebecca with all the venom and hate his soul contained. Yet, she sensed a plea underneath. A plea for what? To be wrong, maybe? She decided to try something. Maybe she could reach him.

'Megan, will you fetch me some fresh water from the spring?' She smiled to Megan with her eyes, trying to convey her message. Leave us for a spell.

Megan seemed to understand as she nodded, grabbed the water bucket and dashed out the door.

Rebecca pulled a chair near the bed. Playing for time, she smoothed the folds of her dress while she composed herself. It was now or never. 'Mr. Penny, I don't understand all you feel, or what you've been told about God. But, I gather you have a very harsh attitude toward Him. I know also that, for the past couple of days, you've listened to your daughter at her reading.' Deliberately keeping her voice low and controlled, she held him with her eyes. 'So you must have heard what the Bible says about God's love and His forgiving nature. Sir, I ask you, which idea of God do you think is real? The Word?' She paused momentarily to give him time to consider, 'Or Brother Zake's?'

'I know what I know. He took my Leona

and left me with . . . with a girl what ain't all there!'

'That's another matter, Mr. Penny. When I first met you, you said Megan was . . . '

'Megan! Megan? What's this Megan business? You keep calling the girl Megan. That ain't her name!'

'She has no other. She needed a name. I gave her one. If your wife was what you say she was, do you think she would want her daughter to grow up without a name? Or, for that matter, to be made to feel responsible for her death? You say God took your wife, yet you punish your daughter. When in truth, sir, neither of them were responsible.' Instead of roaring at her, as she'd half expected, Jacob lay very still, frowning as though he were lost in thought. Rebecca decided to press on while she had an advantage, and hoped he heard her.

'Satan took your wife, Mr. Penny. Not God and not Megan. And your daughter is not simpleminded. As a matter of fact, she's quite bright. She's . . . '

'Leave me. Get out of here.' He didn't raise his voice, nor look in her direction. 'Go.' Something was going on inside that stubborn head of his. Rebecca could almost see thought patterns flying about.

Easing herself from the chair, she quietly

stepped outside, confused by his reaction and the faraway look on his face. Maybe she had gone too fast, said the wrong thing.

'You okay, ma'am?' Davy, the youngest son, approached her with the question. He was a tall, slender young man with fine flaxen hair, open blue eyes, a delicate complexion with a flush on his high cheekbones, and a wide mouth.

'Uh, yes. Yes, I'm fine.' She didn't know what else to say. Then, after a brief hesitation, she said, 'Davy, tell me about yourself, your family. I know so little about any of you, yet we're neighbors.'

'Ain't much to tell, I reckon.' He ducked his head and fidgeted with a loose button on his shirt.

'Well, then, I'll tell you about myself. Sit down.' Rebecca pulled up a rocker near the edge of the porch while Davy sat down on the top step.

Rebecca talked. Davy listened. Then he loosened up and joined the talk. A bit of information here and a bit there. Slowly, Rebecca gathered the pitiful truth. Without exception, they were all afraid of 'Pap,' as they called their father. He was a hard task master; the ruling authority. He and the boys hunted and trapped a bit, just enough to buy the essentials, those things their poor piece of ground wouldn't produce under the labor of the girl in her garden, and the eggs and milk from the chickens and cow she tended. The men folk provided meat for the table by their hunting, but 'the girl' had to dress it out when they brought it home. No one was allowed to help her, and Davy was the only one to offer. Pap allowed that was woman's work, and heaven help the one who defied him.

'I'd help if Pap would let me, but he won't. I bring her critters sometimes, though. She be right fond of critters.' He turned to face Rebecca and a gentle smile warmed his features. 'It takes the sadness from her eyes. And sometimes, I bring her critters what get caught in the traps. She patches them up and makes them well again.'

'You like your sister, don't you, Davy?'

'Yeah, she be okay. For a girl.'

Rebecca laughed about that. He was so serious, yet comical at the same time. 'I'm sorry, Davy. I wasn't laughing at you. It's just that . . . well, it's okay to like girls too, you know.'

★ ★ ★

A few days later, they all received a surprise. Megan and Rebecca were preparing to retire to her room when, unexpectedly, Jacob broke the silence with a gruff request.

'Come read for me, girl. I hear you can read . . . so, read!'

'Read what, Pap?' Megan asked, twisting the corner of her apron into a knot.

'Read me some of that stuff you two's always reading. Might as well hear it from you as some stranger.' His eyes found Rebecca where she stood, transfixed in place. They seemed to say, 'We'll see!'

Well, let the old man have it his way. Rebecca knew that, 'faith cometh by hearing, and hearing by the word of God.' So she didn't care how he heard it, from her or his daughter, as long as he heard it. Rebecca occupied herself with Megan's mending basket in a far corner.

This became the nightly routine for the remainder of Rebecca's stay with the Pennys. There was never any comment or question about the reading, just the command, 'Read, girl,' then, 'Enough' when he grew tired. Nothing more. Rebecca took the liberty of suggesting to Megan she read to her father from the book of Acts. That should give him food for thought.

On the tenth day of her stay, she deemed Jacob Penny mending well enough to no longer require her presence full time. If she expected any show of gratitude for her time there, she was disappointed. Her leave-taking went unnoticed by all, except Megan and Davy. Megan walked part of the way home with her before dashing back to her endless chores. Davy walked with them and shyly thanked her for helping Pap, then hurriedly followed that with, 'I'd be obliged if you'd let me come to lessons with the girl. I wouldn't be no bother. I got me a powerful hankering to read them words like she do.' As usual, he fidgeted with his worn hat while watching his feet.

'I'd like that very much,' Rebecca responded. 'Do join us.'

Davy loped off like a young, healthy buck in his excitement. What would the crotchety old man say about that?

19

On her way home, Rebecca stopped by the old woman's place but found her gone. Her friend must be feeling better. There was no pressing need to hurry home and after being cooped up the better part of ten days, she felt like walking. Overhead, the sky was clear with only a few fleecy white clouds scattered lazily amid the blue, as if for decoration. A warm, gentle breeze caressed her skin and stirred loose wisps of hair across her face.

'It's great to be alive,' Rebecca spoke aloud, tucking a strand of hair back into place.

'Always heard folks that talk to themselves was crazy.'

Startled by the unexpected voice, Rebecca cried out and whirled around. Her startled gaze confronted a man tenderly cradling a shotgun in the crook of his left arm as though it were a child. 'Who are you?' she blurted, unconsciously taking a step backward.

'Are you crazy or just crazy like a fox? What are you doing snooping around here? Who sent you? Well, speak up, woman!' He fired his questions at her as rapidly as Rebecca suspected he could fire both barrels of the gun he held. Clenching her fist, she straightened her spine and tried to force strength into her voice, strength she was far from feeling.

'No one sent me, and I was not snooping,' she replied, in what she hoped was a calm voice.

'You been here before. Why?'

'What do you want of me?' She felt her knees trembling but dared not show it. Numb, paralyzed with shock and fear, she waited as cold, unrelenting eyes held her captive.

'You been prying around here before. I want to know why. You with the law?'

'N-no,' she stammered. A knot of fear wedged in her throat, making it difficult to speak. 'I live near here and I haven't been — ' She didn't finish. She couldn't. He had such a cold, penetrating stare. Her gaze locked on the dark walnut stock of the gun, refusing to meet the glacial, beguiling eyes. When he spoke, she watched the hand gently cradle the stock. Large, powerful hands, yet tender. That thought shocked her, for it was in contrast to the words he spoke. Yet, the thought persisted. His hands reflected a warm, almost maternal quality. What manner of man was this?

'Folks been known to turn up dead around here. They just sort of disappear, and nobody asks no questions. 'Specially when it's known they been poking into other folks' business. It ain't right healthy, if you get my meaning.' His words battered her while he stood like a statue, feet planted firmly apart, shoulders squared, stroking the polished barrel of the gun. The call of a blue jay pierced the air, punctuating his words.

'It ain't healthy, hear? I'd be for staying where I belong if I's you, little lady. Or go back where you come from.' He spit a stream of brown tobacco juice and shifted the wad to his other cheek. Then, in graceful, long-legged motions he strode off, not even glancing back.

Despite the warmth of the day, Rebecca felt a cold chill race across her body as she watched the stranger disappear from view as though swallowed up by the countryside, or like a ghost. 'People disappear . . . it ain't healthy.' She recalled his words. He had threatened her. Who was he, this mysterious and menacing man? Suddenly, she lost the desire to roam the countryside and quickly made for home and safety.

A couple days later, Ole Woman arrived, announcing it was soap making time. She'd had Rebecca saving ashes from the cookstove

206

and fireplace all winter. She hadn't, however, been able to save much in the way of drippings. Most of her meat had been wild game and, therefore, free of fat. But her instructor had attended several hog killings during the fall and had been given the fat, which she'd rendered into lard.

After leaching the ashes with creek water and collecting the residue, which was lye, they were ready to proceed with soap making. Most of the lye and lard mixture was cooked off and molded without benefit of fragrance. A handful of lavender petals were tossed into the last batch cooking in the big, black wash pot. This molding was for bathing.

'Nothing like it for getting a body clean.' This tidbit of information was passed to Rebecca, who was industriously cutting the soap into bars.

'It's lye, won't it be harsh to the skin?'

'Naw! Once we cooked it off, we kill the lye and just left the cleaning properties.' She smiled in answer to Rebecca's ignorance.

While working, Rebecca found herself sharing with the other woman her encounter with the man with the cold stare and the gun. While Rebecca related the incident, her aged helper became quiet. A serious expression settled on her countenance.

'What is it? Why are you looking at me like that?'

'Jethro Bean. That's what be wrong, especially if he thinks you're the law.' She wiped her gnarled old hands on her white apron. Backing up to the workbench, she gently eased her tired old body onto it and, beckoning to Rebecca, said, 'Come here, chil'. Sit next to me. We gotta talk. The time has come, I think, to be letting you know how things be around here. Most of the folks'd be saying I'm talking out of turn, but they don't know you like I do.' That all-knowing gaze settled on Rebecca and studied her for a moment. Placing her wrinkled hand on Rebecca's shoulder, she nodded slowly as if a decision had been made.

'I know you be what you say you are. You ain't no revenoor dog. I'd stake my life on that. So, I'm gonna trust you and tell you about your man with the gun. You see, hereabouts shining be the way lots a folk make they living . . . '

'Shining?'

'Don't go interrupting. Just listen. Shining, moonshining, farming the woods. Call it what you will, it means making whiskey, or white lightning, some calls it. Folks gotta make a living best way they can. 'Course, the law don't see it that way and that causes more than a few problems. Law's always looking for a man's rig or sending someone else to be doing the dirty work of spying around, plum crazy to find a man's fixings. That be what's called a revenoor dog.'

Narrowing her eyes, she gazed intently at Rebecca. Seemingly content with what she saw, she continued. 'Jethro Bean's a shiner. About the best they be in this neck of the woods, too. Jethro takes great pride in his makings, uses only the best. Nothing but white corn for his mash, cold spring water from the north side of the hill, flowing west, and never no sugar. Can't call it pure corn whiskey if you use sugar. Sounds like a heap of work for a sip of whiskey, don't it?' Smiling at Rebecca, she shifted to a more comfortable position. 'Like I said, Jethro be the best moonshiner they is in these hills. Folks come from miles around to buy Jethro's shine. 'Course, Jethro gotta know you before he'll sell you anything. Fetch me a dipper of cool water, will you? All this jawing makes a body thirsty.'

After drinking deeply and wiping her mouth on her apron, she resumed. 'Now, where was I? Oh, yeah. Jethro, he been two steps ahead of them revenoor fellows all his born days, and he don't intend to lose no ground now. So you can see why he be suspicious of strangers. He got good reason to be. Don't go judging him too harshly. He be a fine man at heart. A hard worker, too.

'He got a real fine family. House full of younguns and a wife he fair dotes on. Reckon if Jethro Bean got any weakness in him, it'd be his Rachel. Just does a body good to be around them two. He treats her like a porcelain doll that might break. And her face lights up like a moonbeam when he enters the room. Makes a body wish they's twenty years younger . . . make that forty years.' She chuckled like a schoolgirl, and Rebecca could have sworn she detected a blush.

'Well, now,' she said, rising slowly from the bench and dusting off the back of her dress, 'I get long-winded at times. Back to work now.' She busied herself clearing away their work area. 'I'll have me a chat with Jethro, let him know you can be trusted. Should have done it afore, I reckon.'

That night when Rebecca recorded the day's events and the information given her by Ole Woman about Jethro Bean, his occupation and his family, she tried to compare the man of the story to the man she'd met in the woods. She remembered the cold-eyed stare, the gentle caressing of the gun barrel and the words, 'folk been known to disappear.' Somehow, she couldn't imagine this man and the one Ole Woman talked about were the same. She anticipated and dreaded their next meeting.

20

Rebecca stood at the back door, coffee cup in hand, gazing at the curtain of water that had hung over the area for three weeks. Today was her birthday, the second since coming to the hill country. She had planned to spend it with Ole Woman. Now, glancing at the gray, moisture-laden sky, she abandoned all hope of visiting.

Well, she had to do something or go loony. This kind of weather always made her restless. Turning from the doorway, she noticed the letter from James lying on the kitchen table. Lighting a lamp, she pulled up a chair, sat down at the table and reread the letter. He wrote that he and his family were fine, business was growing, and they were expecting another baby around Thanksgiving. This time they were hoping for a girl.

Toward the end of the letter, James included a bit of news which excited Rebecca very much: Jimmy Johnstone would visit her in May or June. James was sending him to deliver, as he put it, 'a few things to at least provide creature comforts.'

Of course, Rebecca realized what he was

doing. He thought to make her homesick in the hope she would finally 'come to her senses.' Rebecca eagerly anticipated Jimmy's arrival, though she was not in the least homesick. In fact, she had never been so at peace with herself and the world around her as she had been the past year.

The drumming of the rain on the roof had a hypnotic effect. Sitting in the flickering lamplight, she allowed her thoughts to drift, leaving behind the gloom of the dreary day.

The sky remained heavy and gray. Clouds boiled and churned in angry protest at the elements. The ground was saturated, yet it continued to rain, as it had for a month. A constant downpour.

A majestic old oak, growing on the creek bank, finally gave up its battle to maintain its place and toppled into the torrent of swirling water. The embankments surrounding the tree slid away, washed downstream to become topsoil in someone's fields.

The level of the creek rose hourly. A lot of homes would be flooded and property damaged. Rebecca prayed no lives would be lost.

Tomorrow, rain or shine, she was going to check on Ole Woman. With all the rain, she hadn't been to see her in several days. Even though it meant crossing the creek, she felt she should go. Maybe the rain would let up by morning. During the night, her roof developed a few new leaks. She placed pans under them to catch the water. Fortunately, she knew how to repair them once the rain stopped. Diablo was restless from being cooped up in the house so long. He made a few forays across the meadow to visit his friend, Sam, but finally abandoned his trips due to the miserable weather.

★ ★ ★

Her excursion across the creek was slow going and a bit shaky at times. She attempted to step from rock to moss-covered rock at her usual crossing place. The water had receded a little in the night, but still rushed rapidly downstream. Rebecca finally reached the far shore, but not before getting her feet wet several times after losing her balance on the slippery rocks. She was a comical sight by the time she reached solid ground. Her shoes made sloshing sounds but she trudged on, her water-soaked skirt flapping heavily against her shaky legs.

'Land sake, chil'. Ain't you got sense enough to come in out of the rain?'

'I wanted t-to see if you wer-were . . . all right,' Rebecca chattered, shaking with cold.

The rain had commenced again long before she reached her destination and Ole Woman's toasty warm fire.

Her host handed Rebecca a towel. 'Get in front of that there fire and strip, before you catch your death of cold.'

Rebecca didn't hesitate. The chill was already seeping into her bones. By the time she was wrapped in a quilt and fluffing her hair dry before the fire, Ole Woman had a cup of hot tea ready for her. Gratefully, she accepted the brew with trembling hands and took a deep swallow. It left a warm path all the way to her stomach.

'This is delicious. What kind is it?' The warmth radiated throughout her body, and her teeth stopped clicking together.

'It be my special tea for fools what roams about in weather even ducks avoid.' A mischievous grin accompanied the statement.

'It's good, but feels like I've swallowed a fire.' Rebecca continued to sip the piping hot tea. 'I feel a bit sleepy, though.' She felt her head nod forward as the warmth inside became a glow all over.

'Best get you to bed. I see you can't take my special tea.' She chuckled and led Rebecca to the sofa near the fireplace.

When she lay sprawled half on, half off the sofa, she saw wrinkled hands drape a quilt over her and heard herself ask, as if from a great distance, 'What kind of tea?'

'A touch of chamomile and two touches of shine.' The answer floated through the haze in which Rebecca drifted but she couldn't grasp it.

★ ★ ★

'Began to think you'd sleep the day away,' Rebecca heard Ole Woman say. Her arms and legs cramped. In fact, her entire body ached. Glancing about in puzzlement, she stretched slowly to ease the discomfort of her protesting body, then sat up. It had been mid-morning when she arrived, and though it was cloudy and dark even then, she sensed by the fading light that it was now mid-afternoon. It was still raining.

'What happened?' Rebecca asked. Her clothes lay draped over the back of a chair near the fire. She checked them and they were dry. How long had she slept?

'Tea must have been a bit strong' Ole Woman chuckled. 'But it did the trick. You got the rest you needed after that soaking you took. Rested right good, too. You was a-sawing them logs.'

Rebecca finished dressing, tried to digest

that bit of information but failed. 'I was what?'

'Sawing logs . . . uh . . . snoring.'

'I was not! I don't snore,' Rebecca replied hotly, lacing up her shoes. Her head swam slightly, and an odd taste clung to her mouth. She ran her tongue experimentally around her teeth. Strange. They were coated with fur.

'Well, now, don't go getting uppity with me, just 'cause you can't hold your liquor.' She snorted and yanked the quilt from the floor where it had fallen while Rebecca dressed.

'Liquor? What liq . . . ?' Rebecca paused while a faint remembrance floated forward. Chamomile and shine. 'Wait a minute.' Rebecca placed a hand to her throbbing forehead and reasoned it out. This feisty old woman had put moonshine in her tea! No wonder she'd slipped off to Dream Land so suddenly. She couldn't drink alcohol. Her system had no tolerance for it. Of course, her friend had no way of knowing that, and besides, she'd only meant to help. But judging from her behavior and the way she kept flapping that quilt and folding it in a haphazard manner, Rebecca knew she'd hurt her mentor's feelings with her outburst. She wouldn't hurt the older woman for the world, not intentionally, anyway. How was she to mend this breach between them that she'd unwittingly caused?

Laughter burst forth suddenly as a picture of the two of them flashed across her mind's eye.

'What's so funny, missy?' the old woman snapped, tossing the hopeless mess of bedding back on the sofa and turning to face Rebecca.

Upset was probably not the correct term, but it was close. It wasn't chil' or Rebecca, but, *Missy*.

Trying to keep a straight face, Rebecca answered, 'Us. We're both acting like two children, snapping at each other over nothing. At least, nothing worth costing us our friendship. Truce?' She slowly approached the frowning figure, her right hand extended.

Only a second elapsed before a gnarled hand grasped hers, and Rebecca clasped Ole Woman in a hug. She dearly loved this gentle old soul.

'Ain't no fool like an old fool, they say, and this old fool says truce.' She returned Rebecca's hug.

★ ★ ★

Near midnight a clatter awoke them. At first, they thought it must be a loose shutter slapping against the house in the wind gusts. But the pounding was insistent and constant. Ole Woman grumbled and fumbled around for a match. Lighting the lamp, she eased out of the bed they shared.

'Keep your shirt on. I'm a-coming, I'm a-coming.' She padded barefoot toward the front without even taking time to pull a shawl or robe over her flannel gown. But when Rebecca heard a man's panic-pierced voice, she frantically scrambled into her clothes.

The roar of the wind combined with the slashing rain made it impossible to hear all of the conversation. She only heard the man's voice, not the satiny-soft sound of her hostess.

'Hurry up. We got to go . . . now. I don't know. I got Blue Girl, outside to fetch you on. Who? No! No stranger. Oh, awright! But hurry.'

Rebecca gathered there was trouble, sickness, or accident and the man wanted the old woman to go with him, but not her. So what else was new? Rebecca buttoned the last button on her dress, grabbed her cloak, and hurried to get her supplies ready so Ole Woman could get dressed.

They passed in the doorway; she smiled reassuringly and patted Rebecca's arm. 'Get my bag, Rebecca. We got us a sick youngun to tend.'

Rebecca glanced toward the door curiously. And there, framed in the doorway stood the man with the cold-eyed stare and the gun. Though now, he stood twisting his dripping hat between his large hands, his eyes darting from the doorway through which the diminutive figure had disappeared to the darkness outside. A growing puddle formed beneath the waterlogged man. Either he'd come a good distance or it was raining harder, maybe both.

★　★　★

The man gently lifted his fragile burden onto the back of the largest mule Rebecca had ever seen. While the old healer settled herself, Rebecca shivered. Beyond the mule, all she could see was a world engulfed in wet darkness. A slow rumble of thunder slid across the heavens and slowly died away, followed by a vibrant flash of lightning.

Turning to Rebecca, the man gruffly ordered, 'You walk well back of us. Blue Girl don't cotton to strangers much. Touchy, she is . . . like most females.'

Rebecca clenched her jaw, stemming the flow of words, but couldn't help thinking them. His mule was a lot like its master when it came to strangers. And that snide remark about touchy females was unnecessary. Glaring at the man's back, she determined to consider the source and ignore it.

Swinging his lantern high and clasping the lead rope on Blue Girl, he started off through the soggy night with a parting shot slung over his shoulder at Rebecca. 'See you keep up. I ain't got time to be traipsing around looking for you. You can't keep up, you're on your own.'

Clamping her teeth together until they hurt, Rebecca checked her temper. She'd keep up if it killed her. They trudged forward at a pace even the mule found difficult to maintain, slipping and sliding in the gooey mud. Jethro's long-legged stride consumed the miles. By the time they reached their destination, Rebecca was gasping for breath. A spasm of pain knifed through her left side, but she'd die before admitting to him she was in pain. She'd kept up, hadn't she?

Confusion and panic greeted the trio when they dashed inside, dripping puddles of brown muddy water on the clean, but bare floor. Three small, whimpering children huddled together at the foot of the bed where a fourth child lay cradled in the arms of its mother. That child was gasping for air and coughing deeply. The rasping and rattle of the child's labored breathing was audible even across the large room, where the new arrivals busily removed wet shoes and cloaks.

The miniature healer grabbed the wet hem of her long skirt and, without hesitation, wrung the excess water from it. The puddle grew larger at her feet. Then snatching up her bag, she followed quickly on the heels of the young man who had dashed, dripping, across the room to the woman and child on the bed. His concern and love were evident as he leaned forward and placed a tender kiss on the cheek of the woman, and a hand gently caressed the head of the child she held.

'I brought her. It'll be okay now, hon.'

Slinging orders like a general approaching the heart of battle, the tiny woman took charge. Jethro and Rebecca were both dispatched with duties. Even the children were given small chores to do. This was to keep them busy and out from under foot, and to calm their fears and allay the panic which was almost a visible presence in the room. They all had their work cut out for them this night.

With the smell of camphor heavy in the air, Ole Woman huddled beneath a makeshift tent, cradling the sick child in her arms as the steam rose thickly from the kettle at her feet.

The wheeze and rattle filled the room, jarring their nerves. All they could do was stand by, feeling helpless, while the youngster fought for each breath. Then, without warning, it stopped. Silence dropped like death in the room. No one spoke. No one moved. The child wasn't breathing.

Without giving thought to her action, Rebecca dashed beneath the sheet tent. Snatching the child from the old woman's frail arms, she frantically slapped the heel of her right hand between the small shoulder blades, and prayed. Every fiber of her being prayed. Rebecca didn't intend that this child should die. Not now.

She continued to pray and to pound that tiny back. The silence was heavy, the only sound in the room that of her hand connecting with the tender flesh. As if from a great distance she heard her own voice, gaining strength, as she continued, 'Father, Your word says, 'What things so ever ye desire, when ye pray, believe ye receive them, and ye shall have them' and again it says, 'Whatsoever ye shall ask the Father in My name, He will give it you.' Hear me now, Father, for in the name of Jesus, I pray for the healing of this child. And because by faith I believe this child is healed, I give You thanks for it.'

Suddenly, the silence was broken by a soft splatter, a gasp, a quick intake of breath, a cry. Pandemonium erupted as everyone in the room released the breath they'd unconsciously held. The frightened young mother grabbed the child; the man grabbed them both. Three tiny tots raced across the room, laughing, to clutch their mother's hem, wanting to be included and perhaps reassured. Everyone was either laughing, or crying, or both.

Rebecca turned from the joyous scene and slipped, unnoticed, out the front door. She needed to be alone to comprehend the miracle she'd just witnessed. Deep down in her heart, she'd believed. With every fiber of her being, she'd known. Still, it was awesome to see the manifestation of His word in action. Leaning on the porch railing, deep in her prayer of thanksgiving, Rebecca didn't hear the old sage approach. Until she felt the gnarled hand rest over her own trembling hand, she was unaware of anything or anyone.

'You did it, chil'. You saved that youngun's life. I couldn't do a thing for him, but you did,' she spoke softly.

'No. I didn't do it. He did.'

'But if you hadn't acted when you did, that tike in there would have been dead for sure.'

'God did it, not me. You know that.'

'Sure, I know. But it were you who acted. You acted on your faith. I believe, yes, but I didn't act, and faith without action is a dead thing. Because you acted on the faith you possess, God responded and that child was restored to his parents.'

With that, she hugged Rebecca warmly, then patted her hand. 'Come, let's get you in out of this damp air and inside where it's warm. Your skin be cold as death.'

Only then did Rebecca realize she was trembling with cold.

Rebecca properly met the family of Jethro Bean the next morning, though the only way to tell it was morning was the dark was less dense. It still rained.

Rachel, Jethro's wife, was charming. She wasn't what Rebecca had expected after the remarks by Ole Woman about Jethro treating his wife like a porcelain doll. Somehow, Rebecca had pictured a petite, dainty woman. She was neither. In size, at least, she was an excellent match for her husband, and from Rebecca's short observation, in everything else as well. Rachel Bean was a tall, slender woman with the blackest hair Rebecca had ever seen. Raven's-wing black with blue highlights winking through, and clear violet eyes; a great combination. She was a soft-spoken person, yet when she issued an order or request to her young brood; she was instantly obeyed, which in itself spoke loudly of the type person she was. She loved her children enough to train them.

Rebecca noticed that, regardless the circumstance, Jethro Bean had his wife's first and full attention. She attended his every need, even before he was aware he needed. Little things perhaps, but important. It was obvious to even a casual observer they were very much in love. It was a joy to watch them together.

Earlier, she'd caught a glimpse of that love as the two of them stood beside the bed of their sleeping son, who'd been the center of attention the night before. Looking up, their eyes met and spoke volumes. Rebecca felt as though she'd invaded their privacy. They weren't aware of anyone else in the room, only each other.

Then, of course, there was the evidence of their bountiful love, four adoring children: two sons and two daughters; Mark and Luke, Ruth and Hannah. Good, strong biblical names all. Someone in this household was a reader, at least, of the Bible. Rebecca suspected Rachel. She also suspected the young mother was more than a casual reader of it. Her curiosity at work again, she longed to question her. She hoped the young woman's reading had taken her farther than the preaching of Brother Zake.

This house spoke of love and caring. An occasional braided, rag rug adorned the otherwise bare floors bleached almost white from the constant lye-soap scrubbing. The smell of old leather and pipe smoke was present, yet they were not the musty smells you might expect, but pleasant, manly smells. Handmade curtains, crisp with starch, hung over the shuttered windows. Scarred from long use, the tabletop where Rebecca sat on a chair sipping her coffee also showed great care, evident by the high shine of beeswax polishing. Fruit jars filled with early-blooming wildflowers were scattered about the cheerful room.

Running her fingertip across a deep groove in the tabletop, she recalled what the elderly healer had said about this couple. A sigh of yearning escaped her. It was obvious what she'd meant about envying them. They had a lot to envy. Not material things, those were few, yet this family was the wealthiest she'd ever known.

* * *

Rebecca wasn't eavesdropping, actually, just hanging out a few clothes on a line on the back porch with little hope they'd dry, when she heard Jethro Bean's voice mention her

227

name. She was instantly alert. It was easy to surmise she was the topic of his conversation. She glanced over her shoulder and noticed the back door stood ajar. Apparently, she hadn't pushed it closed when she came out with the laundry.

'Still say you're too trusting. We gotta be mighty careful. How you know she ain't law?' His voice rose an octave. "Cause she says so? You don't expect her to come right out and say it, do you?' His questions were fired rapidly and heatedly.

'Jeth, you ought to be ashamed. She saved our Luke last night.' Rachel scolded. 'You ought not to be talking about her like this.'

Rebecca pinned another article on the line and smiled. She had gained at least one supporter.

'Now, hon, I might have known you'd get a soft spot for this woman, 'cause of Luke.' The gruffness left his voice when he spoke to his wife. 'But Ole Woman could have done the same thing, if that other one hadn't grabbed him first and started whacking his back.' Indignation choked the softness from his voice. 'That's what caused that knot of phlegm to dislodge. But no! She rushes in like a house on fire, and now you be going soft for her. I still say . . . '

'Enough! I said, enough. Now, you listen to

228

me, and you listen good. You be a bigger jackass than that mule of yours if you think all that happened here last night was a pounding given your Luke. Or that anyone, even me or you, could have done it. You be a fool.'

Size was no deterrent, as the old woman's own indignation matched his in defense of her friend. 'You best be remembering what else Rebecca be doing 'sides whacking that youngun. She's a-praying. It were the praying, not the whacking, that saved your Luke.' A pause followed while she let her words sink into his thick skull. 'You best be giving thanks where it be due, boy, and stop, just for a minute, looking for the law in everybody you meet.'

Silence.

'You know she's right, Jeth,' Rachel said. 'I knew it last night. I felt it, there in the room with us. God's hand was on our youngun and He sent him back to us. Look at him over there, resting easy. You know it were a miracle, Jeth.'

'I saw what I saw. The boy were choking on a knot of phlegm, was all. You women always jumping on the religion bandwagon.'

'Jethro Bean, you disappoint me, boy. You surely do,' the old woman chided him. 'What really be sticking in your craw, boy, about Rebecca?'

229

'Nothing. Just never you mind.'

Rebecca heard a chair scrape across the floor and his heavy footsteps plod to the front door, then the bang of that door when he stomped outside. Gone to check on his mule, probably. It was time to make her appearance before they forgot her presence. Besides, she was chilled to the bone standing here on the porch with the rain slashing against the house, spraying her with droplets of moisture.

★ ★ ★

By midmorning they were ready to leave, satisfied the little boy, Luke, was out of danger. Ole Woman left a supply of camphor and horehound to keep the mucus loose so he could spit it up and keep his chest from becoming congested again.

Their return was easier only because it was lighter. The rain continued. Few words were spoken as they retraced their footsteps of the night before. When they reached the cutoff to the Penny place, Rebecca decided to drop by and check on Jacob's leg. It might be a while before she could cross the creek again.

Explaining her intent, she refused the offer of assistance and sloshed off on her own in the rain-soaked morning. From somewhere behind her, Rebecca heard the biting words caught by the wind and carried to her.

'Foolish woman. Ought to mind her . . . Get on home . . . No more sense than a goose.'

It was Jethro Bean's voice. What was he doing? Following her? Why?

Jacob Penny was his usual obnoxious self. His leg was mending, though slowly. He'd be laid up for some time yet.

Megan was excited by Rebecca's visit. The only one who was, she gathered. The two older boys, Ted and Leo, shot piercing glances in her direction, but said nothing. Megan fixed hot tea and they chatted a while, catching up on the time they'd been apart due to the nasty wet weather.

The storm outside was gaining in strength and she detected one brewing inside as well. Her departure was hastened due to conditions of both storms. Almost before the door closed behind her, she heard her patient grumbling under his breath.

'Talk to stranger. Can't talk to her Pap . . . all that learning . . . ain't good, I say . . . got work to be a-doing.' Then louder, 'Girl, hey, girl, you can hear me. Get my dinner, I'm starving.'

21

Bundled in her cloak, Rebecca trudged home, allowing her feet to carry her forward while she turned over in her mind the events of the past twenty-four hours. Unaware of her surroundings or of how far she'd traveled; she was jolted into awareness of her situation when her cloak was nearly torn from her shoulders. Clasping the fabric closer, she bowed into the wind.

All around her the storm raged, the air filled with the sound of thunder that vibrated through the soles of her feet as the earth trembled and shook with the violence of the elements. The sky lit up with sudden flashes of light when bolts of lightning followed almost instantly on its heels. There was no time to lose. Her pace quickened. Lowering her head, she fought against the wind-driven rain stinging her skin and blinding her vision. Only a short distance now, then across the creek. Mud sucked at her feet when she stood on the creek bank.

Murky water swirled, surging upward. Soon it would overflow its confining banks. Misgivings tugged her backward. But where would she go? It could be a long time before the waters receded. What would happen to Diablo? There wasn't any other choice.

Before entering the swirling waters of the creek, Rebecca gathered her skirts up, drawing the back hem forward between her legs, tucking it into her waistband in front, like makeshift trousers. She stepped cautiously, picking her way slowly, moving steadily against the swift flowing current. Like an angry monster the water pushed against her, dragging her skirt tail lose, hampering her progress, pushing her farther downstream. Her hair whipped across her face like a wet whip, stinging her cheeks. Her cloak was waterlogged and heavy, plastered to her chilled body. The roll of thunder grew until it resembled a herd of buffalo stampeding across the sky, chased by lighting bolts. The sound of a tree struck by the bolts pierced the air with a wild cry of pain as it split apart and died.

Fighting off panic, Rebecca watched, horrified, as the body of 'the loner's' mule bobbed by, tangled in a floating, swirling mass of debris, causing her to lose her already precarious balance. She felt the black, angry water suck her under, tossing her beneath the swift flowing currents. Coughing and sputtering, she fought her way to a passing log when it raced by. Clinging desperately to the log, she prayed. 'I can't die now, I've only just begun. Not now,' she mouthed. The words were torn from her fear-locked throat to be lost to the rain-swept wind. The log hit a current and rolled, breaking her grip on it, tossing her free. Her fear rose to terrifying heights, her heart lurched. She felt it pounding in her throat, roaring in her ears. When the black water engulfed her once more, she thought she heard a voice calling her name.

She felt herself being plucked from the water, dripping, sputtering, and coughing, then dumped on the ground, face down in the mud. Hands massaged her back. Rebecca knew but couldn't stop her descent when she dropped into the pit of unconsciousness.

★ ★ ★

Inhaling deeply, pulling fresh clean air into her tortured lungs, Rebecca regained consciousness to find a wet, warm tongue licking her face.

Diablo.

'How . . . what . . . ?' She tried to sit up, grew dizzy, tried again. A growl from Diablo caused her to turn in his direction.

'Call that varmint off me, woman.' Jethro

Bean, his back plastered to a nearby tree, pleaded for her help. Diablo held him at bay. The furry animal, teeth bared, fur standing on end, stood between her and the man, poised to leap at any move by his prey. 'Call him off. He's a-gonna be at my throat any second now.'

'Mr. Bean,' Rebecca gasped drawing welcome air into her tortured lungs before she could continue. 'Where did you come from? I thought you . . . '

'Do something with that animal. You can jaw later.' He was losing the slippery grip on his patience. 'Fool woman, anyway.' His eyes never left those bared teeth. 'Where in blazes did that animal come from?'

'Diablo,' she panted for breath. 'It's okay. Down.' She leaned over, stroked Diablo's side and she spoke soothingly. Slowly, the wolf cub relaxed but kept a keen eye on the man he had treed.

Rebecca saw relief flow through Jethro, like a man who had stared Death in the face and been rejected, this time. He grew quite pale and Rebecca noticed his large hands trembling when he snatched his rain-soaked hat from the ground, then slapped it on his head. Water ran in rivulets from beneath his saturated headgear and dripped to his broad shoulders.

'That was a damn fool thing to do.' Jethro's arms stretched toward the raging water. 'Trying to cross a creek in flood. Ain't you got no sense at all? You must be mad to . . .' Jethro jumped back against his tree when Diablo bristled and bared his teeth once more, sensing a threat to his mistress from those flaying arms. 'Ought to kill that animal,' he snapped.

Diablo advanced at the raised voice, his lips curled, revealing his fangs.

Rebecca reached out and grabbed him by the scruff of the neck, speaking to Jethro quietly. 'I wish you wouldn't raise your voice like that. It excites him. He thinks you're going to hurt me. Please, keep your voice down.' Rebecca somehow got to her feet. Though her legs felt like rubber, she managed to stand. 'I want to thank you for rescuing me.' She glanced up, pulling wet hair from her face.

'Ought to have let you drown,' he growled. Again glancing at Diablo, he lowered his voice and finished, 'You got some folk fooled, but not me. If you be what you say and believe all this faith business I be hearing about from folks, how come your God didn't pull you out of that creek? Huh, how come?' He asked his question with a self-satisfied smirk plastered across his features. As if to say, he sure as fire had her this time.

'But, He did, Mr. Bean. He did.'

'I did, you mean. It were me pulled you, puking and gagging, out of that water. Me!'

'You were the hands He used. I prayed to be rescued, and there you were. God uses men to do His bidding, to be His hands.'

'Yeah, sure. I almost drown to save you, and He gets the credit.'

Pulling her wet, clinging skirt away from her legs and shaking out what water she could, Rebecca smiled and asked, 'Mr. Bean, why do you persist in fighting it? You've seen His hand at work twice now in . . . '

'Jethro. The name's Jethro. Mr. Bean was my pa. And don't be telling me what I seen. Just where the hell you get off, coming here telling us what to do and what to believe? Huh?' He removed the dripping hat and gave it a few quick shakes. 'We be doing fine before you come around, sticking your nose in our business. Why don't you just go back to wherever the hell it be you come from?' And with that he sloshed off downstream. Probably looking for a safer place to cross.

Keeping a restraining grip on Diablo, Rebecca watched her angry rescuer disappear into the rain.

22

At last the rain ceased and the surrounding countryside, like a huge, drowsy animal, shook itself, stretched its limbs and came to life after a prolonged hibernation. The profusion of colors was a delight to behold. There was the pale green of the budding cottonwoods, the brighter green of the leafing willows, the strong dark green of the cedars and the soft green of the many oaks, with their lacy fringe dangling beneath the newly-formed leaves. The dogwood, white; the redbud, splashes of pink.

Wildflowers vied for prominence in a kaleidoscope of colors. Fields of pink buttercups competed with the lady's-slippers and wild violets. Seven-sister rosebushes sporting soft, blush-pink blossoms grew wild, their clinging runners ensnaring everything in their path. Wild azaleas in a rainbow of colors hovered in the more shaded areas at the edge of the meadow carpeted with flowering clover. The dew-kissed fragrance of honeysuckle wafted on the morning breeze.

Rebecca's city-bred view of nature's beauty underwent a drastic change as spring arrived in the hill country, creating a paradise of sights and smells. Even the twilight provided a panorama of delight, with ear-pleasing cheeps, chirps, and rustling of insects and night creatures.

Nothing pleased her more than the music coming from the grove when the 'loner's' fiddle greeted each dawn. Ever since the flood, her new neighbor helped with repairs caused by the destructive waters. He neither accepted nor expected payment for his labor.

Her bare feet tucked beneath her, Rebecca was sipping her first cup of eye-opener when a light rapping at the back door sounded. Coffee sloshed from the rim of the cup when she quickly set it on the table and padded across the room.

There stood Sam. 'I'm digging your garden spot today.' Without preamble, he made his announcement. Rays from the rising sun glinted off the metal of the spade slung across his broad shoulders.

'My what?' She wasn't sure she'd heard him right.

'A body needs to be self-sufficient.' He lowered the shovel to the ground. Leaning on its wooden handle, he gazed across the yard as though seeing something only he could see. 'Ought not depend on others for what you can provide for yourself.' He turned to leave.

'A garden, Sam?' She felt odd calling him Sam; to her he was 'the loner.' It fit him.

'Yup. Raise it, kill it, or catch it. I'll be finished by sundown.' If the idea made sense to Sam, that settled it. She'd have a garden.

Rebecca watched his long-legged strides eat up the distance across the back yard. The loss of his mule hadn't stopped him, simply slowed him down. Without the aid of the animal, Sam hand-spaded the garden plot. When he finished, the soil felt like sifted flour, free of clots and clumps. It hadn't been her idea, but she soon wished it had. By May, fresh vegetables abundantly graced her table.

★ ★ ★

'Goshdang, it don't look the same.' Jimmy set his satchel on the porch and stepped back for a better look.

'I could say the same about you.' Rebecca watched the familiar blush stain his neck. It was nearly the only thing left familiar about him. Thirteen months ago he departed for home a gangling, loose-limbed, freckle-faced youth. Those months had brought about a striking transformation. Before her stood a broad-shouldered, slim-hipped, mature young

240

man. His cotton shirt strained to contain those broad shoulders and muscular upper arms.

Rebecca sensed the change was more than surface deep, though she couldn't say how she knew. He appeared to be more serious, more . . . mature. Maturity beyond his nineteen years.

His inspection complete, he surprised Rebecca by swooping her up in a bear hug and whirling her about the yard, his youthful exuberance surfacing once more. 'I was afraid I'd dreamed it. That it would be gone when I got back.' He lowered her to her feet and stepped back. 'Sorry,' he mumbled glancing away from her. He pulled at the collar of his starched shirt. 'I'm just so glad to be back.'

Rebecca reached up and deftly unbuttoned the top button on his shirt. 'Relax and make yourself comfortable. You're home now.'

'Thanks.' Once more his gaze swept the valley. A smile stretched his freckled face. 'I got something for you.' Grabbing his satchel, he bounded up the steps. Rebecca joined him and watched him search through his bag, retrieving several items.

'Mister James sent these. Said he'd have my hide if they didn't arrive safe.'

'Sounds like James.' She set the packages

beside her chair. 'Would you like something to eat?'

'I'm hungry as a bear.'

Shortly after lunch, Jimmy wandered off with Diablo trotting right along beside him as though they'd never been separated.

From the front porch, Rebecca watched them cross the creek. She smiled to herself. She knew as well as he did whom he hoped to find over there. Silently, she wished him luck.

★ ★ ★

One at a time she went through the packages Jimmy brought. She opened the one from James first. Pushing the paper aside, she was delighted to find a pair of galoshes. Apparently, he had heard of their rainy season. Beneath the protective footwear lay a dozen books, a box of stationery, and another of chocolates. Tucked in the corner was a smaller package wrapped separately. She tore the paper away and gasped in sheer delight at the small quantity of quinine. Her tears threatened to flow at this proof of her brother's love for her. He might not approve of her decision, but in his own way he would help her.

Bless him, she thought, wiping the telltale moisture from the corners of her eyes.

Next, she opened the packet from Louise. On top lay several letters. Rebecca's hands trembled slightly as she turned them over and read the names on the envelopes, names of friends she hadn't expected to ever hear from, since they had advised against her move to the hill country. Indeed, they had fought almost as determinedly as her brother and sister against her decision. Nevertheless, she was glad they had written.

Laying the package aside, she tore open the letters, eager to hear from home. As she expected, the letters were filled with repetitious pleas: 'Return home, dear.' 'Poor Rebecca, stuck off in that Godforsaken place.' 'We miss you at our weekly tea.' On and on they went.

Rebecca wanted to laugh at their foolish prattle. She had been more alive and free in her year here than ever before, yet she knew they meant well. Their lives suited them and they were satisfied. She had been suffocated by that life. This was the way she wanted to live. Here, she felt fulfilled, as she never had there, though she knew it would be useless to tell that to her friends.

She laid her letters aside to answer later, then retrieved the package from her sister. It contained linen sheets and pillow slips, hand embroidered and trimmed with tatted lace.

How like Louise. Rebecca could see her sister bent over her tatting, taking special care with the delicate lace as she prepared this gift for her wayward sibling. Her fingers caressed the fragile work, and she wondered how it would survive being washed on a wash board with lye-soap.

★ ★ ★

Much to Jimmy's delight, Diablo shadowed his every move. The pair left together at dawn and didn't return until dusk.

'Still can't believe he stayed,' Jimmy commented one evening.

After several days of his restless roving, Rebecca took her visitor to the pecan grove to meet Sam. To her amazement, the two men took to one another like old friends reunited. She had expected Sam to be as shy with the newcomer as he had been with her.

Later that same day, they were having their accustomed coffee on the porch when Jimmy asked the question she expected sooner. 'That girl still come around?'

'You must mean Megan Penny.' Rebecca smiled, noticing the blush rush up his neck. She knew she shouldn't tease him, but he was so obvious in his subtleties. Apparently, his daily rambles hadn't provided a glimpse of the one he sought.

He nodded. 'She still around?' He repeated his question.

'Yes. You should see her. She's changed a good deal since you saw her last year.' Watching his face in the shadows, she made a suggestion. 'I have an idea. Why don't we go visit her? I need to check on her father's leg, anyway.' His lack of immediate response gave her pause. Perhaps she was wrong about his feelings. If that were the case, she would give him a way out. 'Unless, of course, you have something else to do.'

'Shucks, no,' he blurted. 'I mean, it won't hurt me none to go with you.'

'We'll leave after lunch.'

★   ★   ★

Megan opened the door and her mouth flew open as if to say something, then her glance darted from Rebecca to the young man beside her and back again, then to the man on the bed in the corner of the room just out of sight of the door.

'Well, who be it, Girl? You gone dumb again? Who is it, I say?' Jacob Penny's voice vibrated around them.

'Hello, Megan. I've brought a friend. You remember Jimmy, don't you?' Rebecca tried

245

to fill the awkward moment.

Megan whirled from the door and fled across the floor, disappeared into her room and slammed the barrier behind her. Jimmy glanced at Rebecca in puzzlement and shrugged his broad shoulders. Smiling to reassure him, Rebecca took his hand and led him into the room.

'How's your leg, Mr. Penny?'

'Who's that with you? Another stranger? What's wrong with that fool girl now, acting like a loony again? Well, say something, woman. Don't just stand there.'

Tugging the young man forward, Rebecca said, 'I'd like to introduce a friend of mine, Jimmy Johnstone. Jimmy, this is Jacob Penny.' Rebecca tried to ease the tension she felt building between the two men, as though each sensed a danger from the other. Rebecca busied herself checking her patient's leg. Neither man spoke. She felt her patient flinch with pain when she lowered his mud-encased leg to the bed, but no sound escaped his lips.

'I believe we can remove the cast today and let you start getting up a bit.' She wiped her hands on a towel, more to fill the uncomfortable silence than anything else. 'Only for short periods of time each day, until you get your strength back. You will . . . '

'You gonna take it off, or jaw all day,

woman? Get on with it,' her patient interrupted in his normal way.

Rebecca heard a door creak behind her and turned to see Megan standing in the doorway. The quick gasp of an indrawn breath told Rebecca someone else found the sight breathtaking. And it wasn't Jacob Penny.

Framed in the open doorway, her arms dangling helplessly at her sides, Megan hesitated a moment as if uncertain in her actions. She had changed into her Christmas frock. A matching blue ribbon held her shining tresses in place. And just visible beneath the sweep of her full skirt were unmistakably a pair of shoes.

She was lovely. Rebecca watched the flower of beauty hesitate on the threshold of her room. Jimmy took a step forward, then paused suddenly aware of his action and stood gaping at the girl before him. Apparently, Rebecca wasn't the only one to appreciate the fair maiden.

'Girl, you gone plum crazy or what? Dressed like going to meeting or something.'

No one moved.

'Somebody want to tell me what's happening here? Girl? Answer me!'

Rebecca forced herself to respond. 'Mr. Penny, if you'll hold still and lie down, I'll get this off your leg.' It was a lame attempt to distract his attention from his daughter, but the best she was capable of at the moment. 'Megan, you and Jimmy get me some water from the spring.'

Both young people jumped to do her bidding and dashed from the house, eager to be away from the probing questions lurking in Jacob's eyes.

Rebecca managed to prolong the task of freeing the encased leg, buying extra time for the young couple.

'Have you noticed the change in your daughter since we started her lessons?' Rebecca inquired.

Jacob Penny grunted.

Rebecca persisted, hoping to draw a positive response from him. 'She's advancing in her studies remarkably fast. I'm extremely proud of her, aren't you?' She glanced up from her work. The man on the bed refused to meet her glance. Ignoring his obstinacy, she prodded on. 'Megan is a very intelligent young lady.'

'Okay, woman, you proved your point. So the girl ain't simpleminded after all. She's just hard-headed, not talking all them years.' His eyes narrowed as he forced the words upward and out. It was a bitter thing he was admitting. 'Ungrateful, that's what she be.' His hard eyes sought those of the interfering female behind his most recent trials and tribulations with his daughter. 'And what's this business of Megan? Might as well set it straight here and now. This here is my home. Busybody like you needs to mind your place.' Jacob squinted his eyes as if expecting Rebecca to challenge him. 'That ain't her name.'

It was easy to see he was on the defensive now, and wanting to lay blame on someone. Well, Rebecca would have none of it. It was high time he faced the facts about his daughter and his treatment of her.

'Ungrateful! Pray tell me, what she's got to be grateful for? That you blame her for the death of her mother? That you treat her like a slave, or that you didn't care enough to even give her a name?' Her eyes were now as hard as his. The veins in her neck corded like twisted ropes, her jaw clenched. 'Tell me, what's she got to be grateful for?' Rebecca snapped, her patience frayed.

'You forget yourself, woman. What right you got messing in my family's affairs? You don't know the half of it no how. If it weren't for that girl, I'd still have my woman, my Leona . . . '

'Do you hear what you're saying? You're blaming Megan for something she had no control over.' There was no going back now.

She might as well speak her mind. 'Do you honestly believe your daughter deliberately caused her mother's death? Well, do you?'

A frown of concentration creased Jacob's forehead when he replied. 'Still and all, if she hadn't a-been born, my Leona would be alive today.'

'Did she ask to be born? Or was that your doing, you and your wife?'

'Well, it . . . what's the difference?' he drawled sarcastically. But he was weakening.

Rebecca saw it, pressed her advantage. 'The difference is, you're blaming her for something she had no control over. You've taken it out on her for sixteen long years . . . '

'Seventeen. The girl be seventeen,' he interrupted.

'Seventeen, then. For seventeen years you've not bothered to give her a name. You don't even treat her like a daughter.' Feeling her own heat cool, Rebecca slumped onto a chair beside the bed. 'I can't imagine your wife approving of this treatment of her child. Can you?'

Jacob's gaze dropped; he fidgeted with the corner of the quilt on his bed. Slowly, he lifted his gaze to meet Rebecca's and there was a suspicious moisture in them when he spoke. 'She meant the world to me, my Leona. You just can't understand how I grieve for her. And when I look at the girl, I remember. I . . . no . . . she wouldn't approve. Still, I . . . '

'I wouldn't understand?' Rebecca's eyes met his and she softened her voice. 'I, too, lost someone who meant the world to me. My husband. Oh, yes, I can understand your grief all too well. Yet I don't blame others for my loss, and neither should you.' Her hands idly smoothed the damp towel lying across her lap. 'Satan isn't particular who he steals from us, so put the blame where it belongs. Show your daughter you love her. Treat her as your wife would want you to.'

For the first time since Rebecca had known him, she felt compassion for this grief-stricken man. 'You know, Mr. Penny, I found peace and relief from my grief after I lost my husband in the loving comfort of the Lord. He helped me. I know He'd help you too, if . . . '

'Don't start no preaching at me, woman! I know all about your God!' he shouted, throwing a pillow onto the floor in his outburst. 'I've listened to you talking that trash about loving and forgiving. But don't start that with me, 'cause I know Him.'

Once more, Jacob's pain-filled eyes glared at her in rage. She suspected she had unwittingly torn the scab from his festering

251

rage at the Almighty.

'I know about His anger and His punishing ways. Brother Zake tole me how God took my Leona as punishment for my sinfulness. How I got to hang on while God teaches me my lesson.' Jacob's nostrils flared and his jaw clenched and unclenched while the long-repressed hostilities gushed forth. 'Well, I hung on, but I ain't learned nothing yet. So, don't you start with your nonsense!' He glanced around as if to find the object of his renewed rage. 'Where'd that girl go for that water?'

'How dare he!' Rebecca spat it out before she could stop herself. The ignorance of his words enraged her and awakened that Taurus bull personality her father spoke of. They were a crimson flag waved before her eyes. 'Zake Daniels had no right to tell you such a thing. It's not true, you know. God did not take your wife, Mr. Penny, Satan did. Listen to me. Christ said, 'I came that you might have life and have it more abundantly.' Satan came to steal, kill and destroy. Based on that, who do you think took your wife?'

Jacob Penny lay rigid on the bed, stubbornly refusing to meet Rebecca's eyes as he clenched and unclenched his big hands. He stared coldly and mutely into space. Then, without preamble, he shouted. 'Get out of here! Go. My boys can finish up with my leg.' This time his eyes met hers with a secret gleam in them, as though he knew something she didn't know.

'Brother Zake said you's spouting a false doctrine. I ought to have listened to him. Go on. Get!' Anger replaced the momentary gleam in his eyes. He knotted and unknotted his fist on top of the quilt while he ordered her out of his sight and his home.

'I'll go, Mr. Penny. But you think about what I said. Better yet, prove me wrong. Read the Bible yourself and see how often it speaks of the love of God, and His forgiving nature. Then read the Bible's description of Satan and . . . '

'Can't read!'

'Then have Megan read it to you. That is, if you're not too stubborn to risk being proven wrong.' At his shocked look of surprise, she taunted him. 'Or maybe you enjoy misery, and don't want to find the truth.' Tossing the damp towel on the back of a chair, she picked up her bag.

'I'm going now, but let me know what you find. That is, if you have the courage to find out!' Rebecca marched flatfooted across the floor and out the front door without glancing back.

Just when she started across the yard in

search of the two young people, she heard Jacob let out a roaring yell, 'Girl! Get in here, Girl.'

To think, she had actually felt sorry for that man only a short time ago.

★ ★ ★

Jimmy stayed a week, but Rebecca saw very little of him after their visit to the Penny's. She suspected he was seeing Megan, though he never said so. Megan hadn't visited since his arrival, which was unusual. Or was it? Rebecca wished them luck. They were both very special to her.

23

Jimmy returned home the last week in June. To ease her loss of his company, Rebecca threw herself into activity. Soon she had a settled routine: working her garden early, before the heat became too oppressive; then making rounds to the sick with her mentor. When they weren't visiting their ailing neighbors, they gathered herbs, leaves, and barks for her remedies.

In the evenings, Rebecca took a bar of soap and a towel and retreated to her private bath, a natural spring. It was situated at the base of the hill where runoff from springs higher up the hillside, flowing toward Ten Mile creek, had washed out a depression about two feet deep and four feet around. The water cascaded over the rocks into the pool and formed a small waterfall, then rushed over the opposite side on its way to the creek. Beside the pool was a huge flat rock covered with two inches of spongy moss, which she used as a bath mat. Seclusion was provided by the dense growth of huge cedar trees.

Rebecca's habit was to come to this isolated spot in the early evenings to bathe, wash her hair, and soak away the heat of the day. Relaxing in the pool was the most tranquil part of her day as she lay back, the cool water gushing over her tired body on its scurry to the creek. It was not uncommon for her to spend an hour or more here relaxing, listening to the sounds of evening. Often, if the winds were just right, she could hear the notes from Sam's fiddle in the distance, harmonizing with the birds, the crickets, and the katydids.

* * *

Today the two women stopped to check on Luke Bean. Watching him toddle after his brother and sisters at play, Rebecca found it difficult to imagine how sick he'd been.

Once more, she was struck by the strength of the raven-haired woman. Her tall form filled the doorway when she greeted her visitors. Though her frock was faded and out of fashion, she wore it like a queen. Her large violet eyes echoed her joy.

'You must stay to lunch.' She ushered them inside, sweeping eager children out of her path. 'Outside to play. I'll call you when it's time to eat. Go on, now.' She coaxed the youngsters out the door, then she placed Luke in the center of a folded patchwork quilt where he busied himself with handmade toys.

'Boy looks none the worse for wear.' The tiny woman leaned down and felt the child's forehead, then ran a gnarled finger beneath his chin, enticing a gurgle of laughter from him.

'Never better,' Rachel said. 'I want to thank you again for what you done for my boy.' Turning her glance to include Rebecca, she added, 'You, too. I'm not sure I thanked you proper like. I meant no slight.'

Rebecca returned her smile. 'None taken.'

'You will stay for lunch?'

When neither of her guests responded, she said, 'Jethro won't be joining us. He's busy farming today.'

As one, Rebecca and Old Woman exchanged glances. Neither betrayed their thoughts.

'We'd love to.' Rebecca wondered what the young woman would think if she knew that Rebecca knew exactly what her husband really farmed.

Rebecca enjoyed their visit. Never once while she was there did Rachel treat her as anything but a welcomed guest. The three women chatted away the better part of the afternoon. Rebecca was invited to drop in any time, and she promised to do so. She liked

Jethro Bean's wife and hoped they would be friends.

By evening, the heat settled heavily on everything. Even the insects seemed reluctant to send forth their melodious tunes. Rebecca retreated to her pool to cool off. Sitting on the spongy, moss-covered rock drying off, she was startled by a male voice behind her.

'Mind if I join you?'

Rebecca exploded into a frenzy of activity, snatching up her clothes, draping a towel haphazardly around her; she scrambled behind the nearest tree. A pine tree. A small pine tree.

Glancing around in search of the intruder who had interrupted her peace and invaded her privacy, she observed more of herself exposed than hidden. She heard twigs snapping as someone approached. Hastily, she readjusted the towel, tucking the ends to form a sarong. When she glanced up, she found none other than Zakeriah Daniels standing before her with a grin plastered on his face she longed to slap off.

'Well, if you're not a sight for sore eyes. A lovely sight too, I might add.' He leaned against a knotty bullpine, folding his arms across his chest as though settling in for a comfortable little chat. His greedy eyes roamed at will over her barely concealed body.

'What do you want?' Rebecca clutched the bundle of clothes to her chest. Her heart thumped against her ribcage like a butterfly trapped in a jar. Anger and fright waged a battle within her trembling frame. Anger was winning.

'You know the answer to that.' He grinned and continued to run his eyes like hot fingers up and down her half-exposed body. 'Looks like I got you right where I want you now.'

'What is that supposed to mean?' She was seized with a savage desire to place her fingers about his throat and squeeze that arrogant smirk off his chiseled face.

'Female caught in a compromising situation like this. I mean, you naked, or same as, and a man who isn't her husband being seen with her. Well, what would folks think?' He peeled himself from the tree.

When he took a step forward, Rebecca threw one arm out to hold him off. 'Don't come near me, not another step. No one has seen me but you, so how can that . . . '

'Oh, but I'll tell it differently.' He took another menacing step toward her.

'You wouldn't!'

'Oh, but I would. Of course, a man

wouldn't say nothing about his wife.' He smiled smugly.

'Your w-w-what?' The arrogant boar had said *wife*. How conceited was he? Or was he that convinced?

'Don't play coy, I know women. You know what I'm saying. Marry me, and I won't say anything about this little scene here in the woods.' His arm motioned to encircle the area. 'You with no clothes on, me here and all. You get my meaning?' One brow lifted to emphasis his question. 'You know I've wanted you since you got here, and I don't have time to play silly female games. So just say yes, put your clothes on and let's go make it legal.' Then, with a leer in his husky voice, he added, 'Better still, we can stay here a while, then make it legal.'

Rebecca felt herself blush at his crude words. He again reached out for her and she darted past his outstretched arm back to the pool area, stopping on the moss-covered rock.

Disbelief was written across his dark features. He couldn't grasp that she'd moved away from him. His expression was so comical; Rebecca doubled over with laughter. Holding her sides, she stammered, 'You th-thought I'd actually marry you? Just because you saw me bathing?' She pushed aside her brief comical air and grew serious.

'Nobody marries for reasons like that any more, if they ever did. I can't believe you thought I'd actually marry you. Not now, not ever.'

His big hand closed about her wrist and pain shot up her arm when he pulled her toward him. A scream escaped her as she struggled to free her arm from his brutal grasp. She must get away from this lynx-eyed brute. Out of the corner of her eye, she caught a glimpse of movement like a black arrow flying at the man holding her in his vice-like grip.

With a howl of pain his hold on her arm gave way. Rebecca staggered back, trying to catch her balance, and heard a splash followed by another yell of pain, then a plea for help. Recovering her senses, she snatched up her towel from where it had fallen in their struggle, wrapped it about herself and turned to find Diablo standing guard over a very wet, angry, and frightened preacher.

He lay sprawled on his back in her bathing pool, calling for her to help him. The young wolf stood with fur bristled, teeth bared. Low, deep-throated growls rumbled at each movement Zake Daniels made. While Diablo stood guard, Rebecca slipped behind a huge cedar tree. She dressed slowly, taking her time. The wait in the pool would serve to cool off her would-be attacker, though it probably wouldn't help his disposition.

When she finished, she slowly returned to the scene at the pool. Zakeriah Daniels motioned her back. His movement drew another threat from Diablo.

'Go for help! Get someone out here. Tell them to bring a gun. This animal is going to kill me.' He spoke low and softly, yet anxiously, as the wolf renewed his growls. Never taking his wide-rimmed eyes from the fangs, he moaned. 'I'll probably be dead before you can get help out here.'

Rebecca joined Diablo on the moss-covered rock, then she reached down and petted his side. 'Okay, Boy. You can let him up.' Though her voice remained calm, she pierced the waterlogged culprit with her eyes. With only her palm resting on his back, she led Diablo off the rock and out of reach of the dazed man in the pool.

'What's this?' he sputtered, righting himself. When he could stand, he was almost knee deep in water and looked every bit as ridiculous as Rebecca found him. 'That animal ain't wild, then? And you let me think . . . ' Anger darkened his face; the veins in his thick neck bulged like twisted coils of rope.

'Shut up, Mr. Daniels, before I let him

finish what he started.' Rebecca turned briskly about. Without a backward glance, she strolled off with her protector in tow.

'You'll be sorry for this. Just wait and see. You'll pay for this. Nobody says 'No' to Zake Daniels. Nobody, you hear?' His voice was sullen and brittle.

Rebecca imagined his eyes sparkled with anger as he shouted his contempt and frustrations at her retreating back.

★   ★   ★

Rebecca wasn't left to wonder long what form his retaliation would take.

The bell above the door still tinkled when Bertha hurried across the room, took Rebecca's arm, and whispered, 'Come with me.'

Hustling Rebecca from the main room of the store and up the stairs to her private living quarters, she kept glancing over her shoulder as if expecting the devil himself to be in hot pursuit. Rebecca's attempted inquiry was silenced with, 'Shush, not now.' Once they entered the room, Bertha pointed Rebecca toward an overstuffed sofa covered in blood-red velvet and draped in yards of starched lace doilies.

Glancing about the room, Rebecca found

it, like its owner, big and cheerful. She heard the door close behind her. What was going on?

Bertha returned carrying a tray with two glasses of iced lemonade. 'Go on, sit down,' she ordered. Depositing the tray on a nearby table, she handed Rebecca a frosty glass. 'Now, tell me what's all this talk I'm hearing about you making a fool of yourself chasing the preacher, and . . . '

'I what? Who said I was chasing him?' Rebecca almost dropped her glass of lemonade.

'He did, Brother Zake. And that ain't all he's telling.' Her face was rosier than usual. Tendrils of hair slipped from their confinement and dangled across her florid forehead. 'He's spreading around you got a full grown wolf to protect you. Living with you and all. That you set this animal on innocent folk what come too close to your place.'

'He said that?'

'There's more.' Bertha nodded and her flame-colored curls bounced. 'Say's he seen you parading around the countryside in broad daylight naked as the day you was born, with this wild animal at your heels, and your only covering was your unbound hair, like some kind of pagan goddess.'

It seemed a dry business, repeating all this

tidy news, true or not, and Rebecca watched silently while Bertha took a gulp of lemonade.

'He's telling the folk to stay away from that area and not to associate with you. Says he's knew all along you was Satan's daughter. And only heaven knows what goes on out there.' She took another sip of her drink, running her pink tongue across her full lips. 'He's stirring up the folks real good. That's why I brought you up here. Figured it best to talk in private.' Glancing at Rebecca, she added. 'Not that I believe a word of it, you understand. It's just, I figured you got a right to know.'

'I appreciate that.' Rebecca stood and crossed to the big window, looking out over the collection of buildings below, absently noting that the view from up here encompassed the entire settlement. No wonder Bertha was able to keep tabs on everyone so well. She could see it all from here.

'You awright?'

Slowly turning from the window, Rebecca returned to the sofa, took a slow sip of the soothing drink. 'Yes, I'm okay. It's just . . . well; I don't know what to say. I can't say I'm surprised, except by his story. I mean . . . may I tell you my side?'

'I's hoping you would. Like I said, I didn't believe his tale. But lots of folk will; already do, in fact. You tell your side, maybe we be able to put out the fire he's building.'

So Rebecca told of the incident at the bathing pool, all of it. 'So you see, his story contains some truth, twisted among his lies.'

'And they say hell hath no fury like a woman scorned. Whoever said that must have not met our Brother Zake, who thinks he's God's gift to women.' A hearty chuckle followed her proclamation.

'I'm not interested in the gift!'

'That's the rub. Don't you see? That man ain't used to being turned down. So now he's got to cover his tracks. Make it look like he's the one turning you down.'

'What do I do? I mean, the lies he's . . . '

'Let me handle that. I got some influence hereabouts. I'll put the word out and maybe we can throw enough water of truth to put out his fire of lies. Don't fret none. It'll be okay. Drink your lemonade and relax. I'll go down fill your order then you can ease out the back way.'

'I will not! I'll leave the way I came in. I'm not ashamed of anything I've done.' She snatched up her handbag and headed for the door.

'That's just what I figured you'd say, but I had to offer, anyway. I'll say this, you're a fighter. I like that.' Giving her a quick hug,

Bertha tugged the door open and linked her arm through Rebecca's. They descended the stairs together.

The walk home seemed longer than normal as Rebecca trudged down the dusty trail, sweltering in the July heat and with a boiling rage inside directed at Zake Daniels.

Word traveled fast. The evidence of how fast was visible in the gaping holes where her windowpanes should have been. It was like stepping back in time to the day of her arrival when she stood in the front yard staring at those yawning, empty windows. Glass shards were splattered over the porch and inside the house as well. Rebecca felt tears stinging her eyelids as she stood viewing the senseless destruction of her home. This wasn't the first time this had happened. But it had been a while, and she'd hoped it was over.

Diablo rounded the corner of the house whimpering softly. Instead of bounding to her side, he came forward shyly. His usual wagging tail tucked deeply between his legs as though frightened. He must have witnessed the cowardly visitors who carried out this dastardly deed.

Stroking his side reassuringly, she attempted to comfort him as she longed for someone to comfort her. She felt the warm, soft fur beneath her hand bristle and a low growl rumbled, full-throated, from the young wolf, alerting her they were no longer alone. Whirling around, braced to confront a returning window smasher, Rebecca was stopped short by the sight before her.

'What happened? Looks like a tornado hit,' inquired the vision before her.

And a vision she was. Rebecca had never seen a more strikingly beautiful woman in her life. She was perfection personified, of medium height, slender-framed, well formed in all the right places, her waist impossibly small. Her hair was like ripe wheat and strawberries blended together, neither blonde nor red, yet when the sunlight danced across her long, silky locks, it was like embers of sparkling fire. Her eyes resembled those of a doe, soft brown and fluid. High cheekbones set off a slender nose, classic in shape, above full red lips. She left Rebecca speechless just to look at her, which she realized she'd done far too long.

'I'm sorry, I didn't mean to be rude. You startled me. In answer to your question, I'm not sure, though I've a good idea. Never mind that now. Were you looking for me?'

'If you be Miss Rice,' replied the visitor, gently tugging at a button on her dress.

'Yes, I'm Rebecca Rice, and you are . . . ?'

'Oh, I'm Ruby. That was silly of me, not

telling you my name or nothing. It's just . . . I'm . . . hey, can I help you clean up this mess?' Before Rebecca could reply, the woman called Ruby, dashed up the steps and gingerly commenced picking up the larger pieces of glass. Joining her, Rebecca decided she'd find out sooner or later why she was here.

Working side by side, gathering and sweeping up bits of glass, they finally cleared away the mess and started to remove the window frames when Ruby blurted out, 'I'm in trouble. You gotta help me, Miss Rice.'

24

Ruby twisted her dress hem into a knot, fighting to control the trembling of her young body; tears gushed from her lovely brown eyes. Agony contorted her face, her shoulders shook, and for a second, Rebecca thought the girl would flee. Instead, she collapsed at Rebecca's feet, sobbing uncontrollably.

'Here, here, it can't be that bad.' Rebecca attempted to calm the young woman. She knelt beside the crumpled figure. 'Come on, now, tell me. How bad can it be? Shush, now.' Gently, she coaxed Ruby to her feet. She then led the weeping, nearly hysterical girl inside. Leaving her to gain control of her emotions, Rebecca busied herself preparing a calming drink of chamomile tea.

'Here, drink this. It'll help.' Rebecca set the tea before her, then handed Ruby a napkin. 'Dry your eyes now, and tell me how you're in trouble.'

Rebecca's teary-eyed guest took a sip of the tea, blew her nose, wiped her eyes, and blurted, 'I'm in the family way!' And then she commenced to cry again.

'How wonderful. A baby!'

'But you don't understand.' Gulping back another sob, Ruby raised her blurry gaze. Her napkin grew limp as she tried to stem the deluge of tears flowing down her cheeks. 'I ain't married.' Ruby forced the words past her lips, twisting the damp fabric about her trembling fingers.

It wasn't a statement Ruby would have needed to make to anyone else in the valley. Here, everyone knew everyone else's business. But for this newcomer, she was forced to say the words. She wouldn't have bothered with an explanation except she needed Rebecca Rice's help. Glancing up to judge the effect her claim made, she was surprised to detect none. The only emotion visible was her own. 'I can't have this baby. I can't! You gotta help me.'

'Oh. I — How do you think I can help?'

'Get rid of it! You gotta get rid of it.' The stranger blew her nose again 'You just gotta.'

'But, I-I mean, you — '

'Don't say it. Please, don't say no. I'll die before I have this baby! I'll die. You hear me?'

'You don't mean that. You're upset now, but you'll feel different later. You'll — '

'No! I'll never feel different. Not ever!'

'Ruby, listen to me. Can you tell me why you feel you must . . . do this thing? Have you talked with the father? Perhaps . . . Well, I mean ... marriage, have you considered that?'

'He don't know. He wouldn't, no how. Marry me, I mean.'

'Oh, he's already married, then? I'm prying, I know, but there must be another solution,' Rebecca paused, then added, 'other than what you're suggesting.'

'They ain't.'

Rebecca noticed Ruby hadn't answered about the marital status of the man in question. Perhaps she should leave that for now. Trying a different tactic, she probed, 'What about adoption, have you considered that?'

With a laugh, the strawberry blonde replied, 'Miss Rice, you are new around here if you think anybody would want *my* baby.'

The unavoidable emphasis placed on 'my' baby caused Rebecca a moment of pause, wondering what she meant by the remark. 'I don't understand.'

'I know you don't, or you wouldn't have to ask. Never mind that. Are you gonna help me or not?'

Choosing her words carefully, Rebecca tried to be kind as she explained. 'Ruby, I can't do what you're asking. I can't. That would be ... ' She hesitated, then said the word that to her summed up what the girl was hinting at, 'Murder.'

Ruby flinched as if struck a physical blow by the word. Good, at least Rebecca hit a nerve. Ruby wasn't as indifferent to taking this life as she'd like to be. Given time, Rebecca hoped to persuade the distraught young woman to change her mind.

Softly sobbing, tears forming like crystals in her long, dark lashes as they rolled down the lovely high cheekbones, Ruby hung her head and whispered, 'You was my last hope. Now, I have no one. No one. But then, I never did. I never did.' The chair hit the floor and the napkin hit the table, when Ruby abruptly fled the house and, like a gazelle, flew across the meadow and into the woods.

Stunned, Rebecca remained seated, reflecting on her departed visitor.

* * *

For two days now, Rebecca had roamed aimlessly through the woods, always staying in sight of the house, in case the troubled young woman returned. She turned the story over and over in her mind, searching for answers. There were none. She simply could not do what the young mother-to-be asked of her. Life was too precious to sacrifice even one. Especially one so unable to protect itself.

What if it were her child? What if she were in Ruby's shoes? What if? That was all she had come up with so far. It troubled her every waking hour.

* * *

The morning grew increasingly hot and muggy. By mid-afternoon a suffocating, sultry calm settled over the meadow and creek. The birds fell silent. Not a leaf stirred. The heat grew oppressive. A fringe of dark clouds appeared above the distant hills. Perhaps it would rain and bring relief from the stifling heat. But as Rebecca watched, the fringe became a bulge that swiftly boiled upward until it towered above the sky. The sound of distant thunder rumbled. Then, amidst a grinding roar, the cracking and rending of trees, the storm struck.

Pelted by hailstones, blinded by lightning, and deafened by thunder, Rebecca made a mad rush for home and shelter. Her feet floundered when a tremendous gust of wind struck her. Her dress whipped about her like a wet snake snapping its tail, stinging her legs, hampering her progress. Blindly, she raced on. The sounds of destruction roared in her ears.

When at last she reached the safety of

home, she stood in the shelter of the front porch, clawing at a cedar column for support. She watched, to impress the terrifying scene on her memory. Even though she was on the outer fringes of the assault, she braced herself against the steadfast pillar to prevent being sucked into the maelstrom.

Behind her, the wooden shutters crashed against the side of the house. Like a giant animal laboring for its last breath, the plank flooring beneath her heaved upward, shuddered, then relaxed. Several shingles, ripped from the roof by the tempest, sailed across the yard. The swirling wind was choked with debris, collecting even more as it passed on, bending some trees, uprooting others. Almost immediately, the first violence of the storm was succeeded by a steady, drumming rain. A mist-like smoke hovered just above ground level as the warmth of the earth penetrated the two-inch layer of hailstones. It was like a gauzy mourning veil draped above the path of destruction.

Broken limbs, shredded leaves, and other evidence of the tornado littered the yard and the meadow beyond. Those trees nearest the house were stripped bare of their leaves, like the dead of winter. It was an eerie sensation standing there on the porch, observing the devastating aftermath of nature's fury.

Her neighbor's wagon-home had been blown from its log foundation. Luckily, that appeared to be the only damage in his area, except that the trees in the grove were also barren.

Once the storm abated, Rebecca's first concern was the safety of the others in the area. Snatching up a shawl and her bag of medicines, she dashed off to join Ole Woman, who was probably already on her way to aid the survivors.

It was the same everywhere they went. Homes blown apart. Barns and sheds no longer there. Animals drowned in the creek. Trees uprooted, others splintered like kindling for the cookstove.

Along the way she saw a most unusual sight, a cow in a treetop, legs sprawled over the branches like a cozy-cover for a teapot. Men were busy setting up block and tackle, attempting to extricate the frightened animal. At another place they witnessed a broom driven by the force of the wind completely through a tree trunk.

Fortunately, they found only slight injuries: mostly bruises, cuts, and scrapes. One broken arm. Thank God, no loss of life. Bertha Callahan arrived at daybreak the following morning with a wagonload of supplies for those families in need. There were many.

Big-hearted Bertha, most of these families didn't even trade with her, yet she helped them because there was a need. The Baptist church sent another load of supplies.

Temporary arrangements were made to house those who'd lost their homes with those who were fortunate enough to have been spared. The second day following the storm, the sound of hammers, saws, and axes could be heard ringing throughout the devastated area. People were rebuilding, and like one big family, everyone pitched in.

It was also the second day following the destructive storm that Rebecca once more confronted the young woman, Ruby. They were traveling to areas Rebecca had not previously been, in search of victims of the storm.

'This be Happy Holler. Ain't too many folk live out here, but they be a few. It's poor soil, mostly rocks, can't do no farming. Can't raise much of nothing except goats and hogs, and they be puny.' Wiping sweat from her wrinkled brow, the old healer gazed about, shaking her head as she observed their surroundings. 'The Lees and the Raineys only ones I know of that's stayed. The Raineys got a fair size place and do pretty good. They keep to themselves. Talk is, years back, maybe twenty years now, Mrs. Rainey and her hired man killed ole man Rainey. 'Course, nobody knows for sure, could be just talk,' Ole Woman rambled as they approached a well-tended home site.

Her tale aroused Rebecca's curiosity and she pursued the story. 'What makes people think they killed him?'

'Well, for one thing, he ain't been seen nor heard from in twenty years.'

'But that's not proof he's dead.'

'Nope, it ain't. Kinda strange, though. Rainey was a drinking man, a mean one, too. Hear tell he was bad to beat on his woman and kids when in his cups. And lazy as sin. Zena, that be Mrs. Rainey, did the work on the place with the help of a hired man. Hard worker, she is. Anyhow, Rainey, he'd go off on a toot and be gone weeks at a time. Come in raising cane, cussing, and a-fighting. Sell off a hog or two, usually the ones Zena been fatting out for butchering, then he'd be gone again. Went on like that for years. Then one day he's seen heading home, drunk as usual, and he ain't been seen since.'

'But that still doesn't — '

'I know. It don't mean she kilt him, but a month later the hired man moved in with her and the younguns. They never made no inquiries about her husband's disappearance, just went on as if he'd never been. Neighbors didn't ask no questions, neither. They's kinda glad he was gone. He was always causing trouble, anyhow. This hired man . . . folk still call him 'the hired man,' even though he lives in the big house now. He be a good sort of fellow, hard worker like Zena. They do pretty good, too.' She paused for a breath. Then they descended onto the valley floor approaching the Rainey place.

'What do you suppose really happened to Mr. Rainey?' Rebecca asked, mopping sweat from her brow. It must be over a hundred degrees.

'Folks say the two of them killed him and buried him in the hog pen. Course, if they did, them hogs ate him. Hogs will eat anything.'

Rebecca felt gooseflesh clamber over the surface of her prickly skin at the picture the story presented to her imaginative mind.

'Come on, let's get on down there. We still got one more place to get to today.' The older woman's shoes scraped the rock-covered ground, slowing down in the heat.

There was slight damage to the roof of the house and outbuildings, but no injuries to the occupants. The entire Rainey brood was there, though they were all grown and had families of their own. All had returned to check on their mother, of whom they were obviously very protective. Mack Lewis, the hired man, was treated as the head of the family, as a father and husband would be. If the story was true, no one here seemed to remember, or care. They were all healthy and apparently happy.

Rebecca and Ole Woman's services weren't needed, so they continued their journey after enjoying a light lunch with the Raineys.

The old sage appeared uneasy when she shared details about the next person they would meet, which pricked Rebecca's ever-present curiosity immediately. Usually so open and matter-of-fact with her information, Rebecca wondered what was different this time. She was soon to find out.

'The Lee place is next. Ain't nobody there no more, except the girl. Sad situation. Sad.' Ole Woman shook her head and mopped her brow while looking at Rebecca in a searching way. 'This ain't gonna be an easy visit to make, and I don't rightly know how to explain the situation here.' She paused again, glancing away from Rebecca as though considering how to continue.

'What's so distinctive about this family?' Rebecca prompted.

'No family, just Ruby. And I ain't sure it be my place to be telling her story. But, well, Ruby be what most folk around here calls a bad girl. The women folk, leastways. The men folk don't say much. Can't afford to I reckon, seeing as how more than a few of them wear out the path to her door after dark.'

'You mean she's a — ?'

'Whoa, hold up a bit. Don't go getting on no moral high horse.' The dwarfish figure stopped, straightened her shoulders and gazed through slitted eyelids at Rebecca. 'Before you go judging, you need to know the facts here, and now ain't the time to be telling them. Just keep in mind this youngun got a heap of troubles, is all. Come on.'

Rebecca, properly chastened over her harsh, judgmental attitude, followed silently. Turning over in her mind the words, 'she's a girl in trouble,' wondering if this could be the same girl she'd met a few days ago.

She didn't have to wonder long. They topped the rise that led to their destination and halted in mid-stride. Below, in the rock-strewn meadow where once had stood a house, lay nothing but scattered remains. Approaching carefully, sidestepping the debris, the women spotted a form crouched amidst the ruins, collecting usable items of clothing. When they neared the bent figure, sunlight struck the head that raised at the sound of their approach and doubt vanished. This was indeed the young woman Rebecca had met earlier.

'Looks as if the storm did you dirty. You hurt any?' Ole Woman inquired.

'That ain't my kinda luck. No, I ain't hurt none. Just lost the house, is all. Wasn't much of a house no ways.'

'Gal, I'd like you to meet Rebecca Rice. She's new hereabouts. She's a nurse, sort of.'

'We's met already. Howdy do, ma'am. I'd offer you ladies something to drink if I could find the dipper, or the water bucket.' Ruby's manner was distracted, trying to be polite and sort through the rubble at the same time. She picked up items and discarded them, only to pick up the same article again.

Ole Woman glanced at Rebecca questioningly, as if to find out how they had met. Rebecca shrugged her shoulders in a manner that said, I'll explain later.

'Ruby, what you gonna do now? The house gone and all. You gonna need a place to stay, what with the ba . . .' The old healer stopped in mid-sentence, glancing quickly at Rebecca, then back at the young woman who still rummaged through the remains of her scattered possessions.

'It's okay. Miss Rice already knows about the baby. You can say it out loud. Besides, before long everybody will know.' With that, Ruby Lee began to sob uncontrollably and collapsed amid the ruins of her home and life.

'Here, here now. It ain't good for the little one to be carrying on so. Get hold of yourself now, it'll be okay.' Ole Woman patted Ruby's trembling shoulders solicitously. 'Dry them eyes. Come on, blow your nose and listen to me. You gonna come live with me. That's what you gonna do. Don't know why I didn't think of it sooner. Come on, gather up what you already got sorted out. We got a long way to go.' Ole Woman briskly constructed a bundle of the meager belongings the girl had piled together.

'I won't be going with you. I can't. You don't know what you be saying, asking me to live with you. You know how folks are. They won't go for it. They need you. They don't need me. So, I won't be going with you.' Retrieving the bundle, Ruby sat down on it and continued to cry.

'Would you live with me? I live alone and I get lonely. You'd be doing me a favor if you said 'yes.' '

The troubled redhead lifted her gaze to stare at Rebecca out of tear-blurred eyes. 'You crazy? You don't know nothing about me, yet you'd ask me to live with you? You are a strange one. No wonder folks be talking.' She blew her nose on a rag clutched in her pale hands. Then she smiled weakly. 'I thank you kindly, ma'am, but no.' Ruby slowly wiped her eyes, then stared off into the distance as if the other women weren't present. 'I'll be staying here.'

'But you can't stay here. You ain't go no house, no food, no nothing.'

'Don't matter none, I won't need much.'

'It does matter, to me, leastways. Now, no more of this foolish talk, Ruby Lee. You'll either go stay with me or you'll stay with Rebecca. Take your pick, but you ain't staying here. You hear me? Now, get your things together and let's be off. I'm an old woman, and I'm a-getting tired.' With that, she took the young woman by the arm and lifted her to her feet, took up her bundle of possessions, and started for home.

* * *

By the time they arrived, it was dusky dark. Rebecca decided they should stay with Ole Woman for the night, then leave early the next morning. Ruby collapsed on the sofa and was sound asleep before supper was fixed. Poor thing needed the food, but she must have needed the sleep more.

25

Summer progressed. The days were long, hot, and humid. The heavy, extended rains of spring were over but, they'd left their problems behind to be dealt with in the muggy heat of summer. Mosquitoes, flies, fleas, ticks, and other obnoxious insects thrived. And the snakes. Rebecca had been warned about the 'dog days' of summer.

Snakes be blind in the dog days. They strike by sound instead of sight.

Already, she could envision being attacked by a blind water moccasin as she made her way across the creek or into the berry patch. She learned to be keenly aware of the odor emitted by the water moccasin through its musk glands. That odor, she was told, resembled that of a horse ridden long and hard, and was always a dependable indication that a water moccasin lurked nearby. If there was one living thing Rebecca detested, it was a snake.

The two healers were kept busy treating various bites and infections caused by those assorted parasites. Their ointments, salves, and poultices were in high demand.

Ruby was left on her own for the most part as Rebecca's trips took her further afield. The desperate young woman had chosen to stay with Rebecca until she could make other arrangements, though Rebecca suspected she was chosen for a more personal reason. Intimacy would provide Ruby with the opportunity to plead her case; to convince Rebecca to abort her child. It would be a long wait.

During Rebecca's absence, the young woman either roamed the hillside all day, or she didn't leave her bed at all.

Rebecca tried talking to her about the situation, but may as well have been talking to herself. Ruby erected a mental barrier. She heard only what she wanted to hear. In the end, Rebecca abandoned her earlier attempts to counsel the wretched young woman who daily retreated farther within herself. When Ruby got ready to talk, Rebecca would be there to listen.

In the meantime, Megan and Davy continued their lessons. It wasn't as regular as either of them would like, but they still managed several days a week. Davy proved to be a very eager pupil. Much as his sister had before him, he devoured the lessons Rebecca prepared. Often the three of them took their slates or books down to the creek bank and read to one another. Davy even helped Megan with her chores so they could come together. The three of them attempted to persuade Ruby to join them in their lessons. She replied, 'Be a waste of time. I'll never need it.'

So far there had been no further acts of vandalism. Rebecca's windowpanes and well rope were left unmolested. Perhaps the storm had taken their minds off her for a while. Whatever the reason, Rebecca welcomed the reprieve. Still, she didn't intend to replace the panes until cooler weather, just in case. Ruby argued that she shouldn't replace them at all.

Rebecca refused to allow the incident with Zake Daniels to spoil her pleasure. So she continued her evening trips to the bathing pool, though now she always made certain Diablo accompanied her.

One evening while sitting beside her pool, enthralled by the sounds surrounding her in the growing twilight, Rebecca ran through her mind the options she had in dealing with her houseguest. She watched a ruby-throated hummingbird, wings whirring, sip nectar from a nearby wildflower. The sunset burnished the creek below, causing pink-tinted ripples on the water. Somewhere in the distance a whippoorwill started his haunting cry. Absorbed, Rebecca failed to hear Ruby's approach until she spoke softly.

'Can I talk with you?'

Turning toward the voice, Rebecca indicated a spot beside her on the moss-padded rock. 'Of course.' She noticed again the change in Ruby since their first meeting. Dark purple formed half moons beneath her now lusterless eyes, and her hair hung limply on her slumped shoulders. After settling herself on the rock, Ruby gazed absently at the darkening sky, sighed deeply, turned and said, 'I want to tell you . . . '

'You don't have to.'

'I have to. Maybe you're the only one I can tell. I just know I gotta tell someone, then maybe . . . I don't know.' Listlessly, Ruby brushed lank strands of hair from her forehead. 'Will you just let me talk and not say nothing? Don't ask no questions, I mean?'

'If you don't want me to.'

'I don't.'

'Okay.'

'I'm ashamed. I don't . . . See, I was ten when Ma died. Pa, he took it kind of hard and all, losing Ma. I don't know why, he was always mean to her. Anyhow, he took to drinking more than usual and staying gone a lot.' Ruby paused as if collecting her thoughts. 'Then he quit going away. He'd just sit and drink. One day he called me to him and said, 'Ruby, you gonna have to be the woman of the house now. Your Ma left us, and you gonna have to take her place.' He picked up his corn jug and left the house, walking off into the woods.

'I worked real hard that day, trying to do all the things I'd seen Ma do. I was the woman of the house now, Pa had said so. I cleaned and scrubbed like crazy. I remember I fixed Pa's favorite supper that night. Only, he didn't come home to eat it.' Again she paused, dropped her head onto her folded arms.

Rebecca felt, more than heard, the sob that escaped the girl's throat. Just when Rebecca thought she wouldn't go on, Ruby lifted her head. 'He come to my bed that night. He ... Oh God! He — ' A sob momentarily choked off her words. 'I didn't know he meant ... that! I-I can't. I can't ... '

Rebecca coiled her arms around the girl's shaking shoulders and drew her close, trying to ease the hurt, and felt the sobs convulse through her young body.

'It's okay. You don't have to go on. Hush now, it's okay.'

'No! It ain't okay. It'll never be okay. Never!' She pulled herself from Rebecca's grasp. 'He didn't want a housekeeper and cook. He wanted a ... He kept coming and kept coming to my . . . bed. When I'd cry and beg him to leave me alone, he'd hit me until I couldn't cry out any more.' Ruby stood suddenly and paced back and forth beside the pool. 'Finally, I just quit fighting.' The tears cascading down her memory-tortured face glistened in the moonlight now flooding the area.

She continued to pace and to talk. Each word stripped away layers of the protective shell she'd built throughout the years, exposing the raw, ugly pain. Her thoughts tromped wildly in tight circles of shame and abject misery.

'I don't remember how old I was when Pa brought the first 'Uncle' to visit. 'Uncles,' he called them. All in the family, you see. Like that made it okay, you know. I was to be nice to my uncles. After a while, I quit counting the uncles, too. What did it matter? What good did it do, anyhow? They give Pa money or licker. Besides, if I was nice to the uncles and didn't cause no trouble, Pa wasn't so mean to me, and didn't whup me with the razor strap so often. I learned soon enough that, with or without the strap, Pa would get his way. It was easier without the strap.'

Halting her pacing, the girl of the hills stood before Rebecca squared her shoulders, and said defiantly, 'I kilt him. I kilt Pa, and I ain't sorry, neither.'

This last was uttered almost as a challenge, daring Rebecca to reprimand her actions. Rebecca held her tongue and waited, sensing more had to be said.

'Didn't you hear me? I said . . . '

'I heard.'

Sobbing, Ruby slumped onto the moss-padded rock. 'I ain't sorry. I ain't.' Sobs racked her slender, bloated frame.

Rebecca let her cry, instinctively sensing she must tell it all to cleanse herself of the memories. This time, Rebecca didn't attempt to comfort her. She waited.

'It were winter. Cold as the dickens, and Pa, he didn't come home that night. I found him next day, passed out in the snow. He'd been there all night, I reckon. I finally got him to the house and in his bed. I knew he was sick, real sick. He was coughing a lot and I could hear him rattling in his chest when he breathed. I knew he needed a doctor. I knew.' She glanced at Rebecca, silently judging her reaction. Then she continued.

'I stayed in my room till I couldn't hear that wheezing he made when he breathed no more. I buried him myself, next day. Buried him next to Ma.' She paused a moment. 'I thought, 'Free. I'm free at last.' ' She laughed harshly. 'Free of what? Free to starve? I soon found out. Oh, I tried. I did. I tried to get work from folks around here. I offered to do washing, ironing, anything. They'd have none of me. The good ladies didn't want trash like me doing their washing. Oh, I tried, awright, for all the good it did me.' She laughed again. Only it wasn't a laugh of joy.

The cold, harsh sound caused Rebecca's flesh to prickle and she felt tears sting her eyelids as she listened to Ruby sob beside her, but she remained silent.

'When the 'uncles' started scratching on my door at night, I let them in. Only this time . . . this time it were me in charge. Me. I had food to eat, regular. Clothes to wear. Pretty clothes, too, not cast-offs. If the roof needed fixing, it got fixed. Yeah, I learned. Let the women folk turn their noses up at me. They men folk don't. Even if they do wait till dark, they come to me. Me. 'Pretty Ruby of Happy Holler,' they calls me. And I hate them all.'

Ruby wiped her tear-stained face on the hem of her dress and continued. 'What am I to do now? What? I can't have this baby! Don't you see, I can't? How would I care for it? I won't have my child raised like I was. Not to grow up being nice to uncles to survive. I won't do it. I can't,' she cried, the words ripped from her throat.

'You don't have to. I'll help you.'

The distraught young woman grabbed Rebecca's hand, pressed it to her tear-wet cheek in relief. 'You will?'

'No. Oh no, Ruby. You've misunderstood. I'll help you raise your child. I have some money, not much, but enough. Together, you and I, we can make a home for you and your baby. You'll . . . '

Springing up, Ruby gasped. 'You ain't gonna help me, then? You haven't heard a word I've said. I can't have this baby! He'd never leave me alone if I keep it. He don't want to marry me. I ain't good enough for the likes of him, not to marry, leastways. But a child, he wants a child. I gotta be rid of him.' Wringing her hands in the folds of her dress, she commenced to cry again.

Rebecca was confused more than ever. Who was the he Ruby talked about? Who wants a child, but not enough to marry her? More questions.

Collecting false courage, Rebecca asked, 'Who is it you must be rid of, Ruby?'

'You ain't helping me. It don't matter. Not no more,' Ruby said, then turned and ran blindly into the night, sobbing.

Rebecca sat by the pool listening to the girl's retreating, stumbling footfalls. Diablo leaped to his feet and quickly followed the figure in flight. She'd be all right; Diablo would keep watch over her until she gained control of her tormented emotions and was ready to return.

Slowly, Rebecca got to her feet, allowing the blood to flow freely into her cramped legs, then returned home in the dark.

Ruby and Diablo didn't return until the morning of the second day following her flight from the pool.

Without a word, she went straight to the sofa where she made her bed, lay down and was instantly asleep. She probably hadn't rested since she fled into the night, her soul tormented by hateful memories and a hopeless future.

Life resumed as near normal as was possible. Ruby never again mentioned getting rid of her baby. And neither of them mentioned the story she'd revealed at the pool.

★   ★   ★

Rebecca's garden produced a bumper crop, thanks to Sam's care. He spent more time tending it than she did. Together, she and Ole Woman put up several hundred jars of tomatoes, peas, beans, squash, chow-chow, pickles, apples, peaches, pears, and plums, in addition to a variety of dried fruits and vegetables. Rebecca had never heard of 'leather britches' until that summer. But she and her old friend spent hours sitting in the shade of the big cottonwood in the back yard, listening to it whisper secret messages to the wind, stringing green beans on thread to be hung from the rafters, drying until needed.

Giving her tender fingers a short rest from pushing the threaded needle through beans, Rebecca glanced up to find Ole Woman gazing around, sniffing the air, looking at the sky as if estimating the weather.

'What are you doing?'

'Gonna be a nasty winter.'

'How do you know that?'

'Look around you, chil'. Mother Nature tells you what she's doing, so you can get ready for it. You got to pay attention. Lookee over there at that hornets' nest, see how low they's building it and how heavy it be? See them red ants there?' She pointed her bony finger in the direction of a huge anthill just beyond the rail fence. 'Notice how high they're forming that mound. Take Diablo, for instance; see how his coat's thickening up. Crickets already coming in the house, gathering in the chimney.

'Plants tell us, too. Notice the corn you growed, how the corn shucks be tighter around and further over the ends of the ears, and your onions growed more layers. 'Course, the weather has its own warning signs. A long, hot summer means a long, cold winter. Lots of low, rolling thunder in late fall's a sure sign of a bad winter.' She paused and took a drink of cloverleaf tea before continuing.

'Them ants younder'll also tell you if it's gonna rain. They'll cover the hole to their hill. Earthworms come to the surface just before a rain, and birds fly lower. They all know what Mother Nature is telling them. But folks, they don't pay much mind to her and they get took by surprise.'

'That's amazing.' Rebecca pushed the needle through another green bean pod, flinching when her tender finger cried in protest to the applied pressure.

'Ain't, really. It be the natural way of things. It be much like my herbs, folk don't pay attention. They quit paying attention to the old ways and they're losing a heap of knowledge. They got modern, started reading the Almanac instead of the signs around them.'

26

Suddenly, summer was gone. The heat evaporated. Autumn arrived, crowned with morning fog. The nights were cold, with dew beading the grass blades; trees turned a multi-hued variety of colors. Clamorous honking filled the air, then faded away as a wedge of migrating geese winged southward for the winter and the screech owls held all night meetings.

Due to the weather, they held the last shindig of the season early. Ruby flatly refused Rebecca's suggestion that she attend. In fact, she refused to leave the house any more, though her condition wasn't yet evident. So, Rebecca stayed home with her. One consolation from her decision: she wouldn't have to put up with Zake Daniels.

Megan brought the news of Bertha's husband number five. The storeowner surprised no one by announcing her marriage to the linen salesman, Tim O'Leary.

'He don't stand no taller than Bertha's shoulder, and he'd have to put rocks in his pockets to weigh half what she does. But Bertha's just a-glowing like a new bride. Real proud of him, she is. Funniest thing, he's real bossy-like. Not mean or nothing, just . . . you know, bossy. And Bertha, she's just a-loving it. It was, 'yes dear', 'no dear.' 'You need anything, dear?' A-waiting on him like he was a baby. You should have seen it. Sure enough ain't like the others she done been married to.' Megan bubbled with excitement, repeating the activities of the new bride and groom.

Smiling at her enthusiasm, Rebecca agreed she'd have to make a trip to the settlement and meet the newest catch.

'How's Ruby? I ain't seen her much lately,' Megan inquired solemnly. Her earlier delight vanished when she asked about Rebecca's houseguest.

Rebecca wasn't sure how much Megan knew of Ruby's situation. She'd told her young neighbor only that Ruby was staying with her a while due to losing her home to the storm, which was true, of course. It wasn't her place to explain any more than that. She finished with, 'She's okay, I suppose. It must be upsetting to lose everything the way she did. But I'm sure she'll be all right.' Rebecca changed the subject. 'How's your father doing?'

'He's getting around real good now. Hardly even know his leg were ever hurt. Odd though, just the other day, he asked when you'd be by to check on him. That ain't like Pap. Besides, he don't need no checking on and I told him so, too.'

'Tell him I'll be by tomorrow.' Rebecca suspected she knew why Jacob wanted her to come by. 'Now, will you help me get this tub of hominy down to the creek?'

Since the corn crop had been so abundant, Rebecca was preparing hominy. She'd worked with it several days, soaking it in lye water, working the outer skin off the kernels. Now it required numerous rinsings. Rebecca figured the best way to handle this task would be to transport the tub of corn to the creek.

The following day, Rebecca timed her visit to Jacob Penny when she knew the rest of the family would be occupied elsewhere. 'Well, Mr. Penny, your leg is fine. I don't think there'll be any problems with it, but I'd take it easy for a while longer if I were you,' she said, completing her examination.

'Yeah, that's what I figured, too. Sit . . . take a seat there,' he indicated the rocker next to him on the porch. He leaned over and took up a container of late fall cowpeas and commenced to shell them.

Trying to hide her surprise at his domestic activity, Rebecca made herself comfortable in the chair.

'Wasn't the leg I wanted to see you about.'

'Oh?' Rebecca didn't prompt further. This must be his doing.

While she waited for Jacob to gather his courage, the sound of peas clicking in the pan resembled rifle fire in the uneasy silence. Finally, clearing his throat, the man spoke.

'Been doing some thinking, I have. Ain't saying you're right, but . . . well, it got me to thinking. About what you said. About God being love, and how Leona wouldn't a wanted the girl blamed for her dying.' He paused long enough to lean down and collect a pea that shot out of the pan. 'You know, just thinking. Even had the girl read them passages you told me about. Well, what I'm a trying to say is . . . well, mayhap I been a might hard on the girl and all. I mean Megan, and all.'

He glanced up from his pea shelling and softly added, 'Ain't such a bad name, but suppose it'd be awright if she be called, Megan Leona?' Jacob rushed on as if embarrassed, 'It being her Ma's name, I mean.' He stopped as though out of breath after a long-distance run.

Indeed, he had come a great distance. Rebecca smiled at him and clutched her shawl closer.

'It's a lovely name. Have you told Megan yet?'

Looking out across the yard and fumbling with the peas, he muttered, 'She may not like it. What if she don't want me giving her no name? Now she done got one, I mean. I ain't been too kind to the girl ... Megan,' he amended. 'I'm helping some, though.' He rattled the container of peas to indicate his help. 'And the boys, they're going to start helping, too.' He lifted his misty eyes to meet Rebecca's. 'Am I too late?' Torment and doubt pulled at his features, reflecting the agony within. Rebecca's heart went out to this troubled man as he struggled to right a wrong of seventeen years.

'I don't think so. Megan's a very — ' Rebecca paused, then said, 'Megan Leona's a very loving person, Mr. Penny, and she needs love in return. Perhaps if you shared with her, well, what you feel. Your grief at the loss of her mother. Just love her, Mr. Penny. Love covers a multitude of sins, as the Bible says. Give her love.'

'Sins. That's another thing. You think He'll forgive me? I mean, I done a heap of things I ain't real proud of. I don't know. What do you think?'

Leaving her chair, Rebecca knelt beside Jacob. He dropped his head just as she spotted tears staining his cheeks. Taking his big, trembling hand in hers, Rebecca set the peas aside. 'I know He will. He forgave us all when He hung on that cross so long ago. That's what love is. It's forgiving.'

Another prayer answered.

★ ★ ★

Megan bubbled with joy a few days later when she came to tell Rebecca the wondrous news. Her father called the family together and announced some changes to be made. Megan repeated her father's words for Rebecca's benefit. ' 'From now on, the girl's to be called Megan Leona, proper like. And everybody got chores to be doing. And no back sass about it. Your sister will now do only the household stuff, and you boys the outside chores, that is, after you finish your own work.' Pap sent all three over to the sawmill at Little Grassy. Said not to come back lest they's had a job there.' Megan drew a deep breath and pushed her bangs off her forehead. 'So many changes all at once. Ain't it grand? 'Course, the boys ain't leaping for joy, I can tell you that. I ain't never seen them so upset. They're acting like a bunch of old hens, after the weasel come through.' She giggled thinking about her brothers' reactions to their father's change in the household.

'Ain't it grand, Miss Rebecca? Megan

302

Leona Penny. Just like real folks. I got me a name. And Pap, him a-wanting me to have Ma's name. Ain't it grand?' The young girl fairly danced around the kitchen in her joy.

★ ★ ★

The old sage's winter weather forecast hit right on target. A foot of snow fell before Thanksgiving which, due to the freezing temperatures, stayed on the ground. The drifts were dangerously deep and made traveling treacherous.

The two healers made more calls than usual for this time of year. And as the old woman had predicted, the people hadn't paid heed to the signs of nature and were caught unprepared for the sudden arrival of winter.

Sam laid in a good supply of wood for Rebecca and assisted with the installation of her new windowpanes. With his help she, at least, was all set for the winter.

Croup and sore throats were commonplace ailments. Croup-poultices and hot toddies were dispensed with regularity. Ole Woman had difficulty making the sick calls any distance from home and eventually agreed, reluctantly, that Rebecca should go alone to the farthest cases.

303

Often, Rebecca would be gone weeks at a time. She stayed with first one, then another of the families she treated, traveling on foot as the weather permitted. If she wasn't treated as warmly as she'd like, at least the people accepted her for the medicines she brought. The atmosphere remained cool, but no longer hostile. She always helped with the cooking and dishwashing chores wherever she stayed, and occasionally found herself feeding the farm animals.

Ruby was left more and more on her own. She was melting away. Instead of gaining weight, she lost it. Her clothes hung on her body as if draped on a coat rack. She was all round belly, and big, vacant eyes.

Rebecca tried talking to her about her condition, but the young pregnant woman was beyond caring. Rebecca suspected when she wasn't there, Ruby didn't eat, that she roamed the woods still, even in the bone-rattling cold. Rebecca was beyond knowing what to do for her, though she continued to pray for her. But Ruby resisted her in that as well. Her will couldn't be overridden by Rebecca's desires.

By the middle of December, Rebecca knew she could no longer travel on foot to the far-reaching areas. The cold weather had a tenacious grip and refused to let go. She couldn't continue trudging through knee-deep snowdrifts, struggling against the wind-driven sleet. More and more now, she arrived half frozen, her dress hem stiff with ice crusts clinging to it, her shoes saturated and soggy. Somehow, she must have transportation. She took her problem to Sam.

'I have to have transportation if I'm to continue my calls to the sick in this weather. I don't know which to get, a horse and buggy, or just a horse. What do you think, Sam?'

'Mule.'

'Why a mule? A buggy would let me carry more supplies, wouldn't it? Or a horse. Isn't a horse faster than a mule?' She wasn't thrilled at the idea of a mule.

'Mule. Mule be slower, but more sure-footed. You be going to country that ain't always flat. Horse ain't no good on hilly, rocky ground.' Sam scratched his chin, shook his head and added, 'Buggy, no. Turn it over, or get stuck in the mud. You can't go nowhere hereabouts in no buggy. Mule.' He hugged his old coat closer when a blast of icy wind whipped about them where they stood outside his wagon-home, talking. He never invited her, or anyone else to her knowledge, inside.

'A mule it is, then. I'll go to the smithy's tomorrow and inquire about one. He should know where I can find a dependable animal.' Rebecca, too, tugged her coat closer as the wind continued to assault them with its frigid fingers.

'No need. I can get you one, good one, too. You be needing a saddle. I'll take care of it.' He spat a brown stream of tobacco juice into the wind.

'How much do you think it'll cost for the mule and saddle? I'll go get the money for you.'

'I'll get the mule.' With that statement, he turned and disappeared inside his private domain. He was such an odd creature. But if Sam said he'd get a mule, Rebecca knew somehow he would.

★ ★ ★

Rebecca was awakened at daybreak by the most obnoxious sounds she'd ever heard. 'What in the world?' Almost before her words were out, the noise was repeated. In one fluid movement her feet hit the floor and she snatched up her robe, heading for the back door. She collided with Ruby in the kitchen. She, too, was on her way to investigate the source of their disrupted slumber.

'What's that?' Ruby mumbled, rubbing sleep from her eyes and tugging an old flannel shirt about her protruding belly.

'I haven't the faintest idea, but it has to go, whatever it is. I never heard such a racket.' Rebecca jerked open the door and came to a full halt in mid-stride. There, tied to the porch railing, stood the source of the mysterious commotion. A mule, complete with saddle, braying its fool head off.

'Dear Lord, give me patience,' Rebecca muttered, gaping at the animal.

'Whose is it?' Ruby whispered, joining Rebecca at the open door.

'Mine.' Slamming the door, Rebecca sagged against it for support while she collected herself. 'To think, I asked for that animal! Do they always greet the day in this manner?'

Stumbling to the stove, she stoked up the embers, adding kindling and dry wood. 'I've got to have a cup of coffee,' she said to no one in particular. Automatically, she reached for the pot and bag of coffee beans. Behind her came low giggles. Turning, Rebecca found Ruby ready to burst into full hilarity, supporting her stomach with one hand and covering her mouth with the other.

'What's so funny? I don't see a thing comical about this situation.' Rebecca slapped the pot down on the stove, sloshing water out the spout. She grabbed a tea towel to mop up the mess and asked again, 'Well, what's so funny? I could use a good joke about now.' Forget patience, hers just snapped.

'You. You should have seen the look on your face when you saw that jackass out there. Then you said 'mine' like . . . I don't know — ' Ruby couldn't finish, her contained laughter bubbled over and she collapsed on a nearby chair.

Watching her, Rebecca realized this was the first time she'd ever heard Ruby laugh. It was a good sound. She also saw herself as Ruby must have seen her, and joined in the laughter.

★　★　★

Rebecca named the mule Mercy, for she'd need it to deal with that animal. She had considered calling it Havoc, for obvious reasons, but decided since one should speak the answer, not the problem, Mercy was what she needed.

Ruby gave way to giggles every time Rebecca mounted up and rode away. Rebecca had to admit she made a comical sight, her dress hiked up to her knees, long legs dangling, exposed to elements and eyes alike.

She could have used a ladder to mount up,

for Mercy was at least fifteen hands high, pale gray in color with darker bluish gray splotches along her flanks. It only took a couple of outings to realize the situation needed some adjustments.

*　★　★*

'I know it isn't seemly, but I want them anyway. It's less becoming to ride around exposed from the knee down,' Rebecca told Bertha, paying for her purchases while defending her decision.

'I don't like it. I just don't think it's the thing to be doing. I don't!' Shaking her red head till her curls bounced and rolling her eyes heavenward, Bertha continued to mumble under her breath while Rebecca gathered up her new clothes.

'May I change here? I might as well wear them home.'

'You wouldn't! Rebecca Rice, you'll start a scandal for sure. I just never! I mean, ladies just don't — '

'Well, this lady does. I think it's ridiculous that fashion, and men, dictate what women should, or shouldn't, wear. Now, are you going to allow me to change here, or force me to freeze on my way home?'

Clucking her tongue and wagging her

head, Bertha replied, 'Go ahead. Go on, ruin your reputation . . . and mine.' Her brown eyes swept Rebecca from crown to toe. 'You come riding in here on that blame mule like a mule skinner, and astride at that. Now, you're gonna ride out dressed like one. It ain't ladylike, I say. Women folk don't wear pants and boots.'

Still shaking her head, Bertha turned back to her mail sorting. As Rebecca started upstairs to change, Bertha called after her, 'I don't want to hear about it. When them irate folks ride you out of them hills on a rail, don't come crying to me.' Pausing long enough to read the return address, she continued. 'You got a letter here from your brother.'

'I'll pick it up after I've changed.'

As a concession to Bertha's modesty, Rebecca donned her skirt over her new pants, but she wore her new boots without concealment. Rebecca rode home far more comfortably in her new attire. She might shock a few people, but at least she'd be warmer and more at ease when she traveled.

Ruby didn't know what to say about the new outfit, but from her looks, Rebecca gathered not much.

She wore her new corduroy pants and wool shirt the next day when she rode over to visit her mentor.

'Always wanted to dress like that myself, but never got the nerve,' Ole Woman greeted her. 'Sensible, that's what it is. Good for you, chil'. You got pluck, I'll say that.' The healer grinned, handing Rebecca a cup of hot tea, then offered her pipe.

'Why not? I feel daring today. How do you do it?' Rebecca asked, taking the corncob pipe from her gnarled old hand.

Snickering like a couple of schoolgirls, Rebecca received her first lesson in pipe smoking.

27

The letter from James announced the birth of his daughter on the fifth of December. They named her Elouise Rebecca. Mother and daughter were doing fine.

How like James to name his daughter after her, even though he disapproved of her choice of lifestyle. To indicate her pleasure, Rebecca made a decision she'd been contemplating for sometime. She made out her will and sent it to her brother, leaving all but a small income to her new niece and namesake, Elouise Rebecca. The remainder of her funds, though small, she specified in detail how she wished handled. Once more, James might not approve of her decision, but Rebecca knew she could count on her brother to carry out her wishes.

On Christmas Eve, Sam came by with two pheasants and a fat goose ready to stuff and bake for dinner the next day.

'Sam, what will you do about your Christmas sacks for the children this year?' Rebecca inquired. 'I know the tornado wiped out the pecans, hickory, and black walnuts,

312

because I had a hard time locating enough for my baking.'

'Been whittling. Got wooden toys this year for them younguns,' he mumbled as he dug deep into his old coat and withdrew a wooden horse, which he held out for her inspection.

Rebecca took the delicate piece of art from him. Rotating it in her hand, she admired the lifelike carving. 'It's lovely.' The woodgrain highlighted the mane and tail with its darker markings. She could almost feel the muscles in the chest and shoulders of the figure. 'This is remarkable. I've never seen anything so fine. You could sell this, at a good price, too.' Rebecca said.

Sam took the small horse from her and returned it to his coat pocket. 'I don't sell. I do for pleasure. When you sell, it becomes work. No, I don't sell.'

He turned to leave and Rebecca sensed she'd said something wrong, something which upset him. Though what, she couldn't imagine. 'Sam, I didn't . . . I mean, it's lovely,' Rebecca stammered, unsure of what to say. 'Many people would enjoy your work. I only . . . '

'You don't sell part of your soul, part of what you feel and what you are. Besides, people don't appreciate it, don't even understand. No.'

Before she could think of a reply, Sam opened the door and went outside, marching through the snow to his makeshift home. Diablo trotted beside him in the cold, crisp air. Rebecca returned to her Christmas baking more confused than ever about her neighbor.

The next morning, Rebecca was stoking up the fire in preparation for her morning pot of coffee when Diablo returned, scratching on the back door to be let in to the warmth of the kitchen. The young wolf had been out all night with Sam, delivering his yearly Christmas packages to the children of the area. Making a mad dash for the fireplace and warmth, Diablo sprawled before the fire and quickly dropped off to sleep.

Rebecca bundled up before venturing outside to fetch a bucket of fresh water from the well. The cold bit into her flesh, causing her to draw up her shoulders and pull her coat tighter about her. Glancing up at the morning sky, she found it overcast with gray-bellied clouds, hovering low as though filled with snow. She noticed the wind had picked up and the temperature had dropped. A light mist drifted in the air as the clouds released their abundance of moisture. It would either snow or sleet before the day was out. She could feel it, almost smell it. She noticed the smoke from her cookstove dropped to hover at ground level. The area was devoid of sound; no living creature stirred. They'd already taken refuge from the approaching storm.

Despite the weather, Sam, Ole Woman, and Megan arrived for Christmas dinner. Afterward, they gathered around the tree to exchange gifts and sing carols.

They were deeply engrossed in their activities when a rap on the door interrupted them. Silence descended on the room. They all glanced at each other in surprise, like a group of conspirators caught red-handed. Diablo broke the spell when he barked then raced toward the door to investigate.

When Rebecca opened the door against the tug of the icy wind, she could only stare. Her mouth dropped open in a speechless gape when she recognized her visitor.

Jacob Penny stood on the porch, hunch-shouldered against the bitter cold. Finding her voice at last, Rebecca pulled the door open wider. 'Mr. Penny, come in. Please, come in out of the cold, won't you?'

'Don't mean to be intruding, but . . . '

'Come in, please.' Rebecca grasped his arm and pulled him into the room, shutting the door quickly to stanch the flow of frigid air. Taking his hat, she hung it on a nearby rack and motioned toward the fireplace where the fire crackled invitingly against the chill attacking the walls of the house from without.

Standing on the hearth, Megan's father made much ado over rubbing his hands before the fire. With his back to her, he said, 'I shouldn't be here, I know. But . . . it being Christmas and all, well, I . . . Could I maybe join you? If you don't want me . . . that's okay. I'd understand.' He began rebuttoning his coat as though preparing to leave.

'No, don't go. Join us, please. In fact, I'm very glad you've come, Mr. Penny.'

'Jacob. My name is Jacob. I'd take it kindly were you to call me that.' He removed his coat, then withdrew a bundle wrapped in coarse brown butcher paper, tied with twine. He shoved the package toward her. 'For you.'

Surprised by the action, Rebecca accepted the bundle, then took his coat. Hanging the plaid jacket beside his hat, she turned back to him and said, 'Come, Jacob, let's join the others. This is a wonderful surprise.'

'Pap! What are you doing here?' Megan bounced up from the floor where she'd been reading a poem she had written for Christmas to Ole Woman and Sam. Dashing across the room, she halted before her father and gazed searchingly into his eyes. Father and daughter stood, eyes locked for a long moment before

Jacob looked away, then in a soft, pleading voice said, 'If you don't want me to be here, I'll leave.' He looked back at his daughter. 'But I'd like to stay. It's been a long time, a very long time, since I felt like celebrating Christmas, and the reasons I do now are here. May I stay, daughter?' There was a catch in his voice. Again, his gaze fell away from Megan, who still stood mute, studying him.

The silence was long and loud, their breathing the only sound in the room while they awaited Megan's decision. Then, exploding into action, the young girl wrapped her slender arms about her father, kissed his cheek, and with a laughing sob hugged him to her. 'Merry Christmas, Pap.'

In that final moment of the touching scene played out before them, the group of friends exhaled in unison the breaths they'd held. Then, laughing, they made room for Jacob as they took seats and did their best to make him feel welcome.

'What a Christmas gift! Jacob Penny, I'm right proud of you today. You've made an old woman very happy, and a young one too, by the looks of your Megan. Don't let nobody tell me miracles don't happen. Nosirree, don't go telling me no such thing. I just witnessed one I never thought to see, but mighty glad I did. Let me get you a hot drink to warm your insides as warm as my heart is right now.' When she shuffled off toward the kitchen to fetch the offered drink, Rebecca heard her mumbling to herself. What, Rebecca could only guess.

'It's beautiful. I've never seen such workmanship in lace before. Where on earth did you . . . ? I'm sorry, I didn't mean to be rude. It's lovely, and I'll treasure it always.' Rebecca gently folded the lace tablecloth in her lap.

'My wife, Leona, made it. She worked on it while waiting on her time to come. She loved working on it while she made plans for after . . . She-she was gonna have a big party to show off the baby when . . . meant to use that cloth for the table . . . kinda special like. But she never got the chance . . . ' His voice caught; he couldn't go on. The others fell silent, not knowing what to say. Jacob sat with his head down, his hands trembling.

The gift from Jacob was another revelation of the changes taking place in the man. Acting on impulse, Rebecca jumped up. 'I can't think of a more special time to use your Leona's tablecloth than right now. Megan, come help me clear the table. We'll have our dessert in the kitchen. I think your mother would approve of our using it on such a happy occasion.'

They laughed and talked the afternoon away. Jacob and Sam got off to a slow start, both being the quiet type, but the women had no such problem. Before the day was over, the two men were discussing all manner of things together like old friends.

When Rebecca's guests departed, Jacob Penny made a revealing prediction. 'Ma'am, I put the skids on the pranks been going on around your place.' His face flushed. He refused to meet her gaze as he spoke hesitantly, 'Wild oats. No real harm was intended. Boys just being . . . ' He cleared his throat softly. 'It won't happen again. You got my word on it.'

Jacob Penny, like many others of the hill country, had experienced second thoughts about the widder woman at the old Williams' farm. They had watched like hawks, waited patiently, reserving final judgment. Heads were scratched and nodded in bewilderment, for she appeared to be what she claimed, a healer.

In his way, Jacob was informing Rebecca that the destruction of her windows, well rope, and fence was over. Rebecca suspected what he didn't tell her was that his sons, Leo and Ted, were the perpetrators. Bertha had insinuated that, influenced by Brother Zake, the Penny boys had attempted to frighten off the newcomer, convinced they were doing the folks of the area a favor.

* ★ ★

The only damper on the entire day was Ruby's refusal to leave her room where she'd taken refuge before the guests arrived. All their attempts to get her to join them met with cold refusal.

'Leave her be,' Ole Woman advised. 'I reckon it ain't such a Merry Christmas for her this year. Besides, she be self-conscious about her condition around Sam. She'll be awright. She knows we want her. If she changes her mind, she can join us.'

She didn't.

After her guests departed, Rebecca slipped into Ruby's room to check on her and found her sound asleep. Ruby hadn't eaten all day, and her pallor and listlessness caused Rebecca grave concern.

Rebecca still didn't know who had fathered Ruby's child. The young woman no longer talked about her condition and never mentioned anyone. And no one inquired of her whereabouts since the tornado. Odd.

★ ★ ★

320

The weather continued to be miserable for human and animal alike. At night, Rebecca covered Mercy with a blanket to help cut the cold wind that ripped through the shed, which she used as a stable. She didn't know where Sam acquired it, but just before the hardest of the winter weather hit, he delivered a wagonload of hay for the animal and several sacks of feed as well. Rebecca was glad he'd remembered, because she probably wouldn't have thought of it, especially with all the things she had on her mind lately. The weather matched her mood.

She seemed to be on the move constantly, treating the assorted ailments brought on by the cold. Then there was Rachel Bean, who was expecting again in February. Rachel wasn't doing as well as she should. Rebecca suspected there would be trouble when her time came. Her prayer was for Ole Woman to attend the delivery with her. If her suspicion was correct, the baby was breech. She also prayed for guidance. She'd never delivered a breech birth. 'Lord be with me,' she prayed.

The twenty-third day of February 1897 started out a bleak, dreary day, and progressively grew worse. Sleet obliterated the trees, then switched to snow as the swirling spirals of a fierce snowstorm hit. Boiling and twisting clouds roiled over the shaggy-shouldered hills, rapidly filling the area with snow drifts like white sand.

The bleak, barren trees stood out starkly in the island of white while the pines groaned, bent, and swayed under the battering of the furious winds. Their tortured voices were heard, like music from a mystic song, above the howling winds.

Pounding on the door caused both Rebecca and Ruby to jump in nervous reaction, both from the storm outside and the sudden, insistent knocking. The door was almost jerked from her grasp when Rebecca opened it.

Megan tumbled in, nearly falling in her haste. 'Rachel needs you. Her time has come. Jethro sent me to fetch you. He went on back to be with her.' Megan breathlessly delivered her message, then stumbled to the fireplace to warm her hands before the roaring fire.

'Howdy, Ruby. You be okay by yourself while we be gone?'

Without waiting for Ruby to answer, Megan turned back toward Rebecca. 'I'll go saddle Mercy while you get your things together.' With that, Megan dashed back out into the frigid storm.

Frantically, Rebecca snatched up her bag of supplies, grabbed an extra apron, and her Bible, then turned to find Ruby standing beside her holding her coat, scarf, boots, and pants. Gratefully, Rebecca took the offered clothes. She changed standing in the middle of the kitchen, dropping her skirt over her pants, as was her custom when she traveled. Ruby handed her an extra pair of rough wool socks for her feet and an old flannel shirt Rebecca had never seen before.

'It were Pa's,' she said in answer to Rebecca's glance at the shirt. 'I kept it. Don't know why, but it's warm. Take it.'

Smiling at her, Rebecca seized the shirt and pulled it on over her longjohns. Just before Christmas, she had again scandalized Bertha with her latest purchase. Scandalous or otherwise, the heavy cotton undergarment was quite warm. Bundled up as warmly as possible, Rebecca snatched her gear and headed for the door, almost colliding with Megan as she dashed back inside, breathless from the cold.

'I'm all set. You ready? Let's be going. See you, Ruby.' Back out the door she flew, Rebecca quickly on her heels.

'Be careful!' Ruby shouted above the roar of the storm as Rebecca and Megan neared the corner of the house.

28

Be careful of what? The weather? The birth? What? That disturbing thought scurried through Rebecca's head as they trudged through the snowstorm. The mule whinnied and panted as she struggled through the snowdrifts, her vaporous breath blowing backward along her haunches.

Rebecca's feet and hands were numb. Her teeth chattered. The spreading cold crept through her limbs, but Rebecca knew she must endure. Blinking the freezing snow from her eyelashes, she turned to check on Megan, who rode behind her. She opened her mouth to ask the girl how she was doing and the words were snatched from her lips, lost to the wind, her breath sucked away. Megan nodded, indicating she understood Rebecca's concern, and they plodded onward.

The trip that ordinarily would have taken only an hour seemed to take forever. It grew dark and still they trudged onward in the snowstorm. Rebecca prayed they were not going in circles in the blinding, snow-filled world. Mercy floundered on in the frigid cold of the burning snow, the darkness grew thicker, and the snow heavier. Rebecca felt its bitter kiss on her cheeks.

Abruptly there was a lull in the wind, and out of the blanket of darkness a yellow light flickered through a window shutter, casting a glow on the white snow, sparkling sugar-like in the lamplight. They had made it.

Rebecca's legs felt frozen and stiff when she climbed from Mercy's back and stood leaning into the mule's side for support. Her limbs screamed in protest as the blood rushed through cramped, cold veins. Staggering forward, she approached the house, leaving Megan to dismount and follow.

The door opened slowly, cautiously. Who did Jethro think it was, the law looking for his still? On a night like this?

But it wasn't Jethro. It was the oldest boy, Mark, who stood beside the door peering out. Mark stepped back when he recognized Rebecca, allowing her to enter. An oppressive silence filled the room. The boy reached out to take her saturated wrap, then whispered, 'Ma's in there.' He pointed toward the half-open door of his parents' bedroom.

The only sound came from the woman laboring in the next room. Short, panting breaths and soft moans were barely audible above the howling winds battering the house.

'Megan, put some water on to boil, then

get these children fed and put to bed,' Rebecca instructed. 'I'll go to Rachel.' Rebecca removed her wet boots where she stood, then padded barefoot across the uneven wooden floor toward her patient.

Jethro, crouched beside the bed, clutched Rachel's hand and gently wiped her perspiration-beaded brow, whispering encouragement as he did so. Glancing up at Rebecca's entrance, a look of relief flooded his face.

'Thank goodness, you made it. With the storm and all, I wasn't sure. She's having a rough time. Not like with the others. Help her . . . please.' There was a pleading softness in his voice Rebecca had never heard before, not directed toward her, at least.

Glancing first at the woman on the bed, whose pain masked her loveliness, then at the man beside her, Rebecca recalled Ole Woman's words. 'Makes you envious to watch those two, so devoted to each other. If Jethro Bean got any weakness in him, it be for his Rachel.'

'Of course, I'll help her. I'll do all I can. Now, if you'll leave us, I'll check on the baby's progress.' She opened her bag and withdrew a fresh apron, which she quickly tied about her waist. When she turned back toward the bed, she found the young husband still sitting there, gripping his wife's hand.

'Please, I need to check her. You'll have to leave us now.'

Glancing up as though he'd forgotten her presence, Jethro mumbled, 'Yeah, sure. I'll be right outside the door here if you need me.'

'Mr. Bean, I need you to put our animal in the barn. If you'll take care of that, I'll get on with taking care of your wife. Please . . . go on, now.'

Reluctantly, he left his place beside the bed, glancing back over his shoulder from the doorway. 'Holler if you need me.'

'Everything's going to be fine. Go on, now. That animal will freeze if she stays out in that weather much longer.'

'Yeah, I'm going. She gonna be okay, ain't she? I mean, she ain't gonna die?' Fear and pleading burdened his eyes as well as his voice.

'No. She isn't. Now go!' Rebecca wished she were as confident as she sounded. Making a preliminary check of her patient, who rested fitfully from pain-induced exhaustion, Rebecca heard Megan in the other room reading a story from the Bible to the woman's frightened children. All they could do now was wait.

Rachel spent the night with intervals of pain and wakefulness, then exhausted slumber. Rebecca tried to rest when Rachel did.

She had given up her attempt to keep Rachel's husband away, allowing him back into her room where he remained throughout the long night. Each time Rebecca awoke to check on Rachel, Jethro was there beside her bed, gently stroking his wife's hand.

With morning, her labor arrived full force. Her contractions were severe and regular, yet she made no progress.

Megan fed and occupied the little ones, trying to distract their thoughts from their mother. Jethro left Rachel's bedside long enough to feed and water his stock and bring in wood for the stove. Refusing food for himself, he returned to resume his vigil at Rachel's bedside.

By evening, Rachel was no longer capable of muffling her outbursts of pain. Twisting, bathed in perspiration, her face contorted with pain, her cries vibrated off the walls.

Jethro was like a crazed animal. Simultaneously he soothed his wife and berated Rebecca for doing nothing to help her.

'I'm doing all I can. You need to calm down. You're upsetting Rachel. If you can't be quiet, I'll have to ask you to leave.'

'I ain't going nowhere, woman! You hear me, nowhere! Do something for her. Anything.'

At nine o'clock, Rebecca knew she had to

do more than wait for nature to take her course. The baby would have to be turned. She hoped it would turn on its own, but that hadn't happened. She would have to turn it.

She felt the perspiration bead between her breasts, trickle slowly down her sides, and beneath her armpits. Her hands trembled. It was no use. She couldn't do it. Her hand was too large. She needed a smaller hand. Megan. Megan would have to do it. Though young and untrained, she would have to try.

Turning slowly to the haggard-faced man kneeling beside the bed, Rebecca forced her voice to a level of calm she was far from feeling and informed him of the situation, ending with a request for him to leave the room.

'I know you want to stay, but I need you to be with your children while Megan helps me with Rachel. They need your reassurance and your strength.'

Looking like a man who'd just been handed a death sentence, his gaze dropped to his wife on the bed as she slept between her spasms of pain. Raising his eyes to meet Rebecca's, he voiced the concern on both their minds that until now had not been mentioned. 'If it's Rachel or the baby, save my Rachel.' Shoulders sagging, head down, he left the room.

Megan stood as though riveted to the floor, twisting the corner of her crisp white apron, her eyes wide as Rebecca explained what had to be done and why she was the one that must do it.

'B-but . . . I ain't never even been to no birthing. I don't know if I can.'

'You've got to. You're her only hope. Just do as I tell you and it'll be all right,' Rebecca said with more confidence than she felt.

While Megan followed instructions, Rebecca prayed. While they worked, silence hung heavy in the air. Both women were drenched in perspiration, though the room was cool. Death crouched in the far corner of the room; Rebecca felt its presence. Rebecca would not surrender her patient without a fight. Renewing her efforts, she continued to pray, urging Megan on.

'I feel it! I can feel the baby. What do I do now?' Megan's face glowed as she listened intently to Rebecca's instructions.

Soft moans drew Rebecca's attention to the woman they were working feverishly to help. Glancing up, their eyes met across the mound of Rachel's belly. Her teeth were clenched, her knuckles white as she gripped the rails of her headboard, attempting to strangle the scream forming within her as another, stronger contraction crested. Rachel's eyes beseeched her. To what? Ease her pain, save her life, her baby? Rebecca smiled her reply of understanding.

'Hang on, Rachel. It's almost over now. You'll be fine; your baby will be fine. I promise you. Now, relax.'

Turning back to Megan, Rebecca instructed, 'When her contraction passes, try again.'

'Ain't no use. It won't budge. I . . . '

'It will move! It will. It must!' Rebecca snapped in her anxiety. Recovering quickly, she apologized. 'Sorry. I don't know what got into me. It's just that . . . Megan; I need your faith joined with mine. Matthew 18: 18–20 says, 'Where two or more gather in My name, there I will be also,' and 'whatsoever ye bind or loosen in His name, He will bind or loosen in heaven.' We must agree to loosen the bonds holding this child and bind all forces that would interfere in its safe delivery. Will you join with me in that prayer of agreement?'

'I will.'

Both women jumped at the sound of that voice. Glancing over her shoulder, Rebecca saw, silhouetted in the open doorway, Jethro Bean. Gray-faced, red-eyed, and ragged with fatigue, he stood leaning against the doorframe. Before Rebecca could respond, he said again, 'I will. If it'll help my Rachel, I'll agree

with you. I ain't got much faith myself, but
. . . well, if you believe it'll work . . . then
. . . guess I can, too.'

'Dear Lord, thank you. Let Your power be
witness to this man. Let Thy Spirit fill him
with peace and faith,' Rebecca whispered
under her breath.

'I believe it'll work, Mr. Bean, and I believe
you do, also. Deep down, where it counts.'
When she turned back toward the woman on
the bed, Rebecca caught a glimpse of
Rachel's face. Only moments before it had
been a mask of pain and agony, but now it
glowed radiantly, even in her pain. She
nodded to Rebecca and smiled. Rebecca
returned the smile and began to pray the
prayer of agreement.

Even before Rebecca finished, Megan
shouted, 'It moved. I felt it move. Wait
. . . now . . . I feel . . . Oh! I feel its head.
What do I do now?'

Hot tears of relief flowed from Rebecca's
eyes, cascading down her face. 'Nothing. The
Lord will do the rest.'

Rachel drew her knees up as another
contraction seized her. She gripped the
headboard and whispered, 'Jethro, your son is
on the way.'

Jethro rushed to her bedside, knelt beside
it, took her hand and unashamedly let hot

tears flood his face, while he whispered endearments to his wife.

Rebecca and Megan scrambled to get sheets, towels, hot water, scissors, thread ready. Next they brought in the blankets, warming near the cast iron stove in the front room, to wrap the baby in.

Jethro and Rachel's son was born within minutes with no further assistance. A strong, healthy, black-haired son. A perfect gift from God.

Rebecca wrapped the baby warmly, then handed him to his father. Rachel still required her attention.

Later, Rebecca and Megan changed the bed linens and put a fresh gown on the exhausted mother, making her as comfortable as possible. Rachel dropped off to sleep with her new son lying in the gentle curve of her arm, tugging lustily on the milk-engorged breast he'd already found.

The bedraggled new father stood gazing down at his sleeping wife and son. Swiping tears from his face with the back of his rugged hand, he turned. 'Thank you. I know that ain't much . . . considering. But, thank you. I thought for sure I'd lose her tonight, when things . . . well, when the babe wouldn't turn. I don't think I could live without her.' Glancing at his wife, he shoved his hands into his pockets. When he spoke again, his voice was gruff with emotions. 'You ever be needing anything, anything at all, you just call for Jethro Bean. I'll be there. You got my word on that, ma'am. You too, Megan Penny. God bless you both.'

He scurried from the room as though embarrassed by his emotions. When the bedroom door closed behind him, the outer room exploded with cries of glee from the waiting youngsters at the announcement of their new baby brother.

Together, Rebecca and Megan set the room straight, checked once more on mother and son, then joined the celebration in the other room.

Near midnight, exhaustion fell upon the occupants of the room like a heavy cloak. Pallets were made near the fire for the older boys and Megan. Rebecca took the boys' bed. Jethro placed his pallet on the floor beside his wife's bed. 'She might need something in the night,' he said, closing the door to their bedroom.

Snuggling deep beneath the layers of quilts to get warm, Rebecca drifted off to sleep with that scene on her eyelids: A man sleeping on the floor, in the cold, rather than be separated from his beloved wife.

How blessed was Rachel Bean.

29

The following day, mother and son were fine. Even Jethro survived, though he now avoided meeting Rebecca's eyes when he spoke to her. She suspected he was embarrassed by the events surrounding his son's birth. Almost like he expected her to comment, or force him into a decision about the act of faith he'd taken when he volunteered to the agreement prayer. She didn't intend to do either. That was a decision he alone must make.

Rebecca often found his penetrating eyes on her when he thought her unaware, as though attempting to find a flaw or secret. She suspected he considered her an enigma. If only she could share with him her faith, to say, 'It's okay. I didn't understand it, either, when I first heard.' She didn't, though, because he wasn't ready. Not yet. Jethro must find the answers for himself. He had witnessed the Lord's power thrice now. If he sought the truth, he'd find it.

Though the weather remained bitterly cold, it finally stopped snowing. Two days after his son's birth, Jethro escorted Megan home. The young girl was still in a bemused state at the wonder of birth and the miracle of the righted breech. In fact, she talked of nothing else while she remained at the Bean home.

It would take Jethro all day to make the trip and return. So, donning a pair of Jethro's worn corduroy pants and a flannel shirt, Rebecca bundled up and faced the inevitable. The stock required feeding, no matter the weather. There was no other choice, she would have do it.

A blast of frigid air assaulted her the moment she stepped out the door. It jerked the door from her grasp and banged it back against the house with a force that caused the walls to tremble. Fighting against that force, she managed, finally, to close and latch the door. Then she leaned into the gusty wind and struggled through the snow toward the barn. The cold, crisp air stung her face, her breath puffed steamy clouds.

Once she finished the feeding, she attacked the next problem - water. She had to break the ice on the creek so the animals could drink. Searching the tack room, she found an axe with a broad, flat head and stumbled toward the creek, through knee-deep snow-drifts. The sound of her footsteps echoed as she broke the frozen crust on the glittering, blinding white blanketing the ground.

The gurgling water trapped beneath the

frozen slab was clearly audible as it rushed downstream. When the clamor of cold steel striking ice vibrated through the wooded area near the frozen waterway, it caused rodents, rabbits, and other small creatures to scurry in fear and fright from their snug, warm nests burrowed beneath the snow. After freeing the water of its frozen tomb, she chiseled out a three-foot circle, then wasted no time in heading for the warmth of the house.

While she leaned against the cold plank door, gasping to pull air into her tortured lungs, Mark, the eldest of the Bean children, confronted her. With a bewildered look in those bright violet eyes so like his mother's, the youngster asked, 'Where's the milk, Miss Becka?'

Slumping her shoulders, Rebecca realized she'd forgotten to milk, which meant she must retrace her footsteps and tackle that unwelcome chore. Actually, she would rather face another trip to the frozen creek than have to milk a cow. No two ways about it, she still wasn't very adept at that task. She straightened her weary body and forced a smile across her numb lips.

'I forgot the pail. I'm going now. I'll be right back. You watch the little ones for me, okay?'

His thin chest puffed out with pride at the

responsibility she'd given him. He grinned broadly and replied, 'I can take care of them, Miss Becka. I'll make them mind and stay out of things.'

'I'm sure you can, Mark. I'll only be a minute.' At least she hoped she would. Turning, she once more left the warmth of the house to face the arctic blast of winter. On the way out, she collected the milk pail from the work table by the door.

Rosie was quick to retaliate when it came to icy fingers and cold hands. In a blur, the milk pail sailed across the barn and Rebecca's corduroy-clad bottom smacked the straw-covered barn floor. Righting the three-legged stool from which she'd fallen, Rebecca retrieved the dented bucket.

'All right, Rosie, let's try again.' Slowly, Rebecca approached the animal's side. 'I don't like this any more than you do. But we're in this together, so we might as well get it over with.' She rubbed her cold palms together to force a semblance of warmth into her fingers. Then, cautiously, she crouched on the stool. The cow watched her with big, brown, anxious eyes.

The cow's near-frozen bushy tail slapped Rebecca in the face with enough force to unseat her and send the pail flying. 'Blast it, Rosie!' Rebecca sputtered, sprawled on her back beside the overturned stool.

Brushing dust and straw from her backside, Rebecca again righted the stool and prepared for the next round. Blowing on her hands, then rubbing them briskly, she clenched her teeth to cease their clattering while she slowly circled her opponent. Rosie's fluid brown eyes followed Rebecca nervously. The thick, bristly tail swished from side to side like a lashing whip to discourage any approach.

Acting on impulse more than knowledge, Rebecca filled a box with grain and dumped it into the feed trough standing in the center of the barn, picked up the stool and battered pail, and waited. Just as she hoped, Rosie's greedy appetite overpowered her apprehension and she sauntered to the trough and chomped into the tempting treat.

While the cow was occupied, Rebecca circled her, humming softly under her breath, more to calm herself than to benefit the fractious animal. Yet, she noticed the effect at the same time. The swishing tail slowed and Rosie eyed her less often. *It might work*, Rebecca thought. Singing softly, she took her place at the cow's side. Leaning her head into the cow's soft flank, she gently grasped a teat in each hand, then tugged and squeezed. 'plink-plink.' The first, hard-earned, warm milk collided with the frigid metal. Soon, fervent steam rose from the pail. Patting the broad, red rump, Rebecca collected the full container and made ready to fight her way against the gusty wind and back to the house.

After she latched the barn door, she glanced at the pale milky sky overhead. The wind had died down, yet the cold air burned her flesh. Rebecca made a hasty retreat for the house, crunching through the icy crusted snow, careful not to slosh out any of her hard-won prize.

★ ★ ★

Darkness had just swallowed the day when Rebecca heard the bolt slide back and the door scrape across the bare floor. She turned and saw Jethro Bean framed in the doorway. Blue about the lips, frost formed on his eyelashes and brows, he slammed the door and shrugged his broad shoulders to free them of his heavy coat. His long-legged strides carried him across the plank floor, his hands outstretched to the warmth radiating from the cast iron stove. Immediately, four laughing, bright-eyed children surrounded him, all talking at once.

'Here, this will help warm you.' Rebecca offered him a steaming mug of coffee.

'Thanks. How's Rachel?'

'She's fine. They're both resting now.'

Nodding his satisfaction at the reassuring news, he asked, 'Got any supper left? I'm starved.'

'It's on the stove. I'll fix you a plate. Come on, children, let your father get out of those wet boots and warm up.' She herded them ahead of her. 'Come help me set his supper out.'

'Tarnation, woman, what have you got on?'

Rebecca ground to a halt at the gruffness in his voice. Pushing the children toward the kitchen, she turned to face him. 'They're called pants. As a matter of fact, *your* pants.'

'I can see that! I mean what are you doing wearing pants? Female folks oughtn't to be dressed like no man.'

'Would you rather I go out in this weather and feed your stock, carry water, milk, and bring in wood wearing a dress?'

'Well . . . it's just . . . a woman wearing pants. It's . . . '

Anger welled up within her. 'How would you like to go out in this weather wearing a dress with wind blowing on your legs, your skirt flapping like a sail, hampering you as you walk or work? Good grief, don't you know we women get as cold as you men? Did you ever . . . ?'

'Enough! Awright!' Jethro threw his hands

up as if to ward off her verbal salvo. 'I get the drift of what you're saying. Goldarn, woman, you got a mighty short fuse. You know that?' Jethro ran a callused hand through his damp hair, his taut lips relaxed. 'I was caught off guard seeing you in them britches.' He tossed his hand in her direction. 'And mine, at that. Oh heck, what say we call a truce?'

'Fair enough. I didn't mean to yell at you, but . . . ever since I came here, it seems I have to justify myself or my actions. How about that supper now?'

'After I check on Rachel.' He padded across the room in his stocking feet to the bedroom door.

★   ★   ★

So, a truce was called between Rebecca and Jethro. But, Rebecca continued to wear pants.

The weather moderated on the twenty-eighth and a thaw set in. A weak sun broke through the milky clouds, casting a puny warmth on the world of white, but it was enough. Each day grew a little warmer until the constant sound of melting ice dripped from the eaves of the house. Occasionally, a sudden crash could be heard when a glob of ice gave way and shattered to the ground from treetops or the roof of the barn.

Laughter rang to the rafters every waking moment. Voices were never raised in anger. Everyone shared and shared alike. In all honesty, Rebecca was reluctant to leave the Bean family.

Her trip home was almost as difficult as the trip in the snowstorm. Mercy fought each step through slippery, gooey mud sucking at her hooves and slowing her down. Rebecca dismounted several times to ease their progress when Mercy slipped, nearly losing her balance in the quagmire.

Rebecca arrived home March fifth, having spent ten days with the Bean family.

30

Home at last. It was a wonderful feeling to return to her own place. Tonight, she could sleep in her own bed again.

When Rebecca dropped mud-caked boots just inside the door, she was almost bowled over by an enthusiastic welcome from Diablo. He ran circles around her, wagging his tail, licking her hand, giving evidence of his delight to see her again. Leaning down to rub his side, Rebecca greeted him just as warmly. He was a great comfort to her and she'd missed him.

In the midst of their greetings, Rebecca realized there was a chill in the room. Glancing around the large kitchen, she was dumbfounded. Dirty dishes were strewn across the cabinet and tabletop. Pans caked with dried food were stacked in a dishpan on top of the cookstove. The stove itself was cold, with no hint of fire. Only a few glowing embers remained in a ten-day old bed of ash in the fireplace, and an empty water bucket rested on the cabinet. What on earth was going on here?

Fighting against the knot of fear she felt

growing in the pit of her stomach, she forced herself forward. She knew. Somehow, Rebecca knew before she opened the bedroom door what she'd find. Somewhere deep inside she'd known for a long time. Slowly, she pushed open the door and there was no denying the evidence before her now: Ruby was dying.

She lay sprawled across the bed, partially covered by an old, worn flannel shirt that had once belonged to her father. She was cold; her skin gray and dark violet shadows circled her sunken eyes. Her cheekbones were hollow, her breathing shallow and raspy. Ruby was melting away even as the mound of her belly grew.

Rebecca crossed the cold room, gathered up a rumpled quilt from the floor and covered the frail body on the bed. Clasping Ruby's wasted wrist, she sought a pulse. She found it, faint and thready. At Rebecca's touch, Ruby moaned and mumbled in her semi-conscious state, tossing her head from side to side.

'Ruby, can you hear me? Ruby, it's Rebecca. Wake up, dear.' More alarmed than she cared to admit, Rebecca hurried back to the kitchen. A fire. She needed heat in here. Water . . . hot water, food . . . the young woman must eat. So many things to do, where to start?

Time was the enemy. Rebecca had lost too much already. She should have been here. Shouldn't have left her. What good were regrets now?

It seemed an eternity, but at last she had Ruby bathed, the bed linens changed, and one of her own gowns on the young woman's bloated body. Rebecca even managed to spoon a bit of meat broth into her. She placed hot bricks wrapped in towels near Ruby's feet to warm her chilled, weak body.

Ruby continued to mumble and moan, thrashing about wildly as her demons troubled her rest. 'No! No . . . I will not have it . . . I can't. You gotta help me.' Over and over, she denied the inevitable and pleaded.

Caring for Ruby was a full-time job. Rebecca did the cleaning between feedings, bathing, and bed-changing. It took two days to put the house back in order. Rebecca made a bed on the sofa, but spent most nights sitting beside Ruby's bed in case she needed anything. She watched as the days passed, occasionally glimpsing a soft flutter beneath the quilt covering the taut belly, proof of the tiny life within, struggling to maintain a hold on life.

Boy or girl, Rebecca wondered, setting beside Ruby's bed. Did it matter? What struggle did this child face? Fighting even before its birth. But wasn't that so for all of us? We fight something, big or small, real or imagined, all our lives.

Just past midnight a scream pierced Rebecca's fitful sleep, jarring her ragged nerves. Ruby's labor had started, three weeks early. And the young mother was too weak to be of much assistance with her own delivery. Rebecca was certain by now Ruby had pneumonia. Her fever, the wheezing in her lungs were tell-tale signs. In the days since her return, Ruby had only been awake and lucid a few times and then for only short periods.

The clock on the bedside table ticked away the hours. Her contractions became more regular but she grew weaker, though she was now awake and for the most part alert.

'Rebecca . . . the baby . . . its Pa. Give the baby to its Pa.'

'Hush now, save your strength. We'll talk about it later.'

'Not later. Now!' Taking a deep breath, the weakened woman braced herself for the next onslaught of pain. As the contraction loosed its grip, Ruby started again. 'Promise. And name it Matthew . . . or Mary. Promise me?' Pain again overpowered her.

'I promise, Ruby. I promise,' Rebecca

whispered, bathing the feverish face with a cold, wet cloth. Her breathing grew harsh and shallow. The pain was unrelenting, yet the baby didn't come. Ruby floated in and out of awareness, babbling loudly in her delirium as her fever rose. She grew weaker with each surge of pain, but her contractions remained strong. She was retreating from the pain, her consciousness, her mind, her inner self, seeking refuge deeper within to escape the agony.

Defeat peered at Rebecca out of the pale shadows of the room. With a sinking heart, Rebecca realized Ruby had stopped fighting and was slowly relinquishing her grip on life, letting go as she retreated deeper from consciousness. Rebecca refused to admit defeat. Working frantically and praying, she continued to do all she could to make her patient comfortable. And she waited.

'Please Pa, no more . . . please. I hate it. Don't make me.' Ruby's cries and deep sobs were terrible to hear as she relived all the hell of her past. Her demons seemed to rampage through her subconscious mind.

Gooseflesh clambered across Rebecca's skin as the story unfolded in Ruby's ravings, so much more being revealed than Ruby had been able to bring herself to tell. This once-lovely young woman had been defeated long before she had a chance. Her life devoid of hope or love.

Father forgive her, but Rebecca was glad Arthur Lee was dead. She only regretted he hadn't died sooner, before destroying his daughter. If there was any justice in this world, or the next, Rebecca hoped Lee reaped in the hereafter what he so richly deserved. Love and forgiveness momentarily deserted her as she listened to Ruby's tale of horror.

The inky blackness revealed faint shadows as the weak light of early dawn crawled out of the east. A new day. A new life. Faintly, Rebecca noted it was March 14, 1897.

Ruby's son arrived with the dawn, weak, frail, and tiny. His first cries were as weak as he, more a mewl than a cry. Rebecca wrapped him warmly in blankets she'd kept ready near the stove for that purpose. She lay him near his mother while she turned her attentions back to Ruby.

'No!' Rebecca screamed when she realized Ruby was gone. 'Oh, no. After all she's been through, why this?' She had fought only long enough to deliver her child, then quit. Ruby didn't have to die, but she had.

Standing beside the bed, gazing at the ravaged beauty of this once lovely creature and thinking how futile her life had been, Rebecca remembered a line she'd read somewhere. 'Often men live or die by will.' Ruby had willed to die, feeling she had nothing to live for.

Picking up the delicate, blanket-wrapped bundle, she draped a sheet across the wasted body, already growing cold. She placed the newborn infant in a quilt-lined bureau drawer near the fireplace, slipped on her coat, and headed for the pecan grove to find Sam.

'What you gonna do with the wee one?' Sam asked when she told him about the bittersweet birth. Sam, always so quiet and calm, was visibly shaken by the news of Ruby's death and the orphaned baby boy. 'Its Ma gone, poor tike, how . . . I mean . . . well, what you gonna do, huh?' His eyes were suspiciously moist. He gathered his pick and shovel to prepare a resting place for the young mother.

'I've got an idea, but it will depend on another new mother. I'll be back as soon as I can. If you'll take care of the . . . if you'll . . . '

'Go on. I'll do what's gotta be done here. Take care of the tike.' Sam sauntered off across the meadow ahead of her, his shoulders sagging, but not from the burden of the tools he carried.

While Rebecca prepared her tiny charge for travel, Sam saddled Mercy. Before leaving, she fixed a makeshift feeding of sugar wrapped in the corner of one of her linen handkerchiefs. Dipping the packet in warm water, she placed the dripping cloth to the trembling lips of the infant. Frowning and wrinkling his tiny, red face, he at first refused the sugar teat. But a bit of coaching finally got results, and at last he sucked greedily.

Rebecca used a sheet and formed a sling to strap the infant close to her chest in order to free her hands to guide Mercy over the still-slushy trail. It was slow going. She prayed this wasn't a useless trip. What would she do if they refused her?

★   ★   ★

'Of course I'll take him. I've got plenty of milk for two. He's tiny, ain't he?' Rachel Bean commented as she took the bundle from Rebecca's arms and unwrapped the baby for a closer look.

'Yes. He's more than three weeks early, and his mother didn't take care of herself. She wouldn't eat unless I forced her. Anyway, I hate to ask you, but I have no other choice.'

'Don't be silly. You should have known I wouldn't turn away a poor little fellow who needs milk. Here, sit down while I feed him, then we'll talk. There's coffee on the stove; help yourself.'

351

Rebecca watched as Rachel took her seat in a rocker near the stove and unbuttoned her gingham dress. She withdrew an engorged breast and guided the taut nipple to the puckering mouth of the newborn. There was no hesitation this time to the offer of food, his mouth flew open, then locked around the dripping nipple and voraciously set to filling his empty stomach. With an ache in her heart and a lump in her throat, Rebecca turned from the pair and filled two cups with steaming coffee, then pulled a cane-bottomed chair near them and watched.

As calmly as she could, Rebecca related as much of Ruby's story as she felt necessary to Rachel while she nursed the newborn. Occasionally the raven-haired woman nodded, asked a few questions, and accepted the story as it was told. Rebecca barely finished the woeful tale when Jethro arrived home. Removing his muddy boots just inside the door, he spoke casually before noticing the child at Rachel's breast.

'What's that?' His long legs carried him across the floor to his wife's side.

'Shh, you'll wake the kids. They're all napping. It's a baby,' she replied, smiling with her entire face as she met her husband's eyes.

'I can see that. Whose baby? What's it doing here, and why are you feeding it? Well

. . . somebody say something!'

'If you'll quiet yourself, I'll tell you.'

Rebecca didn't dare open her mouth at this point. She let Rachel handle her husband. Rachel would certainly have better luck with him than Rebecca would. She waited silently while Rachel told Jethro the story she'd been told.

'The Lee girl's kid, you say?' Jethro glanced from the newborn nursing lustily back to his wife's face. 'You ain't keeping it!'

'Why, may I ask?' Rachel's eyes had a spark of fire in them Rebecca had never seen before.

'Why? You daft, woman? You know what that girl was . . . I mean . . . she . . . she . . . ' He sputtered to a halt, red-faced. He glared at Rebecca, the one who brought this trouble to his home. 'It won't be staying.' Then he turned and stormed across the room.

'It stays!' The command in Rachel's voice startled both Jethro and Rebecca when she spoke to her husband's retreating back.

As one, Rebecca and Jethro whirled to face the woman seated in the rocking chair, clasping the orphaned infant to her milk-filled breast. With a look of defiance on her face, she boldly locked her violet gaze on her husband. Glancing briefly from Jethro to Rebecca, she averted her eyes momentarily, as though embarrassed by Rebecca witnessing this confrontation. Then, with resolve, she turned back to her visibly shaken husband. Lowering her voice slightly, she continued. 'Jeth, we can discuss it later privately, or we can discuss it now. But the baby stays. I don't often nay say you. You know I don't. But this time, I gotta. Try to understand.' She paused, gazed down at the sleeping infant in her arms, readjusted his position, then continued. 'It don't make no never mind to me what his ma was, or wasn't. It ain't fair to go taking it out on him.

'Jeth, this youngun won't make it 'less he's cared for. I couldn't live with ... I'll be keeping him till . . . well, as long as he needs me.' Rachel slowly lowered the infant to her lap, buttoned her dress, then gently placed him across her shoulder, patting his back to burp him.

Without a word, Jethro turned, slipped his muddy boots back on, and stormed out of the house. Silence remained behind him. Several minutes passed while Rebecca replayed the scene in her mind, and probably the young wife did the same.

'He'll come around. It's just he ain't accustomed to being crossed.' She stood and gazed down at the tiny sleeping child in her arms before placing him in Rebecca's lap. 'I'll fix him a bed, then we'll talk. What's his name, or has he got one?'

'Matthew. His name is Matthew.'

★ ★ ★

It was finished. Sam and Rebecca laid Ruby to rest behind the fruit orchard on a grassy knoll with a view of the creek. Come spring, the area would be covered with wild flowers, but today it was a cold, lonely place.

31

It shamed Rebecca to put to paper the events of the weeks following Ruby's death. She hadn't handled it well, but if she were to be honest in her journal keeping, it must be recorded.

She slept around the clock the day after the short funeral, where only she and Sam were present. Weak with fatigue from loss of sleep, she dragged listlessly through the next few days, barely remembering to eat and only feeding Diablo at his insistence. She let him in or out only because his persistent scratching at the door drew a listless response from her.

It was so lonely, the house so quiet, even the weather seemed to conspire against her. The days followed one after the other in a cold, misty fog. Dampness seeped into the house despite the heat from the fireplace. Mildew formed on the curtains at the windows. The bed linens were damp to the touch. A black mold took growth in her soul as depression set in.

Ruby's story haunted Rebecca's waking hours. The pain and anguish she witnessed the night Ruby gave birth, then died, tormented her. It gnawed at her. And though Rebecca knew better, she failed to stand strong. She gave way to her emotions. The uselessness of Ruby's pitiful life and senseless death made Rebecca angry and frustrated. Ruby Lee lived a way of life she hated, without hope, without even knowing she had a right, a God-given right, to a better way of life. Ignorance of His Word had been her enemy. These hill folk, and all people, needed more information and less inspiration.

At first, Rebecca was only following her mentor's advice when she poured and consumed a small portion of the elderberry wine. She hadn't even opened the Christmas gift until now. She told herself it was for the rest she so desperately needed, and to kill the images she saw at night when she closed her eyes and found sleep impossible. It wasn't until the jar was suddenly empty that she realized what was happening. She was drowning her pain and sorrow in the wine.

The empty jar had a sobering effect. With new resolve, Rebecca tackled spring house cleaning early. She scrubbed, scoured, and dusted, then retired to her featherbed at night too exhausted to not sleep. She was busy expurgating not only her house, but her spirit as well. Each time her faith flagged, she reminded herself of young Matthew. She had to consider his future. While she worked, she made plans for him. But that would come after he was weaned and she brought him home.

★ ★ ★

Rebecca read Jimmy's letter once more. It said he would arrive the first of May. She scanned the page again, seeking a particular passage. There is was, *I have a surprise for you when I get there, mayhap two.* What on earth could he mean by that?

Whatever it was, Rebecca looked forward to his visit. She needed company. Especially now, because the weather had prevented both Megan and Ole Woman from visiting.

★ ★ ★

Springtime and Jimmy arrived almost together. The days were once again warm and the air filled with fragrances from the many blooming wildflowers sprinkled across the thick, lush carpet of new grass.

Rebecca was on her knees, digging in the flower beds, when Diablo announced a visitor. She pushed the poke bonnet from her head, stood, and dusted the moist soil from the knees of her pants. Ignoring the dirt on her hand, she shaded her eyes from the glare of the sun and spotted a rider approaching. Diablo was already racing down the path toward the figure in the distance. It had to be Jimmy.

Quickly, she dashed inside to change her clothes and wash the grime from her hands. No need to shock him with her new attire his first day back. She smiled, remembering Jimmy's reaction to her openness when she had referred to taking a bath in the creek that long-ago day when she had first arrived here. No telling how he would react to her wearing men's pants. Smiling to herself at the imagined look on his face, she stepped out onto the porch just as Jimmy reined up and dismounted.

Diablo added his welcome to hers, running circles around them, licking Jimmy's hand and wagging his tail while they exchanged greetings. The young man knelt down and scratched the young wolf behind the ears. Then, glancing up, he said, 'I've missed him . . . both of you.' He blushed to the roots of his hair at the admission.

'Come . . . tell me about everyone at home. About you. What you've been doing. But first, the surprise you mentioned in your letter. What's the surprise?' Rebecca realized she was overpowering him with questions, yet she was so anxious for news, for someone to talk to.

Taking a seat on the edge of the porch with Diablo stretched out beside him, Jimmy looked away from her as if not knowing what to say, or how to say it. 'See Sam's still around.'

Rebecca had forgotten until then Jimmy had met her neighbor last year when he visited. 'Yes, he's still here. Still keeps to himself. He never mentions family, friends, or the past. It's as though he has neither.' This was said almost without thought. Partly, she supposed, because she'd pondered about it often. Wondering, but never asking.

'I'm gonna be a preacher.'

Rebecca's mouth flew open, then snapped shut when she realized her reaction. 'That's wonderful, Jimmy. I didn't know. You never mentioned . . . What made you decide?' She knew she wasn't making sense, but surprise was the right word all right.

'I got to thinking, after Diablo being healed, about what you said. I been studying and visiting different churches. Then, something strange happened.' Her young visitor glanced away a moment before continuing. 'I don't know just how to explain it.' He paused again as if gathering his thoughts. Rebecca saw him swallow deeply. 'I heard a voice.' His work-hardened hand fanned the air. 'It sounds crazy, but it . . . this voice said 'Preach.' Not really preach.' This time his callused fingers scratched his head. Wrinkles folded his freckles into bronze lines across his brow. 'No, it said 'Teach.'' He turned until he faced Rebecca squarely and held her with his questioning gaze, 'Does that make any sense?'

'More than you know. Oh, yes, it makes sense.'

★ ★ ★

The sun was sliding into the west before Rebecca and her young friend wound down and stopped talking long enough to eat. Rebecca found sleep impossible that night. She lay awake, going over the plans Jimmy shared with her. His second surprise contained plans which could cause a lot of problems. She prayed there wouldn't be any. But, this time, she'd just have to wait.

Jimmy spent the next day with Sam. He and Diablo left right after breakfast and headed for the covered wagon-home in the pecan grove. Later she saw the trio disappear into the wooded area across the creek, each man carrying a gun, Diablo trotting ahead.

361

Off for a day of squirrel hunting, she supposed.

During Jimmy's absence, Rebecca made a visit to Ole Woman's to invite her to dinner in honor of his return and to share his news. The old healer had recovered from her weakness which set in during the winter months, but she had slowed down visibly. She was no longer as spry as Rebecca expected. Though she flatly denied any illness being associated with her decline, saying, 'Body just tired. It be old and wore out, that's all.'

She perked up immediately upon hearing of Jimmy's plans, though. 'I knowed it. Knowed it all along. Seen it on their faces last summer, I did.' The aged woman chuckled at her own remark. 'Younguns might have a time of it, talking Jacob into letting her marry. The boy be an outsider. He'll be wanting to take her off with him. Shore gonna take some doing.' She shook her head thoughtfully.

'There's also Megan. What if she . . . ?'

'Naw,' the older woman waved off Rebecca's protest. 'Gal's just been waiting for that lad to ask. You'll see.'

Together, the two women made plans for a dinner and exchanged dreams of their hopes for the young couple who were so dear to them both.

The festivities were set for Sunday.

Rebecca would ask Sam to join them, and have Jimmy invite the Penny family. Today was Wednesday. She had time to do her baking, and she'd get Sam and Jimmy to provide game of some sort for the meal. She bubbled with ideas.

Rebecca's strategy left out one key ingredient, Jimmy. Her guest came in late that night and departed before she rose the next morning, so she didn't get a chance to discuss her proposal with him. She spent the day making pies, cakes, and loaves of bread.

Rebecca delayed supper that evening until after dark. Finally, she gave up and had hers, then sat on the porch in the dark, waiting. She felt certain Jimmy had gone to see Megan today and was anxious to hear all the news.

Near midnight, she heard a horse approaching at full gallop. Already nervous over the prolonged absence of her young guest, her heart thrummed in her ears at the sound of the oncoming horse. Jumping up from the rocker and stepping to the edge of the porch, Rebecca scanned the surrounding darkness in an attempt to identify who raced toward the house. A cloud drifted across the face of the moon, leaving the sky shadowless and void of light, except for the stars twinkling like sparklers. The sound of the approaching horse grew louder. She strained to see.

Silhouetted by the lamplight flooding from the open window behind her, Jimmy spotted Rebecca while still a distance from the house and called out, 'Hurry, Miss Rebecca, help me get my things together.'

He reined up beside the porch, leaped to the ground, turned and lifted his arms. Megan slid off the horse and he placed her gently on the porch beside Rebecca.

'What's this about? What are you two doing out this time of night?'

'I'll explain while I pack.' Jimmy brushed past her, tugging Megan behind. Rebecca quickly joined them in the front room and stood silently watching them toss Jimmy's few belongings into his valise. There was a sense of urgency about their actions that sent her mind searching for the cause. The reason wasn't difficult to grasp. Trouble, Jacob Penny, the proposed marriage.

Stepping forward, Rebecca added her assistance, asking questions while they worked. She was right in her supposition of the problem. Jacob Penny ordered Jimmy off the place at gunpoint when asked for his daughter's hand in marriage. The eager suitor waited in the wooded area behind the house until the yelling ceased and the household settled down for the night.

Only when Megan judged her Pap and brothers to be asleep had she gathered together a few personal items and joined him. Davy, who guessed the game plan and stayed awake to assist, if necessary, was the only member of Megan's family to give the couple his blessings.

'He'll be here come sun-up, Miss Rebecca. We gotta hurry. And please, don't try to stop us.' Jimmy flung the request over his shoulder, never missing a beat with his packing. 'We know what we're doing. Ain't the way I planned, but . . . we love each other.' His eyes shifted to Megan, who smiled warmly back at him. 'This be the only way.' Jimmy pleaded for Rebecca's understanding, if not her aid.

'Pap gonna be mighty mad. He's sure to come here first light when he finds me gone. It could go bad for you.' Megan finished folding a coarse cotton shirt. 'I hate leaving you to face him, but I gotta go.' Megan's eyes begged her, implored her to understand.

'I don't agree . . . ' They both started to leave, as though expecting her to try to detain them from their set action. 'Wait, let me finish.' Placing her arms around each and hugging them close, Rebecca continued. 'I don't agree with how you're doing this, and I sincerely wish there were another way. Is it possible Jacob might listen to me if I went to him and . . . '

'No!' The pair chimed in unison.

'You're probably right. I've clashed with him enough in the past to . . . Well, then, if you're set on running away, go, and may God bless you. Now, off with you both. You need all the head start you can get.'

When they headed for the door, valise in hand, Rebecca had a thought. 'Wait just a minute. I'll be only a second.' She hurried to her bedroom and quickly drafted a brief note to her brother, James. Folding the note, she returned to the two frightened young people who stood nervously watching the door, expecting Jacob Penny to come charging through it, gun in hand, no doubt.

Handing Jimmy the paper, Rebecca said, 'Take this to James when you arrive home. He'll take care of everything I've asked. It's my wedding present to you both. Now go, before my better judgment takes over and I attempt to talk you out of this.' Rebecca hugged them again.

While they dashed into the night, Rebecca stood rooted to her place near the door, listening to the sound of the horse's hooves fading in the distance. She said a prayer for their escape and a long and happy life. A life like she and Jonathan should have had. If only — no, she wouldn't have a pity party tonight.

Making a decision suddenly, Rebecca grabbed a shawl to guard against the night chill, blew out the lamp, and stepped outside, pulling the door closed behind her. Carefully, she picked her way to the shed out back and lit the lantern hanging inside the entrance. Hastily, she saddled Mercy. She had a long ride to make tonight and must be there before daylight. It would be a gamble, but it just might buy those two young people some much needed time.

★　★　★

The old healer didn't appear the least bit surprised to find Rebecca on her doorstep at two in the morning. Instead, she ushered her in and put the kettle on to boil water for a cup of hot tea. Not until the steaming mugs sat before them and she had taken her seat across the table did she ask why Rebecca was there.

'Okay, chil', spill it. You ain't just out for a moonlight stroll. Let's have it. What brung you here in the dead of night? As if I can't guess.' Blowing at the vapor rising from the hot brew, she took a sip, then leaned back in her chair. She folded her thin, leathery fingers in her withered lap and waited.

The story poured forth, or as much of it as Rebecca knew. Her mug of tea grew cold before she finished. Grimacing, she took a drink anyway to soothe her dry throat. Her hostess continued to sit, staring off at a distant wall, or perhaps a scene only she could see in her head. Seconds passed, then minutes ticked off on the clock, which provided the only sound in the room as the pendulum swung to and fro.

Finally, those all-seeing eyes refocused on Rebecca and the old woman started as though she'd forgotten her presence. She rose briskly from her chair and announced, 'Don't know about you, but I'm for bed. Gonna need my rest, I'm a-thinking. Coming?'

Her friend's apparent lack of concern left Rebecca dumbfounded. 'But what am I to do? Did you hear me just now? Jacob Penny is going to be searching, and sooner or later he'll come here. You can't just go to bed.'

'Can't do nothing about it tonight. Won't be nothing to it tomorrow. Leave it to me.' Yawning, she padded off to bed, leaving Rebecca to follow.

The next morning, Rebecca was awake and having coffee long before the sun crawled slowly to the treetops. The fiery globe promised a lovely day. It cast a rosy glow amid the newly leafed trees, burning the dewdrops off the grass as it gained strength. The birds were busy greeting the dawn with song. An absolutely glorious morning, and all she could look forward to was the arrival of an irate father. A man in search of a daughter who, until a short time back, he had all but denied existed, whom he now sought to protect.

Ole Woman joined Rebecca in the kitchen as she poured her second cup of coffee. She was in higher spirits than Rebecca had seen her in some time.

'How can you be so cheerful? You know he'll be here. He's going to be furious with them . . . and me.'

The snippet bustled around preparing breakfast, which Rebecca didn't want, couldn't eat.

'Told you last night, don't sweat it. I know how to handle this. Now, one egg or two?' She grinned, cracking the first brown-shelled egg.

★ ★ ★

Rebecca was right. Megan's father was furious. Last year's tornado hadn't roared any louder than Jacob Penny did when he arrived, shouting demands and accusations.

Ole Woman calmly greeted him at the door as though he were a welcome and expected guest. Her unruffled manner crippled his indignation momentarily while he tried to figure out why he was being received so warmly. Then, blustering, he started over.

She looked such a tiny, wrinkled thing standing in front of the big, angry giant. Even so, when she lifted her bony hand for silence, the flustered father stepped back as though struck a blow.

'Take a seat, Jacob.' She offered him a chair in her softest voice, disarming the man further. 'I got a thing or two to say to you, and it hurts my neck to be looking so far up at you. Make it easy on an old woman. Sit.'

He sat. She took a seat near him and motioned Rebecca to join her. Then, clearing her throat, she said, 'You're being a fool, Jacob. It be too late to be trying to bring that gal back here now.'

'What do you mean, I'm being a foo . . . ?'

Holding up that frail, leathery hand, she silenced him in mid-sentence. 'I ain't through yet. I'll thank you to not go interrupting again. I'll say my piece and I'll be telling you when I'm finished.' Her gentle but weathered hands smoothed the fabric of her white apron. 'Now, as I was saying, it be too late. Them younguns been gone *all night*.'

Rebecca caught the emphasis on all night, and wondered if Jacob caught it, too. When she noticed his features blanch, she suspected he had.

'Now, human nature being what human nature is, and I expect it ain't changed all that much since I's a girl — Well, you needn't look at me like that.' The folded wrinkles on her neck stretched almost smooth when she leaned forward and narrowed her eyes at the man. 'I was young once. And yes, I can remember back that far, Jacob Penny. Anyhow,' she relaxed a mite, allowing her body to settle back against the chair. 'Like I was saying, human nature, and two healthy young people what's in love and running off from a Pa what would stop them if he could, I figure it be too late.' She took a slow, deep breath to allow her words to sink in before continuing.

"Course, you could go fetch her back. But it'd be a shame, it would indeed.' Her head bobbed and her lips pursed as she carefully measured her next words. 'The talk . . . you know how folk do love to talk. 'Specially about other folk's problems.'

She paused, rubbed a gnarled index finger across her chin as if considering the comment. 'Yeah, the way I see it, the talk would purely ruin that gal . . . for making a decent match, I mean.' She tilted her finger toward the irate but silent father. 'Well, Jacob, you being a man, you'd know better than me. What feller from these parts gonna want a girl to wed what had to be brung back by her Pa after spending all night with another man? A man who's an outsider, at that. You know any such man, Jacob?'

She paused to let him consider this situation. "Course, you might.' Her head bobbed a time or two as if in agreement with her own statement. 'But then, there's the women folk. They talk, you know. And a tale like this would spread like wildfire.'

Her snow-capped head wagged side to side. A soft noise escaped her withered lips that sounded like, *tish, tish, tish*. 'And the counting off the months on the calendar, figuring how early your first grandchild gonna be borned. Yep, be a shame to put that gal of yours through all that, 'specially when the two of you was just getting close after all them years. And that young man a-loving her like he do. But — ' She paused, then stood, looking at the man seated before her. 'You'd be knowing best about such things. I'm just an old woman, mind. Still, if you're gonna catch up with them two, you best be on your way. They got a right smart head start on you.' With that, she turned toward the door, opened it, and waited.

Jacob Penny proved himself to be a man of action as he quickly sized up the situation as the old woman outlined it, and thinking better of his options, he made his decision. Clearing his throat and twisting his hat between his big hands, he glanced from one woman to the other.

'Reckon I best be going, got lots of work needing to be done and don't seem to be no sense to — You reckon that boy'll take good care of my gal?' His eyes sought those of each woman. 'He didn't seem like a bad sort, did he?'

He was asking for reassurance and they both gave it. If he wasn't exactly approving, at least he was resigned to Megan's choice when he departed. When he reached the gate, he slowly peered back toward the house and asked, 'You reckon she'll ever be coming back . . . to visit at least?'

'I'm sure of it, Jacob. They'll both be back. Soon, I hope.'

Nodding his head, he strode off down the path toward home.

Standing side by side on the porch, the two women watched until he disappeared from view. Then Rebecca could hold her curiosity no longer. 'How did you get him to change his mind? He was ready to tear out after those kids when he got here. Now, he acts like their being together was his idea. I don't understand.'

'You heard what I told him.'

'Yes, but . . .'

'A man's worst nightmare is having a daughter bring shame on herself, or his good name. Jacob there'll go let it out his gal made herself a good catch. Let on like it ain't no surprise to him. Might even come to believe it himself before too long.'

Chuckling and patting Rebecca's arm, she added, 'Same tactic my Ma used on Pa when I run off with my man. It worked on Pa. I figured it'd work on Jacob. Thank God for man's pride. Sometimes it's more helpful than his good sense.'

32

'Well, it's high time them younguns wrote,' Bertha said, withdrawing a letter from the stack of mail she was sorting. 'It's been more than a month since they eloped.'

Rebecca reached for the envelope eagerly. 'I agree.' She took the missive from Bertha and nearly ripped it in half in her haste for news from Jimmy and Megan.

'That pair is mighty special to you, ain't they?'

Rebecca tore her attention from the pages of coarse paper, her hands trembling slightly. She met and held Bertha's gaze. 'Megan and Jimmy are more than special.' She clasped the letter to her breasts, took a slow deep breath before continuing. 'They are probably the closest thing to children I'll ever have.' She noticed the mirth slide from the large woman's rosy features, but only had a moment to ponder the cause for the uncharacteristic gloom.

'Yeah, I know what you mean. Always wanted a brood of little ones myself.' With a flick of her thick wrist, Bertha tossed the fistful of mail on a nearby countertop, ran her hands down the front of her already creaseless apron, then squared her broad shoulders. 'Some things just weren't meant to be, I reckon.' She flipped a weak smile at Rebecca. 'Well, ain't no sense in drowning in a pool of pity.' She took Rebecca's arm and guided her toward the table at the back. 'Let's have a cup of coffee and read that letter of yours.'

Rebecca watched Bertha take two mugs from beneath a cupboard and fill them with steaming coffee. Never had she suspected Bertha's desire for motherhood. What else didn't she know about this woman? Would Bertha ever cease to surprise her?

'Now, then, let's hear what them kids been up to. They been gone a month. Must have a lot to tell us.' Bertha placed the cups on the table and took a seat.

Rebecca would have preferred to read her letter alone. Instead, she smoothed the pages and read it aloud.

Me and Megan got married in Ardmore. We wanted to be man and wife when I introduced Megan to my family. Mr. James has been real swell to us. He found us a furnished house right off. Even helped me fill out enrollment papers so I can take that faith-teaching seminar you suggested. I'm right grateful for all you're doing for us. And just as soon as I can, I plan to repay every cent you've spent on our house and schooling.

Jimmy's words of gratitude brought tears to Rebecca's eyes. If only she could express to this young couple how much it meant to her to be able to help them. She brushed the moisture from her eyes and smiled. She couldn't think of a better way to spend her money. She picked up the letter and continued to read.

Ma treats Megan like the daughter she always wanted. Pa even acts right fond of her though he don't say much. And Megan says she never knew having a mother could be so special.

Having never had a mother of her own, Rebecca suspected Megan would be devoted to her mother-in-law. The news Rebecca hadn't expected, but was delighted to hear, came from Megan herself on the last page.

Miss Rebecca, I want to be a nurse. The birth of Rachel Bean's son was such a special experience; I want to be able to help others as we did that night. Now that

I know there are two ways of doing so, I plan to take nurses' training and study with Jimmy at home on the faith method of healing.

Tell Pap and Ole Woman we have decided to return home as soon as we finish our training.

Rebecca folded the letter, placed it back in the envelope. The needs of the next generation would be met and met abundantly.

★   ★   ★

Summer settled over the hills and even the birds gave up their song. The grass in the meadow grew dry and brittle. A shortage of rain intensified the heat across the land.

Ten Mile Creek was at the lowest level anyone could remember, down to a trickle flowing around the big rocks instead of gushing over them. Rebecca tried carrying water from the creek to her garden in hopes of saving it from the blistering heat, but to no avail. Everything except the okra and purple-hulled peas died anyway.

The heat was oppressive. Heat rash and boils were the main complaint from the young. Cornstarch relieved the rash, and potato scrapings or raw fat meat poultices drew the boils.

The two youngest members of the Bean family were thriving. Young Matthew Lee was holding his own with John Bean. The two boys were separated in age by only nineteen days, and could pass for twins in size, which was amazing since young Matt was premature and undersized at birth. Jethro accepted the boy into his household with no further complaints.

Rebecca didn't know how, but in a month or two she'd have to make arrangements for Matthew. She'd always wanted a child of her own, now was her chance. She knew of no family member to lay claim to the child. Ruby never mentioned any. She had only asked that Rebecca give the child to his father, but she neglected to name the father.

Being a mother would be a new experience, and one Rebecca looked forward to. She spent her free time stitching baby clothes for the boy. Ruby had made no preparations for her child, none of the normal activities of a woman expecting. Rebecca wasn't sure the young woman ever admitted to herself the child was real. She had been so set against having it she denied its existence until the end.

Sam had been exceptionally busy lately, cutting and stacking wood. He must have twelve ricks stacked neatly behind the house. And at his insistence, Rebecca now had running water in the kitchen. Sam installed a pump and dry sink.

'Be easier with the little tike.'

Rebecca certainly couldn't argue with that logic.

Sam staked out a cow in the back yard, then opened the feed sack he'd dropped from his shoulder to the ground to expose a half dozen bantam hens and one young rooster. 'Gonna need fresh milk'n eggs for that boy.'

The yard exploded with activity once the chickens were set free from their sack-prison and ran helter-skelter, seeking safety. Diablo, apparently remembering the episode with the guineas and chickens, scampered beneath the back porch with his tail tucked safely between his legs, emitting yelps of fear as he went.

Mercy broadcast her displeasure of the rude intrusion to her domain when some of the squawking hens dashed into the shed. The mule's braying set off the cow, which was already nervous with her new surroundings. With the Guernsey bawling and straining at her ground stake, Mercy caterwauling, chickens squawking, and Diablo whining, it sounded like McDonald's farm.

Sam shrugged his shoulders, and with a sheepish grin, excused himself from the fracas. 'I best be going now.' He flipped his big hand toward the animals. 'You need anything, just let me know.'

'If I need anyth . . . Sam! I *need* some peace and quiet.' Rebecca shouted to be heard above the racket. 'You can't just abandon me with this mess. How do I calm them down?'

'Uh . . . ain't rightly sure,' he answered, gazing around the yard at the confusion and fumbling with his empty pipe. Then, clamping it between his teeth and shuffling his big feet, he turned and sauntered off toward the pecan grove.

Sam's intentions were great, but what was she to do with those animals? With housework, caring for the sick, and soon a baby, how would she manage?

A week after the arrival of her menagerie, Rebecca awoke to an unusual quiet. She lay in her featherbed, trying to determine what was amiss. What was different about this morning? It was as though the earth was devoid of sound. Even the leaves on the tree outside her bedroom window refused to whisper, the birds were silent.

Then she knew. The music. No fiddle music greeted the dawn. Rebecca had become so accustomed to waking each morning to the mystical music coming from the grove; it was a shock to awaken without it.

Something was wrong. Dreadfully wrong.

Sam hadn't missed a morning since his arrival. Even in the dead of winter his music could be heard drifting, like smoke, across the meadow. Rebecca scrambled into her robe and dashed outside, then froze. Sam's wagon-house was gone. Gone. Where? Why? Not a word of leave taking, no good-byes, just gone. He'd left just as he'd arrived, unexpectedly.

That explained his erratic behavior lately. The stacks of wood, the animals, the kitchen pump, and sink. Sam knew he was leaving. All the preparations had been made with that in mind. In his own way, he'd attempted to ease her burden. Ever thoughtful, ever kind, Sam. He always thought of others before himself.

Standing there on the porch in the predawn light with a soft, gentle breeze playing around her bare feet, Rebecca gazed back to the first morning of his unheralded arrival. The soul-stirring music, the odd wagon-house, and later that stovepipe pro- truding crookedly from it's side. The elusive man who'd dashed into the woods on her first visit. She realized she knew little more about him now than she had on that first morning.

She had come to call him friend, yet she knew next to nothing about him except he had a kind spirit and an enormous heart. He helped so many families in the area in so many ways, never asking anything in return. Then, like wood smoke in a stiff breeze, he was gone. The loner.

Unbidden, a scripture came to mind. 'Be not forgetful to entertain strangers: for thereby some have entertained angels unawares.'

Could Sam be an angel? Rebecca wasn't sure. But she did know she would miss him.

★   ★   ★

The adjustments were enormous, but well worth it. Rebecca brought young Matthew home last month. A healthy, robust baby, he filled Rebecca's days with joy and delight, even while managing to get into everything now that he was crawling.

Diablo had at first reacted with a display of jealousy toward the squirming, noisy young intruder to his domain, resenting the attention showered on the new arrival. Like a spoiled child, he demanded equal time for Rebecca's attention, especially at feeding time. When she sat rocking Matthew, or giving him his bottle, Diablo rubbed against her legs, or lay his head in her lap next to Matthew and whimpered like a child until she reached out and scratched behind his ears.

Soon, though, he accepted the fact the stranger was there to stay and his attitude became protective.

Rebecca often found the animal dragging young Matt by the seat of his diaper out of harm's way. Yesterday, she found the pair at odds over a bone from Diablo's dish. While the wolf cub had learned to tolerate and share most things with the boy, his generosity did not include his food.

* * *

The last pie supper and dance of the year was held a week before Thanksgiving. Rebecca bundled Matthew warmly and treated herself to an outing. She'd been so busy all year, she had almost forgotten how to relax and enjoy herself. It was good to be among the people again. Rebecca wasn't sure if they'd finally accepted her or if it was young Matt's charms, but the ladies weren't as cool toward her as they were at her first dance. Either way, she was determined to enjoy their company.

Young Matthew was passed around with the usual 'ohs' and 'ahs' all little ones received. Of course, speculation on his parentage was to be expected. On more than one occasion Rebecca overheard remarks of,

'Well, he sure enough don't take after the Lees, do he?'

'Looks more like . . . sure is a fine lookin' boy, ma'am.' A pause always followed 'looks like,' as though they knew, then suddenly remembered something, thought better of it and changed the subject.

Jacob Penny arrived late, escorting a middle-age widow from Whiskey Holler. Rebecca met her last year following her husband's death in a logging accident, though she couldn't recall her name.

Things were certainly changing in the Penny household. She'd heard Jacob's two eldest sons moved out and now lived at the sawmill in housing provided for the workers. Davy decided to become a schoolteacher and was finishing his classes while serving his apprenticeship with the teacher here in the Big Grassy community school. Needless to say, Rebecca was quite proud of young Davy's accomplishments.

She was relieved, yet puzzled, by Zake Daniels' behavior: relieved that he wasn't forcing his attentions on her as he had in the past; puzzled because, though he didn't approach her, he stood off to one side of the dance area, just out of the light, and kept his hawk-like gaze fastened on her and young Matthew.

Like a lazy giant, he leaned against an ancient oak stripped of its leaves by the autumn wind. His muscular arms were folded across his chest, his gray, hawk-like eyes hooded as though deep in thought. He barely spoke to those who greeted him, centering his attention in Rebecca's direction. His attitude and stance alarmed her. She couldn't help wondering what he was up to, even though he hadn't bothered her in ages. But he was up to something now; she could almost see the machinery of his mind in motion behind those piercing, gray eyes. Refusing to allow him to spoil the night for her, Rebecca ignored him. But a worm of suspicion burrowed deep in her soul.

Bertha and new husband, Tim, insisted Rebecca and Matthew spend the night with them, or rather, what was left of the night. The two women sat at the kitchen table over numerous cups of hot coffee and caught up on the news of events in the months since they'd last seen each other. Bertha positively glowed with happiness. It seemed Tim was good for her.

Just as the sun crawled to the edge of day, Bertha freshened their cups with more hot coffee and blurted, 'Brother Zake's leaving.'

'Leaving?' Rebecca asked. 'Where? I hadn't heard. You mean, leaving for good?'

'Yep. That's what I hear. Seems he's losing his hold on the folk here 'bouts. Figure you're behind that. So do some others I know.'

'What have I to do with this?'

'Quite a lot, it seems. Folks been watching and listening. Mayhap you thought they weren't, but that's the way of folk here 'bouts. They don't comment nor act 'til they chew on it a bit and check it out for theyselves. 'Peers some of them done found the truth.'

'But, I . . . '

'You be wondering when and why? You remember that juicy little story he started last year, just before the big storm hit?' She took a swallow of her coffee. 'The one 'bout you at the swimming hole?' Absently, she brushed tendrils of red hair behind her ear. 'Anyhow, I hear tell folks was on the verge of running you out of them hills, then wham! The tornado hit. There you was, helping like you's one of them.' The large woman paused in her story and blew on her steaming mug. 'They also took note Brother Zake wasn't nowhere to be seen. Then there was Ruby.' Her voice softened. 'Everybody knew about Ruby and the youngun. But you, you took her in. A stranger did for one of theirs what none of them had.'

'I see . . . I think. Go on, I didn't mean to interrupt.'

'Yeah, well, it come to a head few days back. He, Brother Zake, shows up, asking around for Ruby Lee. Hear tell, the folks ain't talking . . . '

'Why would he be asking about Ruby?' Rebecca blurted, breaking her promise not to interrupt.

"Cause he — ' Bertha paused, looked at Rebecca oddly, then glanced away before continuing. 'All I know for fact is folks ain't telling him nothing.'

The room fell silent as they both thought about what had been said. Morning light stippled the tabletop. Then, rather brusquely, Bertha hefted her bulk from her chair. 'Reckon you'll be wanting to get an early start home.'

Rebecca was being dismissed. Sent home. She wondered, why the rush? She sensed there was something Bertha wasn't telling her.

★ ★ ★

She should have known, should have guessed. But not until Zake Daniels stood on her porch and announced, 'I come for the boy,' did it hit her. Zakeriah Daniels was Matthew's father. Ruby was the redhead she'd seen him with the night of the first dance she'd attended. It all fit now. Now she knew.

Standing inside the room gazing out at him, Rebecca saw a different man. This was not the self-sure, cocky, arrogant individual she'd dealt with in the past. His eyes were red-rimmed and bleary. His face sported a dark stubble of several days' growth of beard. His shoulders were slumped and he avoided direct eye contact.

Before her stood a troubled man, and for the first time in their acquaintance, Rebecca felt a tug of sympathy for him. Though, to be honest, she resisted the tug. She didn't want to feel anything for this person, and especially not now. He had come to take Matthew away. Matthew, whom she'd come to think of as hers.

'I said I've come . . . '

'I heard what you said.' She skewered him with an icy glare. The young wolf greeted her visitor with bared teeth and deep-throated growls and stood protectively beside her. Reaching down, Rebecca stroked Diablo's side soothingly, reassuring him. 'It's all right, boy. Easy, now.'

'That animal don't like me much, does he?'

'Not much. You may as well come in, no need to stand on the porch.' She stepped back and allowed him to enter her home for the first time.

Ambling inside, he removed his hat and stood twisting it between his broad, trembling hands, gazing uneasily at the floor while keeping an alert eye on Diablo.

'Sit down, please. I feel we need to talk.'

'No need to talk. I hear you got my . . . my son. I want him. That's all . . . I want him.' He still would not look at her.

'I think there is. Under different circumstances, you could tell me it's none of my business or that — ' Rebecca faltered, but stood her ground. It was her business. 'I watched that young woman waste away before my eyes; give up her desire to live. Do you know, she wanted me to abort her child?' With satisfaction, she watched him flinch, then continued. 'Where were you all this time? Why weren't you here? You might have made a difference.' She wanted answers, wanted to vent her anger, pain, and frustrations on this man. 'Well?'

At last he raised his head and spoke. 'You don't understand. I didn't know. I didn't . . .'

'Would it have mattered if you had?'

'No. I reckon it wouldn't. I . . . you can see I couldn't have married her.'

'I see no such thing! You fathered a child with her, yet you couldn't marry her. No, I don't see!'

'She was . . . well, she . . . they say what's

born in the blood comes out in the flesh. What do you think people would have said, me marrying her?'

'About the same thing they're saying now, I suppose, or will when they know.'

'They know. Knew before I did even. Nobody would tell me nothing when I asked about her. I couldn't figure it out, the secretiveness and all, until I saw you at the dance with the child. Even then, it took me a bit to put it all together. The last piece fell into place this morning when I found her grave marker out back near the orchard.' He paused, glanced away from her, then took a deep breath and continued.

'Spent a couple of hours out there before I got the courage to come up here to the house. I'm right sorry about Ruby. You may not believe that, but I am. It wouldn't have worked for her and me. Maybe if I was a different kind of man, but . . . well, I am what I am. It's a bit late to change . . . for her, leastways. But the boy, I gotta have my son.'

A silence fell between them for a time. Rebecca remembered Ruby's words, 'Give the child to his pa.' She wanted his father to have him. She'd also known he'd never marry her. Yes, it was too late for Ruby. But Matthew?

As though reading her thoughts, he said,

'It'd be best for the boy. Being with . . . family. I always wanted a son. Now, I have one. I'll be a good father to him. I'm gonna try, leastways.'

This time he was looking straight at her. Rebecca believed he was sincere. She didn't want to believe him, but she did.

'How will you care for him? He's so young, so — ' She waffled momentarily.

'My folks. I'll take him to them. They'll help with him. I'm giving up preaching. I ain't sure . . . I don't know . . . There's a lot of things I don't understand and 'till I find the answers — '

His words rendered Rebecca speechless. Even that thin veneer of arrogance was absent. She examined his eyes. They were lined with pain.

His hands continued to trouble the hat, crushing the brim. His gaze flitted about the large room, avoiding the woman before him. He'd lost every battle to her; he couldn't lose this one. This was the most important decision he'd ever made in his life. For once, he'd found something worth fighting for. Something to give real meaning to his otherwise empty life. A son. He'd go down on his knees if he must, but she had to understand.

'Look, I know you don't think much of me,

and maybe you got the right to feel that way. But can't we put our differences aside and think about what's best for the boy?'

Those gray, piercing eyes beseeched her to understand. And she did; though she wished she didn't. Hands clenched in tight fist, jaws taut with anger, Rebecca gazed searchingly at Zakeriah Daniels. Seeking. A tug of war raged in her heart, struggling against the decision she must make. Her heart told her one thing, her spirit another. Zake Daniels had been her nemesis since her arrival here. He had fueled the fires of suspicion against her, spread tales, rumors, and accusations against her character and her teachings. He'd openly defied her every action.

Her thoughts tumbled wildly, erratically as she raked her ice blue gaze up and down his dejected frame, clutching desperately at the contempt she felt for him. Absently, she shook her head at the thought of what he was asking of her now. After all he had done against her, he was asking her to relinquish Matthew to his care. Her precious Matthew. Hers!

Matthew is his son. The thought came unbidden, and it shook Rebecca. She fought against it, but the thought persisted. His son.

Her shoulders sagged, her jaws relaxed.

Defeated by her own beliefs, she spoke around the lump wedged in her throat. 'Matthew. His name is Matthew.' Her hands hung limply at her sides, resigned. 'I'll get him. He's napping.'

'No, don't wake him. If it's all the same to you, I'll just walk around a bit while you get his things together.'

A softness Rebecca was unaccustomed to filled his husky voice. His words rang with sincerity.

'Look, I know this is gonna be hard on you. I wish it could be different. I want to thank you for all you done for him, for both of them. Well, I'll be outside.' Relief flooded him when he stumbled outside, away from the person who'd caused him to look long and deeply at himself. He found he didn't like what he saw. He'd just won a victory, but it was a hollow victory. It disturbed him to know he was causing her pain. He hadn't expected to feel anything. It was a new experience.

★　★　★

Rebecca wanted to cry. She felt like it. But to what purpose? It wouldn't have changed anything. Zakeriah Daniels left, taking Matthew with him. She might never see the boy again, but she felt blessed to have had him, even for a short time.

She had the best of intentions, but in the end her tears won out. It was a grief akin to that she had suffered when she lost Jonathan, her beloved husband. Only this time, she cried for what had never truly been hers and would never be, a child.

33

The news spread like wildfire. Ole Woman was dead.

Rebecca never discovered how everyone knew, but she'd barely finished dressing her in the dress she had saved for the occasion when they began to arrive.

The hills vibrated with the sounds of human feet, horses' hooves, mules, and wagon wheels. Every form of transportation was used as the people came to pay their last respects to the one who'd tended their sick, birthed their babies, and set their bones. She had been loved and respected by all who knew her and would be missed greatly.

While the activity swirled about her, Rebecca retreated to Ole Woman's bedroom. She needed to be alone for a while. The women prepared the food they'd carried in; the men dug the grave and built a coffin. They felled a huge cedar tree for the purpose, because of its pleasing aroma and its enduring quality, much like Ole Woman herself.

★　★　★

It had been a harrowing two weeks. Rebecca came for a visit to soothe her spirit following Matthew's departure, only to find her friend in bed and not attempting to leave it. In response to Rebecca's probing, the old healer assured her she wasn't sick, just tired.

Rebecca remembered standing near the bed, gazing down into her mentor's age-seamed face. Her white hair streamed across the crisp, white pillow slip as her dry lips cracked a weak smile. Old and brittle, this one, but her eyes were still bright and burning. Reaching up, she placed her leathery palm on Rebecca's arm. 'It ain't the end, chil'. It be the first step of the beginning.'

The hour was at hand. She knew and embraced it.

The days passed slowly, the nights even slower. She told Rebecca where to find her burial dress in the bottom of her cedar chest. Then insisted Rebecca wash and iron it, and hang it near her bed so she could see it. She seemed to take comfort from its being ready.

She'd left instructions for her burial site, next to her man. The passages she wanted read were marked in her well-worn Bible, along with her Will, which she wanted read at the same service. 'So's everyone can know what I want done.'

She grew weaker with the setting of each

sun, as if it drew off her strength as it slid into the west each evening.

Then this morning, in the predawn light, as Rebecca knelt at her bedside praying, she felt the parchment-thin hand on her bent head and heard that velvet voice calling her.

'Rebecca. Chil', don't be doing something I don't want done.'

Rebecca glanced up to find her friend smiling wanly and noticed an urgency in her look. 'What is it? What's wrong?' Rebecca quickly stood, then sat beside her on the bed.

'Nothing. Ain't nothing wrong. It's just . . . I don't want you doing no praying to be keeping me here. I've waited too long now to meet my Maker, and to be reunited with my man and younguns. Alex, that be my man's name. Alex been patient a long, long time now. But lately, he's been calling me to join him, and I'm ready. I can go now. You're here to care for the folk.' Her fingers sought Rebecca's hand. 'Love them and be patient with them.' She stopped and her eyelids closed.

Rebecca thought she slept, but she only rested. Then smiling, she stroked Rebecca's knuckles and said, 'Before I go, I got something I want to tell you. Call it an old woman's vanity if you want. But before I go, I want someone to . . . I want you to know my name. It's been many a year since anybody called my name. Didn't seem to matter so much. I reckon I'm just being fanciful.'

'No. Please tell me. I've often wanted to ask, but . . . didn't.'

'Jessica. Jessica Elaine Breckenridge. Alex called me Jess. He calls me more often lately.' She had a far away look on her face as though even now she heard her husband calling, beckoning her to come to him. Slowly, she turned her head on the pillow and gazed out the window for a moment, then glanced back at Rebecca. 'Remember, I choose to go. I got me some rejoicing to do. Remember also what the word says, 'To be absent from the body, is to be present with the Lord.' ' She gently squeezed Rebecca's hand, took a deep breath, closed her eyes, and was gone.

Rebecca sat beside her, holding her hand, consumed with grief and an aching heart. Her bereavement was for herself, not for Jess. Jessica Elaine Breckenridge had made it plain she was ready to go. Rebecca just hadn't been ready to lose her.

★ ★ ★

Finally, she pulled herself from her own private memories and rejoined the others. She circulated among the crowd of mourners where they stood in groups on the porch, in the yard, and beneath the majestic oak, now bare of its foliage. Rebecca listened to their whispered exchanges among themselves.

Each had a story to relate concerning Ole Woman. Repeatedly, Rebecca heard comments of, 'If it weren't for her, my Becky would have died for sure,' and 'Remember back when ole Jack got kicked by his mule? Figured him a goner for sure, but she patched him right up,' and 'She sit up with my Mabel three days and nights. Wouldn't sleep at all till my girl was out of danger.' Each person present had a similar tale of Jessica's tireless efforts on their behalf.

Since her arrival in the hill country, Rebecca had never seen so many people together in one place, not even at the annual pie supper and dance. They'd come from Big Grassy, Little Grassy, East Lost Prairie, Whiskey Holler, Happy Holler, and other places she hadn't even heard of before. Even the men had suspiciously moist eyes when they spoke of their loss.

Rebecca listened and watched, and once again recalled Hebrews 13:2. 'Be not forgetful to entertain strangers: for thereby some have entertained angels unawares.' Ole Woman and 'the loner'. Jessica and Sam. Why not? It was possible.

The service was over, the Will read, the mourners departing for home. Rebecca doubted the old woman's last instructions surprised anyone. They'd lost her and didn't seem to mind much what was done with what she'd left behind.

Her house, furnishings, and land were left to Jimmy and Megan, provided they returned to the hill country at the end of their training. Her quilts, those lovely handmade works of art, were distributed among the younger women; the farm animals were also divided among the younger families. Even her preserved fruit and vegetables were included in the disbursal.

Rebecca noticed that the possessions were left to those most in need of them. Even at the end, the wise old woman had seen to it that needs were met. To Rebecca, Jessie left her family Bible, her herbs, and recipes for her concoctions and remedies.

Finding it difficult to leave, Rebecca remained that night. Closing up the house the next day was agonizing, like closing up a part of herself. Jessica Elaine Breckenridge, known by the hill folk as Ole Woman, had been her mentor and her friend.

Rebecca returned home with a heavy heart.

It was unseasonably warm for the last of December and Rebecca took her time. Diablo joined her, and together they made their way home, she lost in retrospection, the wolf walked sedately beside her. He whined occasionally and licked her hand, as if sharing her grief.

* * *

Rebecca had little time to mourn, or dwell on the death of her friend. It was near midnight when the pounding on her door awakened her. Horace Snodgrass was to be a father again. Ole Woman had been correct, as usual, in her prediction of the spirit being willing but the flesh being weak. At least Cora Mae had had a short rest between the last baby and this one.

Epilogue

March 10, 1935

Rebecca sat before a comfortable fire roaring in the fireplace and browsed through her journals. She found it hard to believe almost forty years had gone by since she first arrived in these hills. So much had happened, so little had changed. Thumbing through the brittle pages, she read the entry for:

November 15, 1899:

Jimmy and Megan returned to the hill country to make their home. They've both completed their training and enthusiastically returned to start their work. They have a daughter, Leona Jessica, who is one year old and the apple of her grandfather Jacob's eye.

January 1, 1900:

A New Year. A new century. Davy Penny is to be married next month. I haven't met the bride-to-be, but Megan tells me she is Davy's type. Intelligent, shy, and loving. I look forward to meeting her.

April 21, 1917:

My fifty-fifth birthday. It's difficult at times to realize I've lived here twenty-one years. So many boundaries have been crossed. Many of the young people are migrating to the cities, leaving the hills in search of new and different dreams. Our country is at war now and several families have sons overseas. Strange that so many lives are affected by events occurring so far from these hills. Word arrived just last week that Mark Bean was killed in action in a country his parents never even heard of. Jethro and Rachel are taking their loss hard. Both of their other sons, Luke and John, are also in the service of their country. Their parents live in dread and fear for their safety.

August 20, 1919:

Luke and John Bean returned home last week. The family gathered in celebration of the joyous occasion. However, the fly was soon in the ointment. The young Beans brought home new and progressive ideas for 'farming' which Jethro steadfastly resists. Though in his sixties, Jethro still produces the best corn liquor in the area and sees no reason to change at his age.

September 25, 1926:

Jacob Penny died yesterday. Megan is devastated. She and her father grew quite close during the years following her return home. His two eldest sons left home during the war years and never returned. Megan and Davy cared for Jacob lovingly, attempting to make up for the loss of his eldest sons. Forgiveness and love have worked miracles in that family. I still remember my first meeting with Jacob Penny. He was an angry, bitter, and defeated man back then. He became, through the years, a warm and loving father and grandfather, taking great joy in living and in his family. His family was his pride. Jimmy, his son-in-law, was like a son to him. I laugh even now, remembering, Jacob's reaction to Megan and Jimmy's elopement.

October 12, 1930:

How could we have foreseen the effect of the stock market crash last year on our lives? Yet it has had an effect. The arm of poverty has extended to our remote hill country and holds us in its grip. Hunger and sickness creep across the land like a thief in the night. I am constantly called upon to treat an illness I'm unequipped to handle: malnutrition. I have no remedies for miss-meal-colic: that hollow grumble in the gut that screams for food.

July 15, 1933:

The hills rattle with sounds of family after family fleeing their homes, carrying with them only the necessities and leaving behind all else. Only the older folks remain, and many of them simply because they haven't the heart to leave. I share all I have from my

405

garden, which is little enough. My traps rarely net any quail or rabbit any more. The hills have been stripped of wildlife in the vain attempt to feed the hungry. By now, even possum is welcome.

Rebecca turned to today's entry in her journal, having looked back at the written history of her life in the hill country. She realized how good life had been to her and knew she wouldn't have missed those years for anything.

It was doubtful anyone would ever read, or even see, her journals, but if they should, Rebecca wanted them to know she had loved her life here. The work she'd done was not of herself, but of the God she served. He had never left her. If she failed, and she knew at times she had, it had been her failure, not His. Her main regret was that her body betrayed her. There was so much left to do, yet her meager flesh cried out. It was tired. Like Ole Woman used to say, 'The spirit is willing, but the flesh is weak.' Rebecca still missed her. But she knew she would see her soon, sensing that her own time was short. She was ready.

It grew late and Rebecca completed today's entry, poured herself a small glass of elderberry wine, enjoyed a last pipe, before retiring to her lonely bed. She chuckled, imagining Ole Woman's face if she could see her now. Rebecca had acquired her mentor's habit of smoking a pipe for relaxing, and yes, even the pleasure of it. She could see her scrimshawed-face crinkling with mirth when she said, 'Learn to relax, chil'. Learn to relax.'

Well, I did, Jessica. I did. I owe so much to you, dear friend. I'll tell you all about it soon. Real soon. Tomorrow is another day. Tomorrow is for the young.

Megan would be by in the morning to check on her. Rebecca always looked forward to her visits.

★　★　★

Megan was fond of saying to anyone who would listen, 'Rebecca Rice's spiritual contribution to the people of the hill country cannot be estimated. She accomplished a great deal here. To do this, she needed two things, a persistent spirit and a great God. She had both.'

MERMAID'S GROUND

Alice Marlow

It's been five years since Kate Williams' beloved husband died, leaving her with two young children to raise. Now she's built a good life in one of Wiltshire's prettiest villages, and she has her dream job, as gardener at Moxham Court. For the last year, Kate has had a lover, roguishly attractive Justin Spencer, but he won't commit to more than a night here and there. When she takes in a male lodger, Jem, Kate's secretly hoping his presence will provoke a jealous reaction in Justin. What she hasn't reckoned on is exactly how attractive Jem will turn out to be.

HOT POPPIES

Reggie Nadelson

A murder in New York's diamond district. A dead Chinese girl with a photograph in her pocket. A plastic bag of irradiated heroin in an empty apartment. A fire in a Chinatown sweatshop. The worst blizzard in New York's history. These events conspire to bring ex-cop Artie Cohen out of retirement and back into the obsessive world of murder and politics that nearly killed him. The terrifying plot uncoils first in New York — in Artie's own back yard — then in Hong Kong, where everything — and everyone — is for sale.

SECRET OF WERE

Susan Clitheroe

Blessed with wealth and beauty, Miss Sylvestra Harvey makes her debut in the spring of 1812, and she seems destined to take London society by storm. Sylvestra, however, has other ideas; she is set upon marrying her childhood friend, Perry Maynard. What better way, then, to cool the ardour of her admirers than to nurture rumours of a scandalous liaison between herself and the dangerous Marquis of Derwent? This daring plan is to lead Sylvestra into mortal danger before she finally discovers the secrets of her own heart.

ONE BRIGHT CHILD

Patricia Cumper

1936: Leaving behind her favourite perch in the family mango tree in Kingston, Jamaica, little Gloria Carter is sent to a girls' school in England, to receive the finest education money can buy. Gloria discovers two things — one, that in mainly white England she will always need to be twice as good as everyone else in order to be considered half as good; and two, that her ambition is to become a barrister and right the wrongs of her own people. Ahead lies struggle — and joy. The road stretches to Cambridge University, to academic triumph and a controversial mixed marriage. Based on a real-life story.

PROUD HEART, FAIR LADY

Elayn Duffy

Viscount Philip Devlin is not a happy man. From his grave, his father has decreed that the Viscount shall marry a girl he has never met if he is to inherit his beloved Meadowsdene and Kingsgrey Court. For a girl with no dowry to speak of, marrying into one of the oldest, richest houses in England is good fortune indeed. But the Viscount's bride, Kathryn Hastings, faces a grim future for she will be his wife in name only, leaving him to pursue his life as before. Kathryn decides to enact her revenge and turns the tables on Devlin.

DUMMY HAND

Susan Moody

When Cassie Swann is knocked off her bike on a quiet country road, the driver leaves her unconscious and bleeding at the roadside. A man later walks into a police station and confesses, and they gratefully close the case. But something about this guilt-induced confession doesn't smell right, and Cassie's relentless suitor Charlie Quartermain cannot resist doing a little detective work. When a young student at Oxford is found brutally murdered, Charlie begins to suspect that the two incidents are somehow connected. Can he save Cassie from another 'accident' — this time a fatal one?